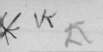

Attention!
—Weather Bulletin—

FROM: National Weather Service
TO: All Region 4 Weather Stations
TIME: 7:10 p.m.

CURRENT STATUS:
    Tornado Watch in effect until 8 p.m.

ADVISORY:
    Upgrade status to **Tornado Warning**

The National Weather Service has issued a
Tornado Warning in effect until 8 p.m. for the
Oklahoma counties of Tillman, Comanche and
Cotton in the southwest corner of the state.

At 7:06, storm chasers led by Dr. Matt Abernathy
from the Center for Tornado Research spotted a
tornado on the ground one mile north of Manitou,
Oklahoma. Doppler radar readings and additional
sightings in the vicinity indicate the possibility of
multiple vortexes. Residents in the **Warning** area
are advised to seek shelter immediately.

The storm is moving to the northeast at
approximately 2.5 miles per hour, and conditions
within this storm cell remain positive for the
outbreak of more tornadoes throughout
the evening.

MEN at WORK

✈️ —MILLIONAIRE'S CLUB   🖥️ —BOARDROOM BOYS   🔆 —MAGNIFICENT MEN

🔗 —TALL, DARK & SMART   🩺 —DOCTOR, DOCTOR   👢 —MEN OF THE WEST

✈️ —MEN OF STEEL   🛡️ —MEN IN UNIFORM

MEN at WORK
CONNIE
BENNETT
WINDSTORM

MAGNIFICENT
MEN

Harlequin Books

TORONTO • NEW YORK • LONDON
AMSTERDAM • PARIS • SYDNEY • HAMBURG
STOCKHOLM • ATHENS • TOKYO • MILAN
MADRID • WARSAW • BUDAPEST • AUCKLAND

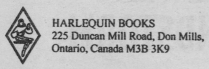

HARLEQUIN BOOKS
225 Duncan Mill Road, Don Mills,
Ontario, Canada M3B 3K9

ISBN 0-373-81016-4

WINDSTORM

Copyright © 1993 by Connie Bennett

This edition published by arrangement with Harlequin Books S.A.

® and TM are trademarks of the publisher. Trademarks indicated with ® are registered in the United States Patent and Trademark Office, the Canadian Trade Marks Office and in other countries.

Printed in U.S.A.

Dear Reader,

Few things are as exciting for an author as being told that one of your books is being reprinted, giving it a second chance to find new readers. I'm particularly proud that *Windstorm* is that book, since its subject is still one of my favorites.

Researching tornadoes and the self-proclaimed "weather nuts" who chase them was a real joy. I read books, attended Tornado Spotter seminars and interviewed storm chasers like *Windstorm*'s daring, sexy hero, Matt Abernathy. I even relied on my own childhood memories of being whisked down to my grandma's creepy old root cellar whenever twisters threatened my little corner of Tornado Alley. (I *hated* that root cellar—the spiders scared me worse than the tornadoes!)

As a result of all my research, I learned more about severe weather systems than most people would ever want to know. Now when storm clouds threaten, I can usually be found searching the sky for the telltale signs that a tornado is imminent. I've even been known to hop into the car and drive out to the flatland east of town for a better look at the cloud's structure.

I haven't spotted a tornado yet, but I'm going to keep looking—from a very safe distance, of course!

Here's hoping that you enjoy *Windstorm* as much as I enjoyed writing and researching it.

Connie J Bennett

P.S. Don't even *think* about going out to chase down a tornado unless you've got an experienced spotter with you who knows how to get you into position and keep you out of danger!

PROLOGUE

THE TORNADO WASN'T a very big one—as tornadoes go. It ripped through the little town of Dry Creek, Oklahoma, about midnight, moving at a sluggish twenty miles an hour, cutting an irregular path less than half a block wide in most places. On Main Street, it demolished Riley's Five and Dime and shattered all the windows of the Merchants' Bank and Trust. On Elm Street, it lifted the Morrison house off its foundation and deposited Grover Smithers's brand-new '72 Chevy pickup squarely in the middle of Myra Brick's vegetable garden.

On Sassafras Street, it hurled debris through solid walls, tore down power lines and uprooted trees. It lifted roofs and carried shingles with it, dumping some of them as far away as Oak Street.

It all happened so fast that hardly anyone had a chance to prepare. By the time the sheriff's department realized that a twister was on the ground, it was too late for the emergency siren at the fire station to do much good. The tornado's freight-train roar woke some of the Dry Creek residents in time for them to seek shelter, but others slept on, blissfully unaware that death was descending on them.

Five minutes later, it was over, and in that brief time twenty-seven people died.

The next day, the stunned, grieving townspeople took stock of what was left of their lives. They mourned the dead and began clearing away the rubble, salvaging what they could from their homes and businesses. Some began rebuilding immediately; others simply gave up and moved away, determined to find a place where wholesale death and destruction wouldn't sneak up on them in the middle of the night.

Some lost more than others that night, but no one in the small community of Dry Creek, Oklahoma, escaped unscathed. The "little" tornado was a specter that would haunt them the rest of their lives.

CHAPTER ONE

THE SKY WAS a sparkling expanse of blue that stretched for miles. A few towering cumulus clouds drifted in that endless sea, but the atmosphere was so calm that their shapes didn't change much as they floated above the rugged desert.

At the edge of a cliff on Shadow Mountain, the air currents were quite different, though. The gentle breeze that wafted over the floor of the California desert began rolling when it hit the base of the five-hundred-foot cliff creating an updraft that gathered enough speed to make the cliff's edge quite windy.

For someone hoping to keep cool in the afternoon sun, it would have been quite pleasant; for a hang-glider pilot looking for a launch site, it was downright dangerous—which made it absolutely perfect in Teddi O'Brien's opinion.

Keeping one eye on the rough terrain and one on a hand-held wind gauge, the tall slender woman walked slowly toward the precipice. About thirty feet from the edge she encountered some serious turbulence—what glider pilots called rotor winds—but closer to the drop-off the air currents became more predictable—gusty, but predictable.

The wind plucked at stray wisps of Teddi's auburn hair and plastered the filmy flame-red fabric of her jumpsuit to her body, but she paid no attention. With the absolute concentration that was her hallmark, she visualized her launch and mentally soared through her flight pattern. She tried to imagine everything that could go wrong and how she would maneuver herself out of it.

Copper Bottom, her landing site, was several miles away, and before she reached it she'd have to gain enough altitude to navigate over two potentially dangerous ridges. Her flight also called for a treacherous 360-degree turn and a landing that fell within twenty feet of a target in the dry creek bed. And she had to accomplish all this under the supervision of a certified observer.

If she made it, she would be well on her way to earning her Hang Five pilot rating; if she didn't, well, the alternatives ranged from mild embarrassment to serious injury to death.

But the risks involved didn't faze Teddi. As a director of action/adventure documentary films, she had built a career out of cheating death and had enjoyed every minute of it. Compared to some of the things she'd done in her thirty-six years on the planet, hang gliding was almost as tame as sitting on a porch in a rocking chair.

She'd been dabbling in the sport for years, but it wasn't until recently that she'd gotten serious about it. Now she was taking lessons from renowned sky-sail instructor Duke Osterman, who demanded that she curb her impetuous tendencies and do things the safe way or not at all. His methods had paid off. Teddi was now ready for something as dangerous as a launch from a five-hundred-foot windy cliff.

"Teddi! Dad's in position!"

The buffeting winds carried the voice away so quickly that Teddi barely heard it. Stepping back from the precipice, she hurried across the uneven ground to where her glider and Carl Osterman, Duke's twenty-five-year-old son and partner in Sky Sail International, were waiting for her. Over the past year, both father and son had acted as her instructors, and in the process the three had become good friends.

"Dad's got the target set up at the landing zone," Carl told her, holding a walkie-talkie out to her. "He wants to talk to you."

"Thanks, Carl," she said as she tucked the wind gauge into one of the zippered pockets of her jumpsuit. She accepted the walkie-talkie and pressed a button on the side. "Duke, this is Teddi. Is everything set on your end?"

She released the talk button, and static crackled until a voice replied, "I'm ready and waiting, gorgeous. How about you? Is the wind holding steady?"

She glanced back at the edge of the cliff and visualized the churning air currents. "It's as good as it's going to get."

"You nervous?"

Teddi laughed, making her bright green eyes sparkle as she winked at Carl. "Who, me?"

"Yes, you," the hang-gliding expert answered. "When are you going to learn that a few butterflies are healthy?"

The words sounded harsh, but Teddi knew from experience that her friend was grinning. "I take vitamins for my health, Duke. I fly for fun. I can't see any reason to spoil a perfectly good thrill with a case of jitters."

"What a nice thought," he said dryly. "I'll have it carved on your tombstone."

"I can think of worse epitaphs."

Static crackled again and Teddi could hear her instructor chuckling. "You're incorrigible."

"And you're a worrywart. Now come on, let's get this show on the road. I want my Hang Five certification so that I can film your tour this summer. I need a job, remember?"

Teddi could visualize Duke shaking his head. "Will you stop worrying about being unemployed?" he said sternly.

"You're one of the best directors in the business, and you have a mantel full of trophies to prove it. I guarantee you'll have an assignment before the month is out. Right now, I don't want you thinking about anything—repeat *anything*—except your glider and the wind conditions. I haven't lost a student yet, and I don't intend for you to be the first. So concentrate!"

"Yes, sir!" she replied with a breezy laugh. He was right, she reflected; it was silly for her to worry. Sooner or later, a job would turn up. One always did, though not every project panned out, as Teddi knew only too well. Her current lack of employment was proof of that. Had it not been for a wad of international red tape, she would have been filming a wildlife documentary in Russia right now, instead of hang gliding in Southern California.

Teddi was still smarting from the cancellation of that project, which had consumed the last six months of her time in extensive preproduction meetings. But another project would take the place of the Russian documentary, and if it didn't, Teddi knew how to "make" her own jobs.

In fact, that was one of the reasons she wanted to upgrade her hang-gliding rating. Duke was planning a major cross-country race this summer, and Teddi had decided to film it as a participant, rather than as a bystander. To do so, though, she had to perfect her sky-sailing skills. If all went well, she'd be a certified expert by the end of the week.

But in the meantime, Teddi needed a job to fill the gap. She abhorred inactivity. She hated waiting, because it gave her too much time to think. She had to have something to occupy the next six months or she'd go crazy.

Duke was right, though—she shouldn't be thinking about that now. Her agent, Larry Harkins, was working on finding her a film to direct. Larry would do his job, and Teddi would concentrate on the matter at hand.

"All right, Duke. I'm completely focused on the flight," she assured him. "I'm going to give the glider a final once-over, then Carl will help me launch. I should be headed your way in about ten minutes."

"I'll be waiting. Good luck, Teddi."

"Thanks, pal." She handed the walkie-talkie back to Carl. "Are you ready?" she asked him.

"Whenever you are."

"Let's do it." She reached for her helmet and slipped it on, adjusting it over the long braid that held her thick mane of hair into some semblance of order. Working methodically, she made her final preflight inspection of the fixed-wing glider. Running her hands along the leading edge, she checked for weak spots in the tubes and rips in the red-and-gold nylon sails. She thoroughly inspected the harness and every pivot bolt, pin, cable and turnbuckle.

When she was satisfied that everything was in perfect working order, she slipped her goggles into place and sidled under the sail. She buckled the harness and ducked her head through the triangular bars that formed the control network of the glider.

Carl made no effort to assist her as she shouldered the control bar and lifted the kite. The turbulent winds buffeted the sails and made moving the glider to the edge of the cliff difficult, but Teddi didn't expect any help; if a pilot couldn't control her glider on the ground, it was a sure thing she couldn't control it in the air. Carl walked along beside her, but it wasn't until they were about ten feet from the edge that he finally turned his back on the cliff and grabbed hold of the nose cables.

They inched forward, and Carl had to exert tremendous pressure on the cables to keep the updraft from toppling the kite over backward. When they'd gone as far as they could go together, Carl glanced at his pupil. "You ready?"

Teddi took a deep breath and nodded. "You?"

"Yes."

The desert valley shimmered in the sun and the sky beckoned. "All right...*now!*" she shouted, lunging forward with every ounce of strength she possessed.

Carl released the cables and instantly the ground fell away from under Teddi's feet. Momentum carried her forward as the wind filled the sails, and within seconds she was gaining altitude. With her feet hitched over the ankle rest and her body completely prone, she soared higher and higher until the updraft played out, then began a lazy, sweeping bank away from the cliff.

Despite the concentrated effort it took to control the glider, a feeling of absolute freedom washed through her. As gracefully as a bird on the wing, she soared above the desert, gathering height and momentum, thrilling to the sensation of no longer being earthbound.

For Teddi, hang gliding was a way of leaving everything behind. She was free to be a creature of the moment, with no cares, no worries, no ties. No future and, best of all, no past. As an added bonus, today she was challenging herself, testing the limits of her mortality—and loving every minute of it.

As she soared, air currents shifted, sometimes subtly, sometimes dramatically, and she adjusted to them, using them when they were beneficial, sidling away when they weren't. An updraft at the first ridge gave her back a little of the altitude she'd lost, but her descent was slow and predictable.

Near the second ridge, a red-tailed hawk appeared, soaring close enough to satisfy his curiosity about the odd creature that had invaded his domain. Teddi smiled with delight, feeling as free as the raptor while he rode the air currents with her. Moments later, though, he flapped his wings and banked away.

Disappointed, she turned her attention to the dry creek bed that was slowly coming into view. Far below her, nearly a mile in the distance, she saw the enormous bull's-eye Duke had staked out as her target. To the right of it, she could just make out Duke's Sky Sail International van sitting on the outskirts of the creek bed. The van was little more than a bright spot of blue, but not far away from it the sun glinted off another vehicle, and Teddi wondered who else had ventured out to Copper Bottom on this beautiful spring day.

Well, she'd know soon enough, she reasoned, quelling her curiosity and returning her full attention to her flight. She had traveled nearly two miles already and had lost a great deal of altitude. To perform a complete 360-degree turn and hit the bull's-eye, she had to be at least a thousand feet aloft, so she banked away from the landing zone, heading for the nearest elevator—a towering cumulus cloud formed by an updraft of warm air.

Sensitive to every change in wind direction, she approached the rim of the updraft and drifted into it. The rising current lifted her up like a master puppeteer manipulating a fragile marionette. It was a strain for Teddi to hold the kite steady, riding the outer rim of the updraft as it carried her toward the base of the cloud, but eventually her sweeping curve gave her the height she needed, and she banked away, heading straight for the bull's-eye.

Exhilarated, she sailed over the target and slipped into a tight arc. Immediately she began losing altitude at a rate that would have been alarming if she hadn't expected it. She caught a glimpse of three people standing near the vehicles, but she paid them no mind. This was the most dangerous part of her flight, and it took her full concentration.

The first quarter of her turn was flawless, but as she went into the second quarter, she felt an unexpected jolt as an air pocket upset the balance of the kite. Shifting her weight on the control bar, she corrected the pitch of the sail, but before she could complete the maneuver, a strong crossdraft struck the kite from behind, knocking the lift out of her sails and forcing the nose down.

In the blink of an eye, the wedge of metal frame and nylon became a death trap as gravity took over and the earth rushed up to meet her.

Teddi's heartbeat thundered in her ears as a surge of adrenalin suffused her veins, but the idea of panicking never occurred to her. Her first thought, in fact, was of how ironic the situation was. The bull's-eye she'd been aiming for was directly below her, and if she went splat, at least she'd land in the target zone.

But of course she wasn't going to go splat. It wasn't even an option. She had defied death before, flirted with it, teased it mercilessly and then danced blithely away. When she landed, she'd be dancing away today, too.

Instinct and training took over, and her adrenaline surge gave her the physical strength she needed to push against the control bar. Gravity was her enemy as she tried to force the nose of the kite up, so she dropped her legs from a horizontal position, letting the momentum carry her sharply against the bar. Miraculously the sudden shift in weight brought the tail of the kite down.

"Yes!" she yelled hoarsely as the sails began fluttering. "Come on, baby, come on!" Fighting the unpredictable and virtually uncontrollable tottering of the kite, she balanced and counterbalanced until she had enough air in the sails to allow them to act as a parachute. Her rate of descent slowed and she began to drop vertically.

She knew it wasn't a particularly pretty descent, but it was a safe one.

If the Grim Reaper wanted to collect on the debt she owed him, he was going to have to wait for another day. Teddi had cheated him again, and it felt great!

Blood was pounding so ferociously in Teddi's head she was barely conscious of the two men running toward her and the third man following more slowly behind them. Her feet connected with solid earth and the kite overbalanced, toppling forward; a second later, she slipped out of her harness, righted the kite and ducked out from under it.

With an exultant cheer, she tore off her helmet and ran hell-bent across the creek bed to throw herself into Duke's arms.

"Did you see it? Did you see that? It was wonderful, wasn't it?" she shouted as Duke whirled her around in circles, his dark bushy beard abrading her cheek. "God, what a rush!"

"You were fantastic!" Duke told her, grinning from ear to ear and talking rapidly as he lowered her back to the ground. "When you didn't correct right away, I thought you were a goner, but I shoulda known you could do it."

Teddi's smile was even broader than his. "Yeah, but I missed the target."

"To hell with the target," Duke replied, hugging her again. "I don't know even half a dozen pilots who could have pulled that out of the fire the way you did."

"But I've still got to do a three-sixty for my certification," she reminded him gleefully. "Come on, let's pack up so I can try it again."

"Are you nuts?" The second man appeared from out of nowhere—or so it seemed to Teddi. She turned to find her agent, Larry Harkins, plucking at her arm. He was still visibly trembling from watching his best client plummet toward the earth. "What the hell did you think you were doing up there? You scared the life out of me!" he howled. "The only way you'll go up again is over my dead body! You got that, kid?"

Teddi's blood was singing and she felt ready to conquer the world. Not even her fussbudget agent could destroy her ebullient mood. "What are you doing here, Lar? Did you see my landing? Wasn't it great?"

"It was not great, it was horrifying. Jeez, Teddi, you could have been killed."

Her eyes sparkling, she gave him a big hug. "Not me, Lar. I'm indestructible, remember?"

He wasn't swayed. "No one is indestructible, Teddi," he told her sternly. "Not even you."

"Oh, don't be a spoilsport," she chided lightly. "What are you doing out here, anyway? Did you come to see me get my certification?"

"Certainly not. I brought a potential client out here to discuss a project with you."

Teddi wouldn't have believed it possible for her spirits to soar any higher, but they did. "Larry, that's great! Talk about the luck of the Irish. Am I on a roll today or what?"

Duke chuckled as he patted her on the shoulder. "See, Teddi, I told you something would turn up. Larry arrived right after I spoke to you on the walkie-talkie. I must be psychic or something."

"Or something," Teddi said with a grin. She turned to Larry, growing more lightheaded by the minute. "So, what's the job?"

Larry was scowling. "Don't get too excited yet, kid. I hadn't counted on having you scare the producer out of his skin. He's probably halfway back to L.A. by now."

"No, he's not," Teddi said as she caught sight of the man strolling toward them. Shielding her eyes to get a better look, she did a quick assessment of him and liked what she saw. He was tall and slender with a very attractive athletic build and dark blond hair that was appealingly unkempt. He had great cheekbones and a straight brow line that gave his eyes a slightly mysterious, hooded appearance.

In the looks department he was a solid nine-and-a-half on a scale of ten, but what Teddi liked most about him was the incredible smile he gave her when their eyes met. Larry might not have approved of her aerial escapade, but this man obviously did. Though Teddi rarely thought about things like eligibility and marital status when she met a man, she couldn't resist a quick glance at his left hand. The fact that he wasn't wearing a ring didn't mean he was single, but it slanted the odds in her favor.

"Hello!" she called out as he approached, darting out a few steps to meet him. "Larry tells me I scared you out of your skin."

Matt Abernathy was having a little difficulty coming up with a rational thought. The forty-one-year-old research meteorologist from Oklahoma, had been looking forward to meeting the renowned T. D. O'Brien for a long time, but nothing had prepared him for what he'd just seen. He knew of her reputation as a fearless daredevil, and her adventure documentaries had backed up that reputation. But this...this was an adventure he hadn't counted on when her agent had escorted him out to the desert. Witnessing her graceful flight and dramatic escape from death was something he wasn't likely to forget.

And neither was her smile as she came toward him. It was a full 250-watt smile that made an already lovely face glow with radiant beauty. Wisps of curling auburn hair that had come loose from her long braid were dancing around her heart-shaped face, and she exuded an incredible amount of energy.

Watching the near-tragedy had left Matt with an adrenaline surge that would have launched a small rocket, but it was clear from the shining emerald-colored eyes he was looking into that her adrenaline rush could have powered the space shuttle *Atlantis*.

It took a second for Matt just to find his voice. "My skin's intact, but my heart's still pounding like a runaway freight train," he told her, hoping he sounded coherent. "That was quite an entrance you made."

"Dramatic entrances are one of my specialties," she said grandly, then extended her hand. "T. D. O'Brien at your service."

Matt took her hand and felt a jolt of excitement shoot through him. "Matt Abernathy."

"Pleased to meet you, Matt," she said, not minding that he held on to her hand a second longer than necessary. "Larry says you have a job for me."

"I do, but I'm sure you'd like a minute to catch your breath before we discuss business," he said, captivated by the dancing lights in her eyes. Matt wasn't sure any woman had ever affected him this way, and he didn't think he could attribute it to the circumstances alone. God, she was gorgeous.

"I'm always ready to talk about work." She made a sweeping gesture that took in the vast expanse of the mountains around them. "Welcome to my office. Sorry I can't offer you a chair."

"That's all right. I'm too hyped up to sit, anyway," he replied with a chuckle.

Teddi winked at her agent, who had hurried up to them. "Knowing Larry as I do, I assume you two have already discussed the practical stuff, and he wouldn't have dragged you out here unless it's a project he knew I'd like, so let's cut to the good part. When do I start?''

Not what's the job or how much does it pay, but when do I start? Matt liked that. A lot. His smile made the corners of his eyes crinkle attractively, and Teddi liked *that* a lot.

''I'm afraid it's rather short notice,'' he told her. ''I would need you to be ready to go to work by the end of the week.''

''No problem. Is it a one-woman job, or do I need to put a crew together?''

''It's a two-camera setup and the crew's already in place, Teddi,'' Larry told her. ''Bryce Lowell and Griff Vandover will be working with you.''

Teddi knew both of them well from earlier jobs. In fact, they were her favorite camera team, but tiny lines formed between her brows as she searched her memory. ''I thought Bryce and Griff were signed up for something Patrick Dennison was directing.''

''That's right. Patrick has been working with Matt in preproduction for the past six months, getting everything lined up for the shoot, but he banged up his leg in a car wreck yesterday morning. He's okay, but he's going to be out of commission for a while.''

''I'm sorry to hear that,'' Teddi said with genuine regret. She liked Dennison and the thought of advancing her own career at the expense of a colleague's didn't sit well with her. Still, she knew better than to question the vagaries of fate. She looked at Matt with pursed lips and a teasing frown. ''So I was your *second* choice, huh? I'm not sure my rapacious ego can handle that.''

''If it's any consolation to your ego, you were my first choice, Ms. O'Brien,'' he told her, keeping his tone as light as hers. "Before I started putting this documentary together, I studied the films of a lot of directors and became a great admirer of your work."

"Thanks. And call me Teddi. All my admirers do," she joked, then turned a scolding glance on her agent. "If that's true, why am I just now hearing about this, Larry?"

"Sorry, Teddi, but when Matt contacted me six months ago you were already committed to the wildlife documentary."

"That's right," Matt said. "I was very disappointed when I learned you weren't available."

"That's better," Teddi said, grinning. "I think my ego can handle that. Of course you realize that Patrick and I have very different working styles," she told him, getting down to business. "He lets his crew do the principal photography while he directs the shots. I prefer being behind one of the cameras myself."

"I understand that and it's no problem," Matt replied. "I've seen enough of your work to know you can handle anything."

"Thanks. Now, tell me about your project. Where do you want me to go and what am I going to be filming?"

Her gung-ho attitude was exactly what Matt had expected. He had known all along, even when he'd had to settle for a lesser director, that Teddi O'Brien was the best person to make a film about his work. Now he was certain. Anyone who could drop out of the sky like a stone and land laughing would understand the adrenaline-pumping thrill he derived from his bizarre occupation. "You'll be going to Oklahoma for two months," he told her, addressing her first question.

Teddi took a deep breath. Oklahoma, where she'd been born and raised. She'd spent the past twenty years suppressing thoughts about her first home, so it took little effort for her to ignore the stab of pain she experienced. Oklahoma was just another state, she told herself firmly. "Oklahoma, huh? You doing a documentary about rodeos?" she asked wistfully, looking Matt over deliberately from head to toe, liking everything she saw. "Funny, you don't look like a cowboy."

Matt's grin widened, but he knew better than to take her flirtatious glance too seriously. She was still riding high. "That could be because I don't know one end of a horse from the other. I'm a meteorologist."

Teddi groaned playfully. "Oh, God, a weatherman! Don't tell me you guys have finally found a way to predict a sunny day, and you want me to document this miracle of modern technology."

Matt chuckled. "Not exactly, but we're working on it. Actually, I'm with the Center for Tornado Research—CTR—in Turner, Oklahoma. We want you to document the activities of our chase team."

Tornado research? His statement hit Teddi like a ton of bricks. She suddenly felt as though all the air had been sucked from her lungs and a black curtain had been drawn around her senses. "Your chase team?" she managed. She spoke more to herself than to Matt, but he didn't seem to notice.

"That's right. I'm in charge of a group of scientists who chase tornadoes two months a year, and we need you to film us in action."

Chase tornadoes? Had she heard him right? This handsome, smiling idiot was actually suggesting that Teddi O'Brien chase tornadoes? The idea was so ludicrous Teddi couldn't do anything but laugh. "You've got to be kidding," she said as a velvet glove of pure terror made a fist in her stomach.

Her reaction was typical, but it certainly wasn't what

Matt had expected from a renowned daredevil, and he was more than a little disappointed. Was he going to have to justify his work to T. D. O'Brien, of all people? "No, I'm not," he said a little stiffly. "This is a very important public-service documentary, Teddi. Not only will it record the activities of my chase team, but it will also contain a section on tornado safety and emergency procedures."

"Tornado safety?" she scoffed, unable to quell her bitterness. "Now there's an oxymoron if ever I heard one."

Matt was completely stymied, unable to imagine where this spate of hostility had come from. Yet there was no other word for it. Teddi O'Brien had gone from exuberant to contemptuous in the space of a heartbeat. "Perhaps you've misunderstood me, Ms. O'Brien. Why don't I explain to you—"

"No, I'll explain to you," she said, feeling a desperate, totally unfamiliar need to escape. "There's not enough money on the planet to get me to do this documentary! Find yourself another director."

With that, she whirled and stalked away, leaving the three men staring after her in stunned silence.

CHAPTER TWO

FEAR WAS A WORD Teddi didn't even consider part of her vocabulary, let alone part of her personality, so it took her a moment to recognize the feeling for what it was. Then she thought she must be mistaken. Teddi O'Brien wasn't afraid of anything. But when Larry Harkins caught up with her as she stormed across the creek bed, the feeling grew, and so did her anger at herself for experiencing something so trivial, so mundane, so…human.

"Teddi! What on earth has come over you?" Larry barked, stepping quickly to keep up with her. "I thought you'd jump at the chance—"

"Well, you thought wrong," she snapped without breaking stride. "I'm sorry you came all this way for nothing, but I'd really appreciate it if you'd get that jerk out of here."

Larry grabbed her arm and forced her to stop. "Jerk? He's a nice guy who's come halfway across the country to offer you a job because he's in a bind and needs the best director available. *You're* the one who's behaving like a jerk. I thought you wanted to go back to work."

Teddi felt hemmed in. Her pulse was pounding with a terror she couldn't put a name to. All she wanted was to be left alone. "I do want a job, Larry. I just don't want this one."

"Why not?"

"Because!"

He looked at her with exasperation. "Oh, good answer, kid. That explains everything."

"Just leave me alone, okay, Lar?" She called out impatiently to Duke, who was standing near Matt Abernathy looking almost as baffled as the meteorologist. "Are you coming? We've got to check the kite over before we can dismantle it and get back to Shadow Mountain. Carl's waiting for us, remember?"

With a bewildered shrug, Duke moved toward her, but Larry wasn't finished. "Teddi, Dr. Abernathy came all this way—"

"Then he can go right back!" she said hotly, stalking across the creek bed. "Find him another director or send him packing, I don't care. Just get him away from me!"

Too stunned for words, Larry Harkins watched as his client stormed away. Teddi was impulsive and stubborn. Where her personal life was concerned, she could be impetuous and occasionally foolhardy, but when it came to her career she was the consummate professional. Her reaction today didn't make sense.

Reluctantly he returned to Matt, who, not surprisingly, looked more than a little perturbed. "I'm really sorry," Larry said. "I've never seen Teddi react to anything that way."

Matt stared after her in disbelief. "What did I say?"

"I haven't got a clue," Larry replied. "Maybe she's just upset because of that near miss in the hang glider."

Matt shook his head. "Are you kidding? She loved every minute of it."

Larry couldn't argue the point. He knew as well as anyone how much his client loved defying death. "Well, maybe if we give her a few minutes to cool off…"

Matt shut him up with a skeptical glance. "Since we

don't know what upset her in the first place, I doubt it would do any good.''

''You've got a point.''

The meteorologist sighed irritably. ''Let's just forget it and head back to town. I've got to figure out some way to salvage this project. I thought Teddi O'Brien was the right one for the job, but I guess I was wrong.''

With a last perplexed look at Teddi, Matt turned away. His disappointment was overwhelming, and it wasn't entirely because he could see all his carefully laid plans for the documentary going down the drain. He was disappointed in Teddi O'Brien, as well. He had admired her work so much that he'd foolishly expected her to be something she obviously wasn't. The best Matt could do was console himself with the knowledge that his project was probably a lot better off without her.

But that didn't make it any easier to walk away.

DUKE OSTERMAN had seen Teddi in just about every emotional state imaginable. When she was happy, her smile could cure a cloudy day. When she was mad, she was capable of white-hot anger that could scar anyone unlucky enough to get in her way. He'd seen her pensive, resolute, depressed—though never for long—and he'd seen her caught in the throes of passionate elation when she was undertaking a new project.

What he was seeing in her now as she examined her glider was completely beyond his comprehension. Tension rolled off her in great, angry waves, and he couldn't begin to imagine why. What he did understand were the paternal feelings that made him want to help her.

''You want to tell me what all that was about?'' he asked.

''No, what I want is for you to help me inspect this kite.''

She grabbed hold of a strut and ran her hand down the length of it. "Does this look bent to you?"

"Forget the glider for a minute, will you?"

"No, I won't," she said, whirling toward him. "You and Carl have to get back to the city tomorrow, so that means I've got less than twenty-four hours to get my certification. I don't want to waste another minute of it. Now, are you going to help me or not?"

"Teddi, talk to me," he insisted, undaunted by her anger. "For weeks you've been complaining about not having a job, and when one finally lands in your lap you turn into the Creature from the Black Lagoon. What gives?"

"Oh, dry up, Duke," she said, turning back to the kite.

He studied her as she began disassembling the glider, and finally he recognized the emotion that she seemed to be trying so hard to control. "You're scared," he said with considerable amazement. "Something Matt Abernathy said scared the living daylights out of you."

"That's bull!" she snapped, not daring to look at him. "I'm not afraid of anything. I just don't want to go to Oklahoma and watch a bunch of lunatics chase...whatever it is they chase. It sounds boring, and I've got better things to do with my time."

"Now who's slinging the bull?" he asked with a shake of his head. When she didn't respond, Duke let a long moment pass before he observed, "You know, I always figured there had to be something."

Teddi didn't want to ask, but she couldn't help herself. "What something?"

"Something you were afraid of," he replied.

She spun toward him defiantly. "I told you, I am not afraid!"

"Oh, come off it, Teddi! I can practically smell the fear. What is it you're scared of?" Considering the conversation he'd witnessed, only one thing made sense. "Is it torna-does? Or do you just have a morbid fear of Midwestern states?"

Teddi glared at him, her emerald eyes shooting fire. "You're close. I have a thing about states that begin with the letter 'O.' You should see how crazy I get when anyone mentions Ohio. You'd better watch yourself, Duke. I feel a real rage coming on and I don't know how much longer I can control it."

"Now, *that* I believe." He placed his hands comfortingly on her shoulders. "Come on, Teddi, it's me, Duke. Friend. Confidant. Sharer of deep dark secrets."

She jerked away. "I don't have any deep, dark secrets."

"Sure you do. Everyone does."

"Well, I don't!"

"Then why did you freeze when Abernathy said he wanted you to chase tornadoes with him for the next two months?"

"Will you leave me alone!" Teddi practically screamed, then whirled away and stormed off.

This is stupid, Teddi, she told herself as her long legs ate up the ground. *You don't yell at friends. You don't turn down jobs for no reason. You don't panic at the drop of a hat, and you're not afraid of anything!*

Except tornadoes.

The realization stopped her in her tracks. Placing her hands on her hips, she took several deep breaths that didn't slow her heartbeat one bit.

It seemed incomprehensible, but it was true. Even after all this time, she was still afraid.

But she'd been so certain she'd conquered that fear. She'd stopped cringing at the approach of black thunder-clouds years ago. Cracks of thunder no longer made her heart pound and her palms sweat. With incredible determination, she had forced herself to ride out storms with a calm, casual attitude that had finally become natural, rather than forced.

Quite simply, storms no longer scared the living daylights out of her. They were just a force of nature to be endured rather than a looming specter of death.

Of course, the fact that tornadoes were practically unheard of in Southern California had helped matters. In the time since she had come to live here twenty years ago, she knew of only three that had come anywhere close to where she was living—and on each of those occasions she'd been out of the state on film assignments. Over the years, she'd seen reports of tornadoes that had struck faraway, Midwestern communities, but she'd steeled herself against feeling anything other than sympathy for those who'd lived through the kind of storm that had so drastically changed her own life.

As she stood in the middle of the dry creek bed, Teddi realized that this was the first time in years she'd been forced to think about a tornado in personal terms. Abernathy's suggestion that she ''chase'' them had brought an image to mind of actually seeing a tornado up close, of confronting a hideous instrument of death.

And her visceral reaction to that image had been to run away. The adrenaline from her exciting flight had enhanced the image and augmented her fear, blowing it out of proportion, but she couldn't deny the fear was there. Obviously she hadn't conquered it; fate had simply allowed her to avoid it.

She didn't like what that said about her as a person.

''This won't do, Teddi,'' she muttered to herself as her pulse finally began returning to normal. ''This won't do at all.''

''If you're going to talk, you should talk to me, not yourself,'' Duke said quietly from the position he'd taken up behind her. "I'm a better listener."

Teddi turned to him, surprised he'd been able to sneak up on her. "Sorry I yelled at you, Duke."

"No problem. You want to tell me what's going on?"

She shoved her hands into her pockets and glanced across the creek bed to where Larry Harkins's BMW was creating a cloud of dust as it edged carefully over the craters in the dirt road. "I made a royal fool of myself, didn't I?" she said.

Duke nodded. "I wish you'd tell me why."

Teddi sighed heavily and pushed aside the remnant of fear still clinging to her. An adrenaline hangover was starting to set in, and she felt completely drained. "You were right. I'm afraid of tornadoes." She shrugged and looked at him. "I thought I'd gotten over it, but obviously I haven't."

It was still hard for Duke to imagine her being afraid of anything. "What caused it?"

She hesitated a moment. "When I was a kid I lived in a little town that was pretty much wiped out by a tornado," she said finally, wondering if he had any idea what it cost her to admit just that much.

"I'm sorry. That must have been a horrifying experience," he said sympathetically.

Teddi looked at him sharply. "Don't feel sorry for me. I lived through it. A lot of people didn't."

Duke raised both hands in a gesture of surrender. "I just meant—"

"I know what you meant," she retorted as she stepped around him to return to her glider. "You've got that 'Oh, you poor thing' look that I despise. That's why I don't talk about it, so do me a favor and can the sympathy, okay?"

"Okay," he said, keeping pace with her. There was obviously a lot more to the story, but Duke knew better than to press her for details. "So, what are you going to do?"

"Disassemble my kite and head back to Shadow Mountain."

"Don't play dense, Teddi. You're no good at it," he told her. "I meant, what are you going to do about Abernathy's offer?"

She glanced at the dust cloud again. "I already did it, remember? I turned him down."

Duke frowned. "That was just a gut reaction, intensified by your adrenaline rush, Teddi. Abernathy took you by surprise."

"That's an understatement," she said dryly.

"But you're still going to run away?" he asked incredulously. "That's not like you."

Her face tightened into hard lines that weren't typical of her, either. "I turned Abernathy down, and that's that. Just drop it, okay?"

Duke nodded slowly in reluctant agreement as they reached the glider.

They went to work silently on her kite, but every so often, Teddi would catch him looking at her with an odd expression on his face. It wasn't just the pity she so abhored. There was something else in his gaze, something that disturbed her on a deeply emotional level because it was what Teddi had seen all too often in her parents' eyes when she was a child.

Duke was disappointed in her. Teddi had spent a lifetime trying to erase the memory of her parents' disapproval. She had worked hard to make them proud of her, even though there was no way they could ever acknowledge her success. In the process, she had gained a reputation as a fearless free spirit, and Duke had once admired her for that. But no more.

For the first time in years, Teddi was ashamed of herself.

BONE WEARY and thoroughly disgusted, Matt leaned forward, ejected another director's work tape from the VCR in his motel room, and tossed it onto the stack of other rejects on the bed beside him. There was only one more tape left to view, which meant that his chances of finding another director had nearly run out.

He'd been at this two days now, ever since he'd returned from his disappointing meeting with T. D. O'Brien. Larry Harkins had given him a list of several other documentary directors he represented, but none of them had been right for the project. Matt didn't want an artsy, esoteric film; he wanted a documentary that combined action with an important public-service message. He also needed a director who could help him put the complicated scientific aspects of his work into language and images anyone could understand.

Teddi O'Brien had fit that bill perfectly and Patrick Dennison had appeared to be the next best choice. Now they were both out of the running, and Matt was in trouble. The storm season in Oklahoma, northern Texas and southern Kansas—the heart of an area known as Tornado Alley—was already beginning. Typically it started in March and lasted through May, and though Matt and his team would be out chasing likely storm systems several days a week during that time, actually witnessing a tornado being born was a rare occurrence. Some years, Matt was lucky if he saw even one. Catching an event like that on film would take diligence, patience and time. He couldn't afford any delay.

Not that CTR would allow him a postponement, even if he wanted to ask for one. It hadn't been easy to get his bosses to fund the documentary, which would cost nearly a million dollars by the time it was finished. If Matt wasn't ready to begin shooting next week, they would cut their losses immediately and cancel. The likelihood that they'd be willing to try again next year was virtually nil. It was now or never, and never seemed to be getting closer all the time.

Irrationally, Matt blamed Teddi for the problem. If she'd listened to his proposal and decided to reject it for logical reasons, he wouldn't have held it against her. But he was certain her reasons weren't logical. She'd had an adverse reaction to something he'd said, and she hadn't had the decency to explain.

Of course, Matt had finally realized that part of her behavior could have been explained by her brush with death in the glider, as Larry had suggested. Adrenaline wasn't something that could be controlled once it was released into a person's bloodstream. It tended to heighten any emotional state; it could blow mild reactions out of proportion, and that could have contributed to Teddi's blowup. It hadn't *caused* it, though.

And now he was desperately trying to salvage the project he'd worked so hard to put together. Once he'd rejected all of Larry Harkins's clients, he'd gone to several other agents who represented directors, and it was their work he was just about finished viewing.

Things were not looking up.

Part of the problem, of course, was that he was comparing every documentary he saw to those Teddi had directed. Nothing he'd seen had even come close to her work. All the really good directors were already committed to other projects, which left only mediocre ones to choose from.

With a weary sigh, he looked at the lone videotape beside the VCR. It seemed to be looking back at him, tantalizing him with one last shred of hope, and he popped it into the machine, praying this would be the one.

Five minutes into a pedantic dissertation on communism in China, Matt was grateful for the interruption of someone knocking at his door. He crossed the small motel room and glanced through the security peephole.

Teddi O'Brien?

Matt took a second look, wondering if he was seeing things. It hardly seemed likely or even possible that she would come calling on him, yet the proof was indisputable. There was no mistaking that lovely face or the mane of auburn hair that framed it.

What on earth was she doing here? Had she reconsidered, or did she just want the pleasure of insulting him some more? Squelching simultaneous bursts of irritation and expectation, he ran a quick hand through his hair and opened the door.

CHEWING NERVOUSLY on her lower lip, Teddi lowered her hand to her side and waited. Knocking on Matt Abernathy's door had been harder than she'd imagined. Not that making the decision to come here had been a picnic in the park. For two days she'd thought of little else but his job offer, her reaction to it and Duke's disturbing looks of disappointment.

She'd done a lot of soul-searching—something she wasn't very good at—but she had come to a surprising conclusion. There were worse things in the world than being afraid of tornadoes—things like living with her own cowardice. Once she'd realized that, she'd known she had no choice but to face Matt Abernathy. And the job he'd offered her.

As the door creaked open, though, Teddi's resolve slipped a little, and she did what she always did when her confidence flagged. She smiled her brightest smile and summoned all her bravado to bluff her way through.

Abernathy looked like he'd had a worse two days than she'd had, and he wasn't bothering to cover up any of his emotions. He clearly wasn't overjoyed to see her.

"Surprised, Dr. Abernathy?" she asked brightly.

"That's something of an understatement," Matt replied guardedly. There wasn't a hint of apology in the sparkling eyes that lighted on him, and that irritated him. She'd wasted his time, insulted him, made him feel like something lower than dirt and, worst of all, shattered his illusions about how wonderful she was. If she was going to appear at his door out of the blue, the least she could do was have the grace to look properly humble and contrite. "What can I do for you?"

Teddi gestured vaguely toward the room behind him. "Mind if I come in, or would you prefer I take a flying leap into the nearest sizable body of water?"

Matt tried not to smile, but it was difficult. He'd just gotten accustomed to not liking her, and he didn't particularly want to change his opinion. "I'd opt for the flying leap, but you'd probably enjoy it too much." He stepped back and cleared the way for her to enter. "Come on in."

"Thanks."

She moved past him, and Matt caught a whiff of something tantalizing—not a perfume, exactly, but a clean soft scent that affected him on a purely primal level. She was dressed in white: tennis shoes, crisply pressed trousers, Windbreaker and tank top. If she had hoped the color of purity would make her seem innocent and vulnerable, though, she was sadly mistaken. Teddi O'Brien wore sensuality the way other women wore cologne. He'd noticed it two days ago when they'd met, and he'd liked it a lot. Now, it only compounded his irritation with her.

"Well, once again, what can I do for you, Ms. O'Brien?" he asked as he closed the door.

"First off, you can call me Teddi," she suggested. "You had the hang of it the other day, but you regressed after I threw my little tantrum."

"All right, *Teddi,* what can I do for you?"

She glanced around the room and her eyes landed for a moment on the rumpled bed and videotapes. She recognized the packaging instantly because her own work sample looked just like everyone else's in the industry—on the outside, at least. "I take it you're still looking for a director."

"Yes." Matt moved to the television and shut off the documentary he'd left running.

"Good." She took a deep breath and prepared herself for the scariest dive she'd ever taken in her life. "How would you feel about giving T. D. O'Brien another shot at it?"

Matt looked at her sharply, not daring to believe what he was hearing. "I thought you weren't interested."

She shrugged negligently. "I changed my mind. That is a woman's prerogative, you know."

"Did Larry browbeat you into coming here?" he asked suspiciously.

Teddi smiled at that. "Matt, take my word for it—no one browbeats me into doing anything I don't want to do. This was entirely my idea. Though I will admit that Larry was only too happy to tell me where to find you. He agreed with me that at the very least I owe you an apology for the way I behaved."

"Frankly, I'd rather have an explanation than an apology." He thought a moment. "Though an apology would be nice," he added wistfully.

She smiled at his attempt at humor. "I am truly sorry,

Matt. I have a lot of faults, but being obnoxious usually isn't one of them.''

"Apology accepted," he said magnanimously. "Now, about that explanation…"

She gestured toward the room's only chair. "Do you mind if I sit?"

"Oh, of course not. Sorry. Make yourself comfortable." She did, and Matt swept the videotapes on the bed aside and sat facing her. The size of the room made for a feeling of intimacy the situation didn't call for.

Teddi felt it, too—that exciting spark in the air that hinted of very promising chemistry between a man and a woman. Under other circumstances, she would have welcomed the sensation, but not tonight. This visit was all business, and she wanted to get down to it. "I called Patrick Dennison yesterday. He's out of the hospital and as grumpy as a grizzly bear, but he was happy to tell me about your documentary."

Matt was surprised. "Why did you go to him, instead of me?"

"Because I needed information and I wanted time to think it over before talking to you. Patrick offered to share his preproduction notes with me, so I can be up to speed on the project very quickly. Of course, I won't do everything the way he would have done it," she warned him. "But based on what he told me, I'm confident I can do a good job."

Matt didn't doubt that for a moment, but he wasn't ready to make a commitment yet. She'd obviously gone out of her way to find out more about his film, but her about-face was a little too abrupt. Matt couldn't afford to hire a director who wasn't seriously committed to his project. The stakes were too high. And there was still a big question to be answered. "You're not going to explain what set you off the other day, are you?"

She flashed him a bright smile. "Only if you give me no other choice."

Matt refused to be moved by her charm, but it wasn't easy. "Why not?"

Her smile faded a bit. "Because it involves something very personal, and I don't make a habit of exposing my private life," she replied quietly.

"That's perfectly understandable, Teddi. I certainly don't want to pry, but you have to admit that your behavior was a little strange. Larry assures me that you don't normally display Jekyll and Hyde personality traits, but he's your agent. He gets paid to stand up for you."

"And he does it admirably," Teddi said generously. "In this case, he happens to be telling the truth though. I do have a temper, but I try very hard to keep it under control."

"Then why couldn't you the other day?"

This was what Teddi had dreaded the most. "I blew up because you offered me a job chasing tornadoes."

Matt nodded as though she'd given him a perfectly reasonable explanation. "Well, that certainly clarifies everything," he said dryly. "I should be taken out and shot in front of a firing squad."

Teddi chuckled and decided that she really liked Matt Abernathy. Despite his irritation, his humor and his easygoing manner were obvious. That would make him a lot of fun to work with, but it didn't make it any easier to explain things to him. She'd spent too many years trying to keep the past buried. "I don't blame you for being confused. I was, too, until I figured it out. You see...I knew someone who was killed by a tornado when I was a kid."

Matt felt an automatic stab of sympathy. "Someone close to you?"

Teddi nodded. "It left a pretty bad impression on me, to say the least."

Though her tone was light, Matt saw a shadow darken her eyes that said a lot more than her words. He understood the meaning of that shadow only too well. "I'm sorry."

"It was a long time ago, and I really thought I'd overcome my grief and...well, some other emotional baggage," she hastened to reassure him. "But I was wrong. Living in California, I've never had to think much about tornadoes. When you suggested the possibility of actually confronting one, it seemed like...like..." Words failed her, but Matt supplied them.

"A cruel joke?"

That wasn't exactly what she meant, but it was close enough. "Yes."

"Why on earth didn't Larry tell me about this? Surely he knew that you'd have reservations about doing a documentary on this subject. The least he could have done was prepare you, rather than just letting me blindside you with my suggestion."

"Larry doesn't know. I tend to keep my professional life separate from my personal life. And frankly, it isn't something I talk about very often to anyone."

Matt understood a lot of things now, and he could sympathize on a number of levels. He compartmentalized his own personal life—what there was of it. Hobbies, casual interests, even relationships usually took second place to his work. And he knew a lot of people who had lost loved ones to tornadoes, so he thought he understood the resentment, bewilderment and pain Teddi felt. For a long time, he'd even felt some of those things himself. Like Teddi, he had ghosts in his own past that he rarely discussed with anyone.

"I'm really sorry about your loss," he told her, then

admitted with some reluctance, "My best friend was killed by a tornado about fifteen years ago, so I have an idea of what you must have gone through."

Teddi's delicately arched brows shot up in surprise. "And you still chase them for a living?"

Matt nodded and pushed away the haunting memories of Joe Cochran and how he had died. "Yes. It took me a while to come to grips with the tragedy and get on with my work, but I did it."

"That's very commendable," she said, feeling a mounting respect for him because he'd done something she hadn't been able to do. "But why chase them at all?"

"Because what I do has saved a lot of lives and has the potential to save more in the future. A tornado is one of the most powerful forces in nature, and one of these days I'm going to understand where that power comes from."

"And control it?" she asked shrewdly.

Matt laughed. "Hardly. Man will never exhibit that much control over nature. No, what I want to do is *predict* tornadoes—when they'll strike and where—so that no one will ever be taken by surprise again. There are too many lives lost every year."

Teddi certainly couldn't argue with that. If Matt's work could save lives, maybe her work on a documentary about his work would save a few lives, too. Now she had two powerful reasons to convince him to hire her.

Teddi leaned forward intently, resting her elbows on her knees. "I want to do this documentary, Matt. Forget about what happened at Copper Bottom. Forget I made a fool of myself and that I offended you. I've done nothing for the last two days but think about this, and I know what I want. Hire me and you won't be disappointed."

Her offer was like a bright light at the end of a dark tunnel, but Matt was too much of a professional to jump blindly at the ray of hope she offered. "Have you ever seen a tornado?" he asked. "Not just photographs or videos, but a real living, breathing tornado?"

It was a miracle, but she was unable to meet his gaze steadily. "No."

"It's an incredible experience, and based on what I've seen of your work, it's an experience I was certain you'd enjoy," he told her. "Now, I'm not so certain. Why would you want to subject yourself to something that might arouse painful memories?"

That was the easiest question he'd asked her. "Because I'm not a runner," she replied, straightening in her chair. "I'd rather face something head-on and conquer it than live with the knowledge that I ran away." She spread her hands. "It's really that simple."

Matt believed her. The sincerity in her eyes and voice made it impossible for him not to. In that instant, his respect for Teddi O'Brien, the woman and the filmmaker, finally returned in full measure. But it wasn't quite as simple as she seemed to think it was. "How can I be sure it won't affect your work?"

Teddi's smile looked a lot more confident to Matt than it felt to her. "Matt, I once did a short subject on men who wrangle rattlesnakes for a living. Needless to say, I didn't fall in love with the snakes, but it was an effective little film."

She'd made her point admirably, and Matt grinned. "I know it was. I saw it."

"Then you know I don't allow my distaste for a subject to affect my work."

"But has anyone you know ever been bitten by a rattler?" he asked quietly.

"Yes." Teddi met his gaze steadily. "Me. On that film, as a matter of fact." She flashed him a dazzling smile.

"Hire me for this job and I'll tell you all about it sometime. I can do this, if you'll give me the chance."

Matt didn't see how he could refuse. If he'd had another brilliant director vying for the job, he might have given it more thought, but there was no one else. If he didn't hire her, he would most likely be forced to cancel the project. She was ready and willing to begin on schedule.

His choice seemed obvious.

"All right, Teddi," he said as he rose and extended his hand. "Let's go for it."

She stood and accepted his hand. "You won't be sorry, Matt."

As their hands clasped firmly, the same jolt of excitement he'd felt the first time he touched her coursed through Matt again, making him wonder if there'd been another reason for his decision that had nothing to do with budgets and mediocre directors. Then he dismissed the thought as foolish. The fact that she was beautiful, vivacious and smelled sinfully sexy had nothing to do with hiring her.

Did it?

CHAPTER THREE

"GOD, MY HEAD HURTS," Teddi moaned, pressing her palms against her temples as she fell back into an overstuffed armchair. Books and papers were strewn around her like fallen leaves, making her Venice Beach bungalow even more cluttered than usual. "I'm sorry, Matt, but if I look at one more weather chart I may run screaming onto the freeway."

Matt chuckled as he dropped the sheaf of papers onto the oak coffee table between their chairs. "Is that your subtle way of suggesting it's time to take a break?"

She cocked one eyebrow at him. "Haven't you figured out yet that I'm never subtle?" For emphasis, she pivoted, flinging her long legs over the arm of the chair. "Yes, we are taking a break." She dropped her head back, spilling her auburn hair over the side.

"You won't get any objection from me. We've been at this for ten hours straight." Matt eased back in his own chair and tried to ignore the havoc her pose of complete abandon wreaked on his senses. It was a battle he'd been fighting—and losing—all day because everything about Teddi O'Brien attracted him. He'd never met anyone like her.

After they'd sealed their agreement with a handshake last night, they had arranged to meet at Teddi's this morning for a crash course in meteorology and storm chasing. Matt was flying back to Oklahoma tomorrow, and Teddi would begin driving out the day after, so there wasn't much time for her to prepare. What they had covered so far wouldn't have filled a thimble, but Matt didn't expect her to absorb in a day what it had taken him a lifetime to learn.

Still, he had to confess she was an excellent pupil. He had brought a mountain of data with him, and she had pored over it with fierce concentration, but after ten hours, she'd reached saturation point. And so had he.

Now, she was sprawled on her chair, her eyes closed. Supposedly she was relaxing, but even in repose there was an aura of restrained energy about her, as though she might erupt into action at any moment. She had thrown her whole being into studying, and now she was putting an equal amount into resting. Matt didn't know how that was possible, but it was true. After all these hours with Teddi, he still didn't know her any better than he had last night, but the idea of understanding her intrigued him.

There were clues around her house, of course. Matt just wasn't sure how to interpret them. The cozy two-bedroom bungalow was spacious enough, with high ceilings, white stucco walls and an attractive fenced-in yard beyond a bay of windows in the living room. Matt sensed that at one time she had made a stab at decorating in the Santa Fe style, but whatever effect she'd been aiming for had been lost amid the clutter of knickknacks and souvenirs that occupied every surface, nook and cranny. Elegant African tribal masks competed for attention with beautiful Native American baskets and woven rugs. A tarnished bronze conquistador helmet sat on the top of a bookcase beside a huge stuffed mouse wearing a EuroDisney T-shirt.

Everything in the room, she had told him this morning, was a memento from her travels, and by the looks of it, she'd been around the world more than once. The memorabilia gave her home character—a rather eccentric one.

Perhaps that was the biggest clue Matt had to who Teddi
O'Brien really was. She was definitely one of a kind.

"Teddi?"

"Hmm?"

"I'm glad you changed your mind about the documentary."

She didn't open her eyes. "If I'd known what a slave
driver you are, I might not have."

Matt chuckled. "Don't worry, you'll have plenty of time
to rest in Oklahoma. Storm chasing isn't a full-time occupation, even during the height of the season. Sometimes a
full week or more passes between chases."

"During which time I will be conducting interviews,
writing copy, filming all this background information we've
been working on and editing the miles of footage we'll
have shot." She finally opened her eyes and looked at him.
"That certainly sounds restful to me."

Matt grinned. "I have the feeling that rest is the last thing
you need on a regular basis. You thrive on action, don't
you?"

Though his comment was entirely accurate, Teddi found
herself growing uncomfortable. She always did when Matt
smiled at her, and her discomfort was growing because she
liked his smile and the way it made her feel. Matt was
charming, easygoing and fun to be with, and if he'd been
anything in the world but a tornado chaser, Teddi would
have been delighted by the attraction she felt for him. As
it was, though, she'd spent the entire day trying to pretend
that the air didn't sizzle every time he smiled at her.

"Actually, I thrive on food," she said, coming to her
feet. A nagging feeling of cowardice clung to her, but she
ignored it. "I'm starving and you must be, too. Come on,
let's go eat."

She moved so abruptly that Matt was startled. He

shouldn't have been, though; another thing he'd learned about her was that she hated talking about herself. "All right. Since you're the native, I'll leave the choice of restaurant in your capable hands. Where are we going?" He stood and began stacking some of the papers and books while Teddi disappeared into her bedroom.

"To a great sidewalk café down on the boardwalk. It's not far," she told him from the other room.

"Within walking distance?" he called back.

"Yes. It's about a mile from here."

"I didn't think anyone in L.A. walked anywhere."

"They don't, but you're not in L.A. This is Venice. We do things a little differently out here."

"Why doesn't that surprise me?" he asked dryly.

She reappeared wearing the same khaki safari shorts and *Jurassic Park* T-shirt she'd worn all day. Now, though, the strap of an enormous canvas purse stretched across her torso, bisecting the head of a menacing Tyrannosaurus rex. It also defined and outlined the fullness of her breasts, but Matt tried to ignore that aspect of her outfit.

"I take it dress is casual at this restaurant," he commented as she closed and locked the patio door.

"On the boardwalk, always. In fact, you may find that we have completely redefined the concept. Come on. Let's go soak up some local color." She let him out the door, locked it with two dead bolts, then followed him down a short walkway. A quiet neighborhood of stucco bungalows shaded by palm trees stretched out around them, and there was surprisingly little traffic on the narrow street. They turned west, and Matt found himself staring directly into the first colorful splashes of a hazy red-and-gold sunset reflecting off the ocean.

"It's beautiful," he commented.

"Just wait, it gets better. An hour from now it'll be glorious," Teddi assured him. "Smog may be bad for your health, but it creates very surreal sunsets."

"It's kind of...otherworldly."

Teddi laughed. "You ain't seen nothin' yet. Venice Beach is about as otherworldly as you can get."

When they turned a corner a few moments later, Matt saw exactly what she meant. The twenty-foot-wide boardwalk that stretched out in front of them was a carnival of color and motion. Rollerbladers clad in neon spandex whizzed along the walk, skillfully dodging hundreds of tourists and street performers of every description. Beyond the walk, a bicycle path followed the contours of the beach, where a few dedicated sun worshipers were taking advantage of the last hour of sunlight.

Matt felt as though all his senses were being assaulted at once. The wail of heavy-metal rock from a passing boom box clashed with the performance of a classical guitarist, who in turn clashed with the haunting chords being strummed by a harpist farther down the boardwalk. Beyond that, a daring young man had drawn a huge crowd to watch him juggle three buzzing chainsaws, and beyond him an audience of gawkers sat on the bleachers behind a platform crowded with body builders pumping iron.

Homeless transients with overflowing shopping carts rubbed elbows with wary tourists, and vendors sold everything from soy burgers with alfalfa sprouts to Greek pita bread and pizza. A deeply tanned woman wearing the skimpiest bikini Matt had ever seen coasted by on roller blades, her momentum sustained by the three sleek Afghan hounds trotting in front of her.

"Amazing," Matt murmured, trying to look in four directions at once.

Teddi had to laugh. "I didn't mean to send you into terminal culture shock."

"I'll survive. I think."

"Come on." She took his hand on impulse and led him through the sea of moving bodies toward the beach where it was a little quieter and a lot less crowded. On the way, they met at least a dozen people Teddi knew. One of the street performers stopped her to talk a moment. A bedraggled old woman pushing a shopping cart flashed her a toothless grin.

She greeted them all with friendly enthusiasm, and Matt quickly realized that she possessed the remarkable ability to make everyone she met feel special.

Their most unusual encounter was with a sand sculptor named Clooney who was dressed in purple Bermuda shorts, an obnoxious Hawaiian shirt, wraparound sunglasses and unlaced high-top tennis shoes. To top off the ensemble, he carried a big yellow pail complete with shovel. He looked like a deranged refugee from an old beach-party movie, and the wild mane of gray hair that dangled to his waist only heightened the impression.

Clooney greeted Teddi with a big hug and insisted on showing her his latest creation—a life-size female sunbather, perfect down to the last detail. The sculpture was so lifelike that Matt felt almost voyeuristic—and he said so.

"She's beautiful," Matt told him. "I half expect her to get up and walk off at any minute."

"Good. That's what you're supposed to think," Clooney said, then winked at Teddi. "The man knows good art when he sees it. You have my permission to invite him to the party I'm throwing this weekend."

Teddi looked genuinely disappointed. "Oh, Clooney, I'm sorry, but I'm leaving for a shoot day after tomorrow."

"That's great!" Clooney exclaimed. "You finally got a

job. What is it this time? Sharks on the Great Barrier Reef with Jacques Cousteau?"

She shook her head. "Storm chasing in Oklahoma with Matt."

Clooney's scraggly eyebrows went up. "Now that's a new one on me." He looked at Matt. "What do you do when you catch one?"

Matt laughed. "I watch it to see if it will spin out a tornado."

"And people say I'm crazy," he muttered, then sighed. "Well, Teddi, happy hunting. Give me a call when you get back, okay?"

"Will do," she promised, accepting a parting hug from her friend.

Teddi and Matt stood watching him, swinging his shovel and pail, as he disappeared into the crowd. "Are all your friends so..." He fumbled for the word, and Teddi helped him out.

"Crazy?"

"Colorful."

Teddi chuckled at his diplomacy. "Not all of them, but I do like variety."

"Is that why you live here? For the variety?"

She thought it over as she began strolling down the beach again. "No, it's for the sense of community we all feel. Once you get away from the furor of the boardwalk, Venice is really just a small town that happens to be surrounded by a big city."

"Is it an artists' colony?"

She nodded. "Pretty much. Movie people, mostly. We like Venice because there's a feeling that the rules that bind the rest of society don't apply here. We're free to be who we are and do what we want." She gave him a sheepish smile. "It's an illusion, of course. Still, down here you can be an oddball and not stick out. I like that a lot."

Matt was surprised. Not by what she'd said, but by the fact that she'd actually said it. It was the first personal revelation she'd made all day. "Well, I have to admit, you do fit in," he told her.

Teddi shot him a suspicious sidelong glance. "I can't tell if that's a compliment or not."

"It's a compliment," he assured her. "This place has an energy and excitement about it that's totally unique. It's almost a rhythm, like a pulse or a heartbeat. The only difference is that you are contained energy waiting to be released, and out here, the energy has already exploded."

Teddi was flattered by the assessment, but she couldn't resist teasing him. "You mean I'm like an accident waiting to happen?".

"Not at all," Matt said with a chuckle. "I just meant that you're very...vibrant, very intense."

"That's why some people find it exhausting to be around me."

Matt thought it over. "I suppose. I find it very exciting."

Teddi felt a little flutter of excitement herself as she looked into his warm brown eyes. "Thanks." She didn't dare say any more than that. Doing so, she reflected, might lead them in a direction she wasn't quite ready to go in yet. "Considering what you do for a living, you'd fit right in around here, too."

"I don't think so," he said doubtfully. "California doesn't have enough tornadoes to suit me."

Which is why it suits me so well. The thought hit Teddi so suddenly that it wiped out the chord of sexual tension humming through her. She quickly changed the subject. "Are you originally from Oklahoma?"

Matt shook his head. "Kansas. I was raised on a farm

in the middle of nowhere. Nothing but low rolling hills and cultivated fields for as far as the eye could see. I loved it. What about you? Were you born in L.A.?''

"No, I moved here from Anaheim when I started college," she said, hoping he wouldn't ask if she'd lived anywhere before Anaheim. She didn't want to lie to him. She'd skirted the truth too much already. "How did a Kansas farm boy become a meteorologist?''

If Matt noticed that his question had made her uncomfortable, he didn't show it. "It's not as big a leap as you might think. Weather is the single most crucial element in a farmer's life. Everything we did—everything we *had*— was based on whether or not it rained. Too much, and the crops molded in the fields; too little, and we watched them burn to a crisp. We were obsessed by the weather out of necessity.''

The sun was sliding closer to the ocean and the crowd on the boardwalk was beginning to thin. Vendors were closing up shop, musicians were packing away their instruments, and the rhythm Matt had noticed earlier began to change drastically. The booming, cacophonous heartbeat shifted to a murmur that was gradually overpowered by the languid hammering of the surf.

As Matt and Teddi strolled along the increasingly deserted beach, the change in the atmosphere suffused their conversation with an intimacy that crept up on them before they realized it.

"You know, you city folks really don't have any concept of what weather is all about," he told her. "You know that it's either cold or hot, rainy or sunny, humid or dry, but you're not really...connected to the weather. You hear on the six-o'clock news that it's probably going to rain tomorrow, but you don't see it coming. You don't sense the subtle shifts in the way the air tastes and smells. You don't see the clouds gathering on the horizon sixty miles away. You don't feel the power accumulating out there.''

"You make it sound almost poetic," she commented, enjoying the quiet, mesmerizing quality of his voice.

"Sorry. I didn't mean to wax rhapsodic."

"It's all right," she assured him. "I need to understand what makes you tick."

Matt was experiencing the same needs, but he was astonished she would admit it. He stopped abruptly and Teddi turned to him. The sun turned her hair to flame and her skin to gold. It was a breathtaking sight. "Why?"

His look was so intense, so personal, that it nearly took Teddi's breath away. An ache of longing blossomed inside her, and she had to fight for a rational thought. "So that I can capture the essence of who you are on film," she answered as casually as she could.

Matt held her gaze intently. "And that's the only reason?"

Teddi recognized a moment of truth when it struck her in the face. She'd been retreating from Matt all day, but he wasn't going to let that continue. "You mean, am I attempting to explore the...attraction we seem to feel for each other?"

He nodded. "Are you?"

"Maybe just a little," she confessed, hoping she didn't sound as breathless as she felt. "The attraction is there. It would be silly for us to deny it. But I'm not so sure it would be a good thing to act on it."

Matt was disappointed but not at all discouraged. "You don't believe in mixing business with pleasure, is that it?"

"That's right," she replied, feeling an overwhelming sense of guilt because it was the first out-and-out lie she'd told him. Actually, Teddi had no compunction at all about mixing business and pleasure. She normally devoted so much time and energy to her work that if she didn't mix business with pleasure from time to time, she'd never have any pleasure.

No, this time what held her back was Matt's unusual profession. But if she revealed her reservations about becoming involved with a tornado chaser she would have to tell him why. Last night, Matt hadn't demanded a detailed explanation of how one particular storm had changed her life, and Teddi didn't want to explain, because it was no one's business but her own.

As she held his gaze steadily, Matt considered her answer, weighing it against the strand of magnetic attraction that seemed to be binding them together despite her veto of a relationship that didn't even exist yet. "Is that a hard and fast rule or just a general guideline?" he asked.

Despite her reservations, Teddi couldn't stop herself from telling him wistfully, "It gets a little fuzzy around the edges sometimes."

"Good," Matt said with a grin as he started down the beach again. "That leaves us a little room to maneuver. Now, let's go back to your original question. What did you want to know about me? Professionally, that is," he added with mock gravity.

"Anything you'd care to tell me," she answered, getting back to business as she fell into step with him. "We've spent the whole day discussing the technical aspects of your work, but I also need to know about you as a person if I'm going to build a film around you."

"Ah, but the film's not supposed to be about *me*, Teddi," he said lightly. "It's about my team and the value of the work we do."

"But it also has to be about why anyone would take the risks you people take. Face it, Matt, you are utterly fascinated by something that most people view with fear and dread. To understand *what* you do, an audience will have to understand *why* you do it. You can talk about saving lives and reducing property damage all you want, but your love of storms goes way beyond that. I've heard it in your voice and seen it on your face all day. *That's* what I have to understand.''

Matt couldn't deny it. He was so accustomed to people thinking he was crazy for being passionately in love with tornadoes that he had developed a surefire defense mechanism. Focusing on the good his work did deflected criticism and made his job more palatable.

But Teddi had seen beyond that, and she wanted her audience to see it, too. He wasn't about to argue with her artistic vision. ''All right,'' he said finally. ''I'll try to tell you anything you want to know.''

''Good. Tell me why you're so passionate about them.''

''Storms in general, or tornadoes?''

''Both.''

Matt thought a moment, trying to put his feelings into words. ''That controlled power fascinates me. You can feel a thunderstorm coming long before you see the first clouds, you know. There's a heaviness in the atmosphere that's almost oppressive, and you can actually taste the electricity. When I was a kid, I'd be out on a tractor in the fields, and I could sense the change. That's when I'd start looking for the cloud towers in the distance.''

As he talked, his voice took on a reverence and vibrancy Teddi found captivating. It was like listening to a master storyteller. ''Huge clouds on the horizon would slowly start drifting together like giants gathering for a town meeting. Over the years I began to see patterns in the types of storms produced by different cloud formations. The storms that spun out tornadoes were the most majestic and terrifying of all.''

Teddi was surprised. "You found them terrifying?"

"In a wonderful, compelling sort of way," he said with a nod. "They have so much power they seem alive. I can't describe how it feels to watch a storm coming toward you that's so huge it covers half a state. The white towers shoot sixty thousand feet into the air and slowly turn to a deep midnight blue. Then the anvil starts spreading…"

"Anvil?"

"It's a shelf of blue-black cloud that stretches forward from the top of the storm because a cap of cold air above it won't let the warm air rise any higher. The whole thing becomes a gigantic pressure cooker, and when enough pressure finally builds up, the warm air punches a hole in the cap. All that trapped energy starts churning faster and faster, until it finally unleashes a tornado because there's just too much energy to be contained by one cloud.

"I swear, Teddi, it's a living thing. It writhes and twists like a giant sea serpent, roaring down on you, inhaling everything in its path. I've seen the spectacle a hundred times, and it never ceases to leave me awestruck."

Teddi found it difficult to breathe and even harder to swallow, and she hated herself for having prodded him into this discussion. He had described the process to her earlier in the day, but then his narrative had been scientific and analytical. This was a visceral description that fired Teddi's strong visual sense. Her knack for composition helped her imagine the scenes he described, and she found the artist inside her warring violently with the part of her that had nearly been destroyed by the very thing Matt found so compelling.

The filmmaker in her wanted to capture and share the excitement Matt felt, her daredevil side wanted to experience the danger, and her seldom-acknowledged rational self wanted to run like hell. Teddi suddenly realized she'd never been so conflicted about anything in her life.

"It must be a very powerful emotional experience," she managed to say.

"It is. There's nothing quite like it in the world."

"I don't doubt that," she said, trying to keep her voice even and neutral so that Matt wouldn't see how rattled she was. She wanted desperately to change the subject, but Teddi didn't run away from things that scared her—she ran toward them. "Do you remember your very first experience with one?"

"Oh, definitely. It's one of my earliest memories, in fact."

"Somehow that doesn't surprise me," she said, striving for a light tone.

"I was hiding in the root cellar with my parents and two brothers as a tornado roared overhead, and I remember sitting on a sack of potatoes thinking the world was coming to an end. The ground shook and at one point it felt as though all the air had been sucked out of the cellar. I was absolutely terrified, and at the same time I was wishing my mom had let me stay outside to watch it."

Teddi swallowed hard, trying not to remember the sound of that roar—the sound of death. "How old were you?"

"Five, I think. Maybe six."

"Did it do much damage?"

"It flattened our barn and broke some windows in the house, but that's about all." Matt shook his head. "I can't really describe how seeing the destruction made me feel. Until that moment, I thought my parents were the most powerful force in the universe, but when I saw the pieces of kindling that had once been our barn, I realized that people were insignificant compared to tornadoes. After that,

I began watching for storms, studying everything about them.''

"So that you'd feel less insignificant?" Teddi asked quietly.

Matt glanced at her. "What?"

Teddi looked away from him, wishing she hadn't asked the question. She'd just learned something very important about Matt, but she didn't want to think about how it applied to her own life. He had taken a terrifying experience and turned it into something constructive. She had simply run away.

"Knowing everything there is to know about something gives you power over it," she explained. "Maybe learning about storms was your way of controlling something that would have seemed totally uncontrollable to a five-year-old child."

Matt mulled the insight over for a moment and was amazed to find that it fit. "You're absolutely right. I'd just learned that my parents couldn't keep me safe, so I found a way to protect myself." He looked at Teddi and found her profile unreadable. "Are you a psychologist, as well as a filmmaker?"

At that moment, Teddi didn't want to talk about what she was or wasn't. Matt's narrative was filling her with too many conflicting emotions that wouldn't bear up under scrutiny. "Every good filmmaker has a little psychologist in her—or him. Does that bother you?"

"Not at all." Matt would have given anything to be able to tell what Teddi was really thinking. For the first time since he'd met her, she wasn't exuding anything. She seemed self-contained and quiet, almost withdrawn.

"Here's the restaurant," she said with considerable relief.

As they walked, they had been drifting slowly back to

the boardwalk, which was nearly deserted now. Just ahead, a huge awning covered an outdoor dining area that was separated from the boardwalk by a low, plant-laden brick wall.

Unlike the boardwalk, the café was still busy, but they didn't have to wait long for a table that provided them with a glorious view of the sunset. The palm trees along the bike path were black silhouettes against a crimson sky, and the ocean shimmered like molten gold.

"You're very quiet all of a sudden," Matt said once they were seated with their menus.

"My energy usually sags about this time of day," she told him.

"Uh-oh. That's not good."

"Why?"

"Because this is the golden hour for storm chasing. Most tornadoes form in the late afternoon just before sunset, when the ground starts releasing all the heat it's been storing up during the day. That's one of the factors that gives a tornado its power. You're going to need all the energy you can get at this time of day."

"If the experience is as exciting as you claim, I expect my adrenaline will give me all the energy I need and then some." Her tone was teasing, but Matt didn't smile because he suddenly realized that for all of Teddi's outgoing charm, there was something infinitely unknowable about her. Somehow, that realization only challenged Matt to find a route past the veneer. "This discussion bothered you, didn't it?"

All Teddi's defenses went on alert. "No. Of course not."

"I don't think I believe you," he replied, watching her face carefully. "We've already established that this is a difficult subject for you, Teddi. If it's going to cause you problems, I need to know about it."

Teddi looked down and found that she was toying with her silverware. She forced her hands to be still. "I'm sorry. You're right, it is a little hard for me to take. Obviously your love for storms borders on passion, while I despise them with an equal intensity. That leaves me a little...torn."

Matt frowned. "Would it help to talk about what happened, Teddi? You told me someone you knew was killed by a tornado, but that's all I know. Maybe if you told me—"

"No," Teddi said quickly, then added, "But thank you. It's really not worth going into, Matt."

"Do you want to change your mind about doing the film?"

Teddi was shocked that he would even suggest it. "Of course not. Once I make a commitment, I don't back down from it, Matt. Not ever. I'll give you a hundred percent, and if everything you've told me is true, I'll create a documentary that's as compelling, exciting and horrifying as the subject we're depicting. Just don't ask me to fall in love with the storms."

But could you fall in love with the storm chaser? he thought. The question came to him so suddenly that it rocked him back in his chair. How on earth could he be thinking about love with a woman he'd known only a few days? A woman who was as mercurial as the weather and just as hard to predict?

"I don't expect you to love tornadoes, Teddi. But I don't want them to depress you, either."

"I'm not depressed," she assured him. "It's just that you've given me a lot of information today, and I have to digest it. There's still so much I don't know, but I have to go to work in three days, whether I'm ready or not."

"I realize that, Teddi. From where you sit, the project must seem pretty overwhelming."

"I've handled worse, but there are a lot of technical details I have to address if I'm going to film you and your team at work. I've barely had a chance to glance at Pat Dennison's equipment requisitions, and my crew left for Oklahoma yesterday before I could discuss anything with them."

Those were just excuses and Teddi knew it. Pat's requisitions were fine, and Teddi knew the crew he'd hired so well that discussing anything with them was irrelevant. It did bother her, though, that Bryce and Griff would be expecting guidance from her, and she was still fumbling around in the dark. She was gradually developing a feel for what the film should be, but the concept wasn't fully formed yet. Until it became a cohesive vision, she would be off balance. Her personal conflicts only added to the problem, but she wasn't going to tell Matt that.

"I don't want you to worry about the technical side of this," she told him. "I'll do my job, you do yours, and at the end of two months I'll present you with a rough cut of a film that will knock your socks off."

"I don't doubt that, Teddi," he replied.

"But you are doubting me personally."

"I didn't this morning. I guess that's because this is so important to me that I need to believe you can handle it."

"Then believe it," she said, but at that moment Teddi wasn't sure which one of them she was trying to convince. To cover her uncertainty, she picked up her menu and smiled her most dazzling smile. "Now, shall we order? They make the best omelets in the world here. I personally recommend the Amelia Earhart—black olives, mushrooms, sour cream and ham. It's heavenly."

She was doing it again, keeping him at arm's length using nothing more than a smile and radiant energy. For the next two months he was going to have to resist the incredible appeal of that smile—or find a way to penetrate it.

Either way, it was going to be a long, very interesting storm season.

CHAPTER FOUR

THE AMELIA EARHART OMELET was as good as Teddi had promised, and she hadn't overestimated the sunset, either. They watched the reds and golds on the horizon slowly fade to deep hues of purple that blended dramatically with the midnight blue of the sky above. By the time they finished eating, the beach was bathed in darkness that was interrupted only occasionally by pools of artificial light from the streetlamps on the boardwalk. The ocean beyond was a murmuring black void.

Matt sensed that the area was no longer as safe as it had been during the day, so they didn't dawdle on the walk back to the bungalow. With Teddi beside him it was hard to think about the physical dangers of the city, though. The personal dangers of her charismatic personality were much more absorbing. During dinner he'd tried to get her to talk about herself, but all he'd gotten for his efforts were anecdotes about her travels that were sometimes amusing but more often hair-raising. Teddi had done things that made Matt's occupation seem tame and boring.

"So there I was," she was saying now, "hanging literally by a thread over the gorge. It was fifteen hundred feet straight down, with thin air behind me and a sheer wall of unbroken ice in front of me."

She was holding Matt spellbound with her description of her ascent of an Arctic glacier. He'd seen the documentary she'd shot on that trip, but the escapade she was describing hadn't been included. While she and her camera crew had been hauling equipment to the top of the glacier, Teddi lost her precarious footing and dropped thirty feet. The jolt caused her harness to fray and she'd been in imminent peril. Obviously she had survived.

"What did you do?" Matt prodded anxiously.

"I ver-r-ry carefully swung into the wall, jammed both picks into the ice face, and hung on for dear life until Bryce dropped me another rope. After that, I was shaking so badly he practically had to haul me to the top."

Matt didn't believe that for a minute. She was just being modest. "The Bryce you're talking about is Bryce Lowell? The one who's working on our documentary?"

Teddi wasn't sure when Matt's documentary had changed from "mine" to "ours," but she liked it. It was good to know she hadn't shaken his confidence in her too much with her ridiculous reaction to his storm descriptions. "That's right. Bryce is an excellent cinematographer—and a damned good mountain climber, thank goodness. He's pulled me out of more than one tough spot." She slanted a grin at Matt as they strolled along the deserted boardwalk. "And I've pulled him out of a couple, too. Get him to tell you about our kayak trip through the Grand Canyon sometime."

Matt searched his memory. "I don't guess I've seen that documentary."

"Oh, it wasn't a working trip. That one was just for fun."

"Ah." Matt didn't risk saying any more for fear of betraying his disappointment. He hadn't met Bryce Lowell yet, but apparently Teddi and the cinematographer had more than just a professional relationship. How much more Matt didn't know, and he wasn't sure he wanted to find out. "Is Bryce going to work on the hang-gliding film you were telling me about?"

"I don't know yet," Teddi replied as they turned the corner onto the narrow street that led to her bungalow. "The last time I talked to him about it his agent was trying to get him a job on a feature film that's set to shoot this summer. That was a couple of months ago and I have no idea whether it panned out or not."

Matt felt a little relieved. If it had been a couple of months since she last saw Lowell, their relationship couldn't be too serious—if there was any "relationship" there at all. To keep himself from asking, he changed the subject. "Why don't you direct feature films?"

She chuckled ruefully. "Oh, I'm not cut out for that end of the business. I've done a few commercials and a handful of music videos, but feature films don't hold any appeal for me. They're much too structured."

"What do you mean?"

"A movie is built around a script, so it has an inherent structure that you really can't stray from. A documentary is entirely different, though. Like yours, for example. I'll go to Oklahoma and record whatever happens, then turn it into a film."

"You make it sound so simple."

She grinned at him. "It is when you compare it to a feature. It's a far more spontaneous process."

"And that's what you like about it, isn't it? The spontaneity."

She nodded and began digging in her purse for her keys when she realized they were only a few steps from her front walk. "I like a small mobile crew, instead of hundreds to manage. I also like the control. On a documentary, I'm the writer, director, cinematographer and editor. Anyway, it's what I do best, so I see no reason to change."

"I certainly can't argue with that," Matt replied.

They turned up the walk just as Teddi found her keys. Matt was close beside her when she stopped on the porch to unlock the door, and she suddenly got that awkward "first date" feeling. She was much too aware of Matt Abernathy as a man.

"Well, what now?" she asked as the second tumbler turned over. She pushed the door open, leaned against the frame and looked up at Matt. She hadn't left any lights on, so only the faint glow of a streetlamp illuminated him. The shadows on his face made him seem mysterious and very sexy. "It's only about eight-thirty. Do you want to shove some more data down my throat, or shall we call it a night?"

Storm data was the last thing on Matt's mind as he looked at Teddi leaning negligently against the doorframe. Her face was tilted up to his, and her bright eyes held a hint of challenge.

Challenging him to do what, though? Did she have any idea what kind of effect she had on him? Matt wondered. Was she being deliberately flirtatious, or was this the way she was with everyone—seemingly open and carefree, vibrant, and more alive than anyone Matt had ever known?

Did she know that he wanted very much to kiss her?

He had to take a step back to keep himself from doing just that. "We'd better call it a night," he said after a long, uncomfortable moment. "I have an early flight tomorrow and you have a lot of packing to do. I will need to get my briefcase, though."

"Come on in." Teddi stepped over the threshold and began turning on lights.

Matt stopped just inside the door. He had forgotten what a mess they'd left earlier. "My God, this room looks like it was hit by a tornado. Did we really do all this?"

"No, I pay a couple of elves to come in every night and destroy the place."

"Let me help you straighten up," he offered, moving to the coffee table.

"It's really not necessary."

"I don't think I have a choice if I want to find my briefcase."

"Oh, it's around here somewhere," she assured him. While Matt collected the papers on the coffee table and returned them to their original file folders, Teddi knelt by the chair opposite him and began stacking the books and scientific journals he'd brought. She found the canvas bag they'd arrived in behind her chair, and eventually the briefcase surfaced.

"I'm going to leave all of this material with you," Matt told her once they'd achieved a semblance of order. "You probably won't have time to study much of it before you arrive in Turner, but it will come in handy later."

"Gee, thanks," she said dryly, and Matt chuckled.

"You're welcome." He dug into a pocket in his briefcase and produced a hand-drawn map. "Here, you'll need this. Instructions on how to get to Turner from Oklahoma City. The Westwind Motor Lodge is on the southern end of town. You can't miss it. And directions to the tornado research center are on the back."

Teddi accepted the map. "Thanks."

They were kneeling on opposite sides of the coffee table, and neither of them made an effort to rise. "You've been a good sport about all this work, Teddi. I appreciate it."

"Hey, it's my job," she replied with a shrug.

"And I appreciated the tour of Venice."

She grinned at him. "No extra charge."

He nodded through a long pause. "Well, then...I guess I'll see you at the center on Thursday."

"I'll be there."

"My home number and office number are on the map. If you have any questions or problems, just give me a call."

"Don't worry, I will."

Another pause stretched between them, and Teddi finally stood up. Matt followed suit, snapping his briefcase closed as he rose. Teddi escorted him to the door, where he stopped and looked at her.

He didn't want to leave. Matt knew it, and Teddi knew it. He was trying to decide if it was appropriate to kiss her; Teddi knew that, too. She also knew that she didn't want him to leave and she did want him to kiss her. Despite all her efforts to ignore the attraction between them, he made her feel good. So good, in fact, that he was almost as scary as his tornadoes. That was why she'd been keeping him at arm's length all day.

If she'd been anyone but Teddi O'Brien, that fact might have made her take a step back and close the door. But she *was* Teddi O'Brien, and she didn't back down from anything. Instead, she took a step toward him.

"What the hell," she muttered, taking the briefcase out of his hand and setting it on the floor at their feet. When she looked up at him again, Matt was grinning. "We might as well get this over with."

She took another step toward him and Matt slipped his arms around her waist. "You make it sound so romantic."

"Romance has *nothing* to do with this, Matt," she murmured as she lifted her face to his.

He brought his lips a heartbeat away from hers. "You don't think so?"

"Shut up and kiss me," she whispered.

His lips closed over hers, and sparks sizzled up and down Teddi's spine. When his tongue brushed hers lightly, Teddi wrapped her arms around his shoulders and wove one hand into his hair, encouraging him to deepen the kiss. He understood the gesture and complied. His lips slanted across hers and he probed deeper, with Teddi meeting him touch for touch, sigh for sigh.

They strained feverishly to get closer as the kiss intensified. Matt's hands clutched at her waist, fitting her body snugly against his, then one hand slid down her thigh. Teddi groaned and arched into him as a wave of dizzying heat spread through her and finally centered in the core of her womanhood. It was the most powerful feeling of arousal Teddi had ever experienced, and she realized she'd never wanted this much this quickly from any man.

Giving in to that need would have been as easy as breathing.

When the kiss finally ended with Matt reluctantly dragging his lips from hers, Teddi slipped out of his arms and took a step back. Breathless and aching, she leaned against the doorframe and watched as Matt mirrored her position on the other side. He never took his eyes from her face, and his look was as sensuous as his touch had been.

"That may have been a mistake," Teddi said breathlessly. Her breasts were tingling, and she wished he'd reach out and caress them.

Matt grinned at her, but his eyes were still dark with the passion they'd just uncovered. "You think so, huh?"

Teddi nodded. "I'm pretty sure of it."

"You want to try again just to be absolutely certain?"

A laugh bubbled in her throat. "We'd better not. You have a plane to catch."

"Not till morning."

Teddi caught her lower lip between her teeth, then let it go. She could still taste Matt. That made it a lot harder to tell him, "Sorry, but I don't fix breakfast on the first date."

"Ah, but this wasn't a date," he reminded her.

"I know. It was *supposed* to be business."

Matt shook his head. "Teddi, we're going to have a very hard time remembering that. Especially now."

She certainly couldn't argue the point. Kissing Matt had been playing with fire—something Teddi excelled at. She just hadn't counted on getting singed in the process.

Fighting the urge to get even closer to the blaze, she pushed away from the doorframe and picked up his briefcase. "Say good-night, Matt. I'll see you on Thursday."

His hand closed over hers on the handle. She didn't pull away or allow her eyes to leave his face. "Will we continue this...discussion then?" he asked.

"I don't know," Teddi replied honestly. "It could be very dangerous for both of us."

"Ah, but you and I both thrive on danger."

She nodded. "That's the problem in a nutshell."

"It's only a problem if we let it become one." His hand remained on hers, and the briefcase still dangled between them. Matt pulled it slowly toward his body, bringing Teddi along with it. Her head was angled up to his, and he pressed the merest hint of a kiss to her lips.

When he raised his head, Teddi let him have possession of the briefcase and stepped back. "Good night, Matt."

He nodded reluctantly. "Good night."

With considerable difficulty, he moved onto the porch and down the walk, resisting the urge to look back at her. When he finally gave up fighting and turned, Teddi had already closed the door.

MATT TOSSED THE LAST of his clothes into the suitcase and closed the lid. Except for his shaving kit, the suit he'd wear on the plane tomorrow and the bathrobe he had on, he was all packed and it wasn't even ten o'clock. Now what?

Too restless to sleep, he turned on the TV, flipped

through the channels and switched it off again when nothing captured his attention. He looked around the impersonal motel room. In his briefcase he had notes for a journal article he was supposed to be writing, but diving into his paper on computer-generated mathematical tornado models didn't hold any appeal at the moment. Nor did the paperback novel he'd picked up at the airport in Oklahoma City five days ago.

Nothing, it seemed, was going to take his mind off Teddi O'Brien and the kiss they'd shared. An icy-cold shower hadn't helped, but if he didn't wipe out the memory of that kiss soon, he might try the remedy again.

Wishing he knew what the hell was going on, Matt threw himself onto the bed and stared at the dark television screen. He'd never had such intense feelings for any woman. It just wasn't like him to go overboard this way.

Am I star struck? he wondered. Would that explain his outrageous attraction to a woman he barely knew? Teddi wasn't a movie star and she wasn't famous by most accepted standards, but she was certainly bigger than life, as well as a celebrity that Matt had been anxious to meet. In fact, he had built her up in his mind so much that he'd been crushed when she hadn't met his expectations. Then she'd done an about-face, convinced him to hire her for his documentary and spent a full day keeping him tied in knots as he tried to figure her out.

But the sparks between them had been genuine. Matt was certain of that. It was probably because they were a lot alike in so many ways. He wouldn't go so far as to call them kindred souls, but there had definitely been something special at work between them, something that simmered just beneath the surface. And when they had kissed, that something had broken the surface and exploded.

So what do I do about it? was the next question, and it

was a doozie. It had only been one kiss, after all—filled with promise and overloaded with passion, but just a kiss, nevertheless.

Logic told him to expect nothing, but his body was in complete disagreement. Teddi had claimed not to like mixing business with pleasure—then she'd kissed him. Was the next move his, or should he be a gentleman and wait for Teddi to set the pace? When he saw her again, would she pretend it hadn't happened, or open the door for a repeat performance?

Matt came up with a lot of similar questions before he finally drifted off to sleep, but ultimately he realized that where Teddi O'Brien was concerned, there was only one logical answer.

He should expect nothing, and be ready for anything.

THE NEXT DAY Matt returned to the Center for Tornado Research and spent most of the afternoon answering questions about his week in Hollywood. No, he hadn't seen any movie stars or visited John Wayne's footprints in front of the Chinese Theater. Yes, he had hired T. D. O'Brien. Most of his friends and colleagues who'd been in on the planning of the documentary knew that Teddi had been his first choice for director; they knew this because he'd forced them all to watch at least one of her adventure films.

His enthusiasm had been contagious and his praise of Teddi generous. Everyone was now anxiously awaiting her arrival—Matt most of all. This season was shaping up to be one of the most active storm seasons in recent years. Winter in Texas and Oklahoma had been unusually wet and warm; in the northern states, it had been dry, with temperatures below normal. As the jet stream began edging its way north those disparate weather patterns would come into conflict, creating some spectacular storms. In fact, the short-range forecast showed that one was already brewing. With any luck, Chase One would see its first good storm of the season by the weekend.

There was a ton of paperwork waiting for Matt, but it was late afternoon before he had a chance to address any of it. Chasing tornadoes was just a small part of his job at CTR. Most of his time was spent analyzing weather data, conducting lab research, creating computer models of weather patterns and supervising the research of other meteorologists. It kept him busy—particularly during storm season.

Wanting to catch up with everything before Teddi arrived on Thursday, he closed his door and asked the receptionist to hold his calls, but apparently he wasn't meant to get any work done today. He'd barely started opening his mail when someone knocked on his door.

"Come in," he said patiently, tossing his letter opener aside with a flourish.

Laura Cochran poked her head cautiously through a crack in the door. "Hi there, stranger. Can you spare a minute for a long lost friend?"

Matt laughed as he moved around the desk to welcome her. "I didn't know you'd been lost, and it hasn't been that long. Come on in." He gathered her into his arms for a friendly hug, then escorted her to a chair. "I was going to call you tonight to tell you about my trip."

"That's good to know. I thought you'd forgotten all about me."

Matt could tell she was joking by the teasing light in her clear blue eyes. Laura had been one of his best friends since their days in college when she, Joe and Matt had been the three musketeers of the University of Oklahoma. Joe and Matt had competed for the affection of the attractive blond coed, but Joe had won hands down. Matt hadn't minded being best man at their wedding, and he'd been honored when they'd made him their son's godfather.

Joe was gone now, but the commitment Matt had made to his friend's family would last a lifetime.

"What brings you down from the big city? I'm sure it wasn't just to give me a hard time," he said as he returned to his desk. Laura lived up in Norman, where she divided her time between running a catering business and working on the county Disaster Planning Commission.

"Actually, I have three reasons for being here," she told him, digging into her briefcase. She pulled out two files and handed one to Matt. "First, I want you to look over the final draft of the new Tornado Safety brochure. If you've got any suggestions, I'll need to hear them before the commission meets next Wednesday."

Matt glanced through the file, then placed it on top of the stack of other work he had to plow through this week. "I'll have a list of comments to you by Monday," he promised.

"I'd really appreciate it. You've already done so much work on it I feel a little guilty about asking for more."

"It's no problem," he assured her. "And besides, you're going to repay me by giving us a very informative interview on safety planning for the documentary, right?"

She rolled her eyes. "Only if I absolutely have to. The last time someone interviewed me on TV, I looked like a beached whale."

"You did not," he argued. "And you're not getting out of the interview. Next item?" he said before she could continue her protest.

She opened the second file. "We have to discuss the menu for your party Saturday night." When Matt groaned, Laura gave him a impish grin. "I knew you'd like that."

"Just do what you usually do," he told her. Every year

he hosted a party for all the visiting meteorologists and CTR staff to celebrate the beginning of the storm season. Laura hated the party—or at least the reason for it—but she catered it for him, anyway.

"That's what you always say, Matt, but you forget that I have to know a few little details. Like how many to plan for?"

"Right." He reached for a pen and did some quick calculations on a notepad. The center was expecting twelve visiting meteorologists and five amateur storm chasers who always arranged their vacations around the tornado season. Fifteen CTR staffers plus spouses and a couple of professors from the university brought the total to forty. Not all of them would come, but he gave Laura that number just to be on the safe side.

She shook her head. "This thing gets bigger every year. If you're going to keep it up, Matt, you need to think about changing it to an afternoon barbecue," she said as she made notes. "As it is, I'll have to set some tables and lawn torches off the back deck. You can't possibly accommodate that many in the house."

"Whatever you think best."

"What about the movie people? Did you include them?"

Matt couldn't believe he'd forgotten about Teddi. He hadn't thought that was possible, because he hadn't been able to get her out of his mind since he'd left her house last night. "Oops, make that forty-three."

Laura revised her note and closed the file. "And that brings me to my third reason for being here. What happened in Hollywood? Did you see—"

"—any movie stars?" He finished the question with a chuckle. "No, I didn't. I tried to make a date with Kathleen Turner, but she was otherwise engaged."

"That's too bad," Laura said dryly. "Did you at least get to meet that director you were so hot for?"

She meant that in the professional sense of course, but to Matt the comment had a double meaning. "Uh, yes. Teddi O'Brien. We got off to a rocky start, but she finally agreed to direct. She's going to be great."

"What do you mean a rocky start?" Laura asked, and Matt explained the circumstances and disastrous results of their first meeting. He also told her about Teddi's change of heart and their marathon work session. He left out the part about their good-night kiss, but Laura knew him well enough to read between the lines.

"You like her, don't you?" she said with a knowing smile, which Matt chose to ignore.

"Of course I do. She's a very talented filmmaker."

"That's not what I mean," Laura said patiently. "Is she young and attractive?"

Matt sighed. Obviously Laura wasn't going to let him off the hook. "She's about thirty-five and gorgeous."

"Is she equally attracted to you?"

"I think so. With Teddi, it's a little hard to tell. I've never met anyone quite like her before."

"Well, for you, that's a pretty big enticement in itself. Just watch out, okay? I don't want to have to mop up the mess if some glamour puss breaks your heart," she said with a teasing grin.

"Teddi's not exactly glamorous," Matt countered.

Laura's eyebrows went up questioningly. "But she *could* break your heart?"

Matt chuckled. "Lord, I hope not. I've done a pretty good job of avoiding that possibility for a long time now."

"Maybe too long," Laura replied, growing serious. "Isn't it about time you settled down, Matt?"

Uh-oh. He'd walked very neatly into that trap. With a

heavy sigh, Matt leaned back in his chair. "By 'settle down' do you mean get married and have kids, or give up tornado chasing?"

"Both," she said firmly. "I know you want a wife and family, Matt, but you can't have them and your insane career, too. No woman could live with the kind of chances you take. It's just too cruel."

It had taken Matt a long time to reach that same conclusion, but over the years he had come to agree with her. He'd seen what Joe's death had done to Laura, and he knew in his heart it wouldn't be fair to subject any woman to the uncertainty and fear Laura had suffered while Joe was alive—or the devastating loneliness she'd endured after his death.

But Matt couldn't imagine giving up his career. He'd seriously considered it only once, but even then he hadn't been abandoning his career out of love.

"Laura, my work is a part of me. You know that better than anyone," he said finally. "I could no more change what I do than I could change the color of my eyes or my shoe size."

"Not even for someone you love?"

Matt shook his head. "Not even then." He gave her a gentle smile. "Why don't we table this discussion for some other time?" he suggested.

"You can't avoid the truth forever," she insisted.

"But it's your truth, Laura, not mine. You've got it in your head that tornado chasing is one step away from inevitable death. I understand why you feel that way, but it's not true."

"Yes, it is! You just don't want to believe it," she said hotly, then calmed herself. "I don't want to have to bury you, too, Matt. You mean too much to me, and I've already had enough grief to last a lifetime."

"I am not going to die, Laura," he said slowly and succinctly, putting emphasis on every word. "At least, not in a chase and not anytime soon."

She looked at him, her eyes glazed with sadness. "That's what Joe used to tell me," she said quietly.

"Laura, I'm not Joe," he reminded her gently.

"No, but you have that same insane desire to live on the edge that he had," she countered. "You love to chase storms *because* of the danger, not in spite of it."

He couldn't deny that, but he'd had about all he could take of this dissection of his personality and his career. Instead of arguing, he gave her a teasing grin and threw her a bone that he hoped would distract her. "Well, if that's true, then Teddi O'Brien is the perfect woman for me. Some of the things she does make tornado chasing look tame by comparison."

"Oh, great," Laura said, rolling her eyes. "Just what you need—someone to feed your lust for danger."

Matt wiggled his eyebrows comically. "That's not the lust she feeds."

Laura laughed in spite of herself. "I can't wait to meet her. If she's anything like you, I may throttle you both just to save the world from a couple of lunatics."

That's better, Matt thought with relief, grateful that Laura's sense of humor had been restored. "You'll have a chance to meet her at the party Saturday, and you'll like her, I promise."

"If you don't mind, I'll reserve that judgment for myself. And speaking of the party—" she returned her files to the briefcase "—I'll be at your place about two o'clock Saturday to start setting up."

Matt was relieved that she was preparing to leave. "Do you need me to drive up to Norman and give you a hand with the tables and torches?"

Laura stood. "No, the tables are already in the van, and I'll try to shanghai Corey into helping with the rest. Just do me one favor."

"What?" Matt asked as he came around the desk.

"Tell my son that if he doesn't help set up, he can't come to the party. These days you have a lot more influence over him than I do."

There was a time when Laura could have said that and meant it as a joke, but she wasn't teasing now. She and her twenty-one-year-old son were having big problems, and Matt was caught squarely in the middle. "I'll tell him," he promised. "I expect he'll drop by my office after he finishes classes this afternoon."

"Naturally," she said tersely.

"Corey *does* work here, Laura."

"Don't remind me."

Matt stopped with her at the door. "Did you two have another fight while I was gone?"

She sighed heavily. "No. Just more of the same. I have a charming, personable son who can hardly stand to be in the same room with me. If he could afford grad school *and* an apartment, he'd move out of the house in a flash."

"He'll get over it, Laura," Matt said without much conviction.

She shook her head sadly. "Not until I give in or he decides that what I want doesn't matter. Either way I'm going to lose him."

Over the years, Laura had retained the girlishly pretty face of her youth, but when she talked about Corey she looked a lot older than her forty-one years.

"It'll all work out for the best," he said lamely, because he didn't know what else to say.

She looked up at him with sad blue eyes. "Yes, but your idea of what's best has nothing to do with mine. You don't see anything wrong with my son wanting to follow in his father's footsteps.'' She stretched up on her toes to kiss Matt's cheek. "I'll see you Saturday.''

"Bye, Laura. And thanks.''

She took off down the hall, and only a good friend like Matt would have noticed that her step didn't have its usual buoyancy. He ached for her, but he had no idea how to help her. He'd already done everything he could.

In fact, he sometimes wondered if he'd done too much.

CHAPTER FIVE

TURNER, OKLAHOMA, wasn't much more than a wide spot in the road. Situated thirty-five miles south and slightly east of Oklahoma City, the little town was expected to someday become a bustling suburb of the ever-expanding state capital, but as near as Teddi could tell, urbanization was still a few years away. According to the sign at the city limits, Turner had 2,367 residents, and they were all quite proud of their annual Frontier Days Rodeo and Wild West Show, if the gigantic billboard she passed on her way into town was any indication.

On the main drag of the small business district she spotted a midsize supermarket and a restaurant called the Chat 'n Chew. There was also a variety store, a hardware store, several clothing shops, a used-car lot and the usual assortment of professional establishments: a medical clinic, dentist's office and one law firm.

All in all, it took less than five minutes to drive from the northern city-limit sign to the shiny silver water tower that stood near the southern boundary.

"Get used to it, Teddi-girl. This is going to be your home away from home for the next two months," she murmured as she took another look at the directions Matt had given her three days ago.

After he'd left her Monday night, Teddi had started packing with all the efficiency of someone who'd been through the same drill a hundred times. The next morning she had picked up the editing equipment Patrick Dennison had rented and taken care of a dozen little details that had to be attended to before she could leave home for two months.

The incredibly busy day had been a relief, because it had kept Teddi from thinking too much about her encounter with Matt the night before. But yesterday at dawn she'd climbed behind the wheel of her Bronco and set out on the long drive across Arizona, New Mexico and Texas. With nothing to do but navigate the boring interstate, she'd had too much time to think.

Had it been a mistake to kiss him? she'd wondered a dozen times. Had she led him to expect something that wasn't going to happen? Or *was* it going to happen? Did she even want an intimate relationship with Matt?

Obviously she did, or she wouldn't have kissed him at all. Teddi had always been a creature of the moment, impulsive to a fault. Usually her instincts were good, and if she made mistakes she accepted them and didn't look back.

That included all her relationships, romantic or otherwise. Plunging headlong into the uncharted waters of romance didn't bother her in the least. In fact, she rather enjoyed it, and it had been a long time since she'd even thought about falling in love. But did she want to become involved with a tornado chaser? Teddi liked an element of danger in her relationships, but this bordered on suicidal.

Ultimately, she had no idea what to do about Matt, but somewhere in New Mexico she'd decided she was looking forward to figuring it out. She certainly hadn't forgotten what it had been like to kiss him, and speculating on what it would be like to do more had been deliciously tantalizing.

All that speculating had had a very positive result. Primarily, it had helped Teddi avoid thinking about what was in store for her in the coming weeks. Intellectually, she had resolved to conquer her fear, but she hadn't even begun to confront it emotionally.

It had started to catch up with her about halfway across Texas, though. A feeling of unease and an odd sensation of detachment had grown more profound with every mile she covered. She'd spent a restless night in a motel on the Texas-Oklahoma border and crossed into her home state this morning at dawn for the first time in twenty years.

She hadn't seen an Oklahoma sky since the day every resident of Dry Creek had turned out for the mass funeral for the twenty-seven victims of a killer tornado. Three of those graves had held the most important people in Teddi's life, but all she'd been able to think about was leaving the pain and devastation of her shattered life behind. She had climbed on a plane to Anaheim, California, where her only aunt was waiting for her, and had spent the next twenty years doing her best to forget.

Now, she was back. There was a hard knot in her stomach, but it still didn't seem real. She couldn't possibly be in Oklahoma—but she was, and there was no escaping it. The best she could do was avoid thinking about it.

A quarter of a mile past the Turner water tower she spotted the Westwind Motor Lodge exactly where Matt had told her it would be. Journey's end—almost. The motel was old, an obvious holdover from the time before the interstate had left Turner high and dry, but it was well kept. The neon sign out front boasted a pool, cable TV, kitchenettes and no vacancies.

That surprised Teddi. The Frontier Days Rodeo was in June, according to the sign north of town, so what monumental event now in tiny little Turner could have prompted sell-out crowds in the town's only motel?

Tornado season, of course, she realized as she pulled into the parking lot. The Center for Tornado Research was less than three miles away. At this time of year it served as a magnet for dozens of lunatics who chased tornadoes for a living or as a hobby.

She whipped her bright red Bronco into a vacant parking space near the office, shut off the engine and took a deep breath. "Welcome to the Westwind Motor Lodge and Insane Asylum," she muttered.

If I can joke about it, it mustn't be that bad, she told herself.

Grabbing her suitcase-size purse, she jumped out of the Bronco and checked the sky for the hundredth time that morning. It was a transparent, nearly cloudless blue, but she found no comfort in that. She knew how quickly blue skies could give way to roaring black death. It was only ten o'clock, but already it was hot and humid. Just the kind of weather that lunatics like Matt Abernathy probably prayed for.

"Good, Teddi, that's good. You're being very objective. I'm sure Matt would be delighted to know what a wonderful opinion you have of him."

"You talkin' to me, lady?"

Startled, Teddi glanced toward the office and saw an old man in a chair just outside the door. What little hair he had was completely white, and his thin face was a network of deeply tanned lines and wrinkles. His sharp blue eyes were studying her with undisguised suspicion.

She flashed him a hundred-watt smile that contained a hint of sheepishness. "No, sir. I was talking to myself."

"That's a mighty bad habit."

"But it's one I can't seem to break. Are you the manager here?"

The old man nodded. "Manager and owner. Gus Hanley's the name. You must be T. D. O'Brien."

Teddi was surprised. "That's right. How did you know?"

He gestured toward her Bronco. "California license plates. The freeway's only a couple of miles away, but the Westwind don't get too much business since they built that fancy motel right on the exit. This time of year I get mostly tornado nuts, and you're about the only one who ain't checked in yet."

Teddi chuckled as she closed the door of the Bronco and leaned against it. Obviously she wasn't the only person in Oklahoma who thought that chasing tornadoes for a living was a screwy occupation. "How many nuts do you have staying here?"

"We got eighteen rooms and they're all booked up through June. 'Course, not all of the weather people stay the full season, but as soon as one of 'em leaves another one arrives." His eyes squinted as he studied her. "Accordin' to my reservation list, you're here for the long haul, ain't that right?"

"That's right. I'm directing a documentary about a chase team."

"I know. Two guys with a whole truckload of movie cameras checked in day before yesterday." He said it as though it was a common occurrence—which perhaps it was. Matt's documentary certainly wasn't the first that had ever been made on the subject.

"That would be Bryce Lowell and Griff Vandover."

"Yep."

Teddi glanced around the parking lot but didn't see Griff's blue mini-van. "What rooms are they in?"

"Fifteen and sixteen, around on the back side," Gus told her. "They been askin' about you, too."

Teddi frowned. "Too? Who else has been asking about me?"

Gus hitched his thumb in a general southerly direction. "Matt Abernathy. He's called up from the center three times already this mornin'. You're a mighty popular gal."

Teddi grinned, pleased to know that Matt was anxious to see her. "Then I'd better get checked in and let him know I've arrived," she said, pushing away from the Bronco.

Gus sighed heavily and began the laborious process of rising. He muttered something about "damned arthritis," and Teddi resisted the urge to give him a hand. She followed him slowly into the office and waited while he shuffled around the front desk. He gave her a card to fill out and handed her a key. "You're in number ten, down on the northeast corner," he told her. "Best room in the motel."

Teddi looked at him in surprise. She had expected adequate accommodations, but she hadn't imagined that Matt would arrange anything special for her. "Really? What makes it better than the others?"

Gus cracked a mischievous smile that splintered his craggy face into even more lines and wrinkles. "The northeast corner. Most tornadoes come in from the southwest, and that makes room ten the safest place to be at this time of year."

Teddi felt her heart skip a beat. "Do you get many in Turner?" Amazingly, her voice sounded normal.

"The Westwind has been hit twice in the last thirty years," he said as though it was something to be proud of. And maybe it was, Teddi realized. He'd weathered two tornadoes and survived. "The first was in '61—that was a monster, lemme tell you. Damn near leveled the whole town. Then a little fella whipped right through here six years ago and took the roof off the south end."

A mental picture of the scene he described flashed into

Teddi's head and she repressed a shudder. "Why do you keep rebuilding?"

Gus shrugged. "This motel is all I got to leave to my kids and my grandkids. Why shouldn't I rebuild?"

"No reason, I guess," she said, but her voice didn't sound quite so normal now. Striving for a nonchalance she scarcely felt, Teddi tossed her room key into the air and caught it. "Thanks for the safe room, Mr. Hanley."

It was only a short drive to Teddi's "safe" room at the end of the building. She backed the Bronco into the parking slot in front of it and began unloading her belongings.

There wasn't much to unload, though Teddi felt she'd packed extravagantly. Two suitcases held her clothes, and since she wasn't much of a gourmet cook, one small box had everything she'd need for the kitchenette. The spacious cargo area of the Bronco was still full when she finally shut the door, but it was all equipment that would be unloaded at the Center for Tornado Research, where Matt was setting up a work space for her.

She unlocked the door and was pleased to find that her new quarters were going to suit her just fine. The double bed on the left wall had a firm mattress, and near the front of the room was a small sitting area with a love seat and chair clustered around an old color TV. The bathroom door was to the right, and the kitchenette in back had a two-burner stove, a small refrigerator and four cabinets—two above the sink and two below.

For someone who was accustomed to spending months at a time living out of tents in remote parts of the world, it felt like the Taj Mahal.

"Where do ya want these bags, ma'am?"

Teddi whirled at the sound of the gruff voice and found an old friend leaning against the doorjamb, his muscular frame silhouetted by the bright sunlight. Smiling happily, she propped her hands on her hips and looked him over from top to toe—all six feet of him. "Well, as I live and breathe, if it isn't my favorite cameraman!"

Bryce Lowell grinned as he stepped into the room. "Awe, shucks, ma'am, I bet you say that to all the cinematographers."

"Only the ones who look as good as you," she replied. Bryce opened his arms and Teddi happily stepped into them, giving him a big hug. "It's good to see you, Bryce."

"Same here, Teddi." He stepped back and smiled down at her. "You look great."

"Thanks. So do you." And he did. The cameraman was nearing forty, but that was impossible to tell from the way he was aging. There wasn't a single hint of gray in the long dark hair that he wore pulled back into a ponytail, and regular workouts kept his big, rawboned physique from becoming paunchy. His broad face was tanned to a perfect bronze that made his blue eyes more vivid than anyone's eyes had a right to be.

He was a handsome man, and he was one of Teddi's best friends. At one time, they'd toyed with the idea of making their relationship more than that, but a romance had never really materialized. "So where's Griff?" she asked.

"Outside in the van. We were on our way to the center when we saw your car."

Teddi feigned shock. "You were going to the center without your fearless leader? Now that's what I call loyalty."

"Hey, we stopped for you, didn't we? And I'll even play valet." He stepped to the door and picked up Teddi's suitcases. "Where do you want these?"

"On the bed." She retrieved the box of kitchen supplies. "Did you and Griff go by the center yesterday?"

"Yep. Dr. Abernathy gave us the grand tour."

"What did you think of the place?"

"Pretty impressive. Everyone seems eager to cooperate with us."

"Good." Teddi dumped the box next to the sink. "What did you think of Dr. Abernathy?" she asked a little too casually as she turned.

"He seems like a nice guy." A couple of frown lines creased Bryce's tanned face. "Why? What do you think of him?" he asked with a touch of suspicion.

Teddi feigned all the innocence she could muster. It wasn't much. "Same as you. Nice guy."

Bryce nodded slowly. "I see."

He packed the simple comment with so much innuendo that Teddi couldn't let it pass. "What does that mean?"

He feigned a little innocence of his own. "Nothing. Just 'I see.'"

Teddi put her hands on her hips and pretended to be irritated with him. "Okay, wise guy. I know what you're thinking."

Bryce grinned at her and shook his head. "I'm thinking exactly what you wanted me to think, sweetheart. Otherwise you wouldn't have asked the question. You're about as subtle as a Mack truck. So, is this a serious relationship?"

She sighed impatiently. "I've known him less than a week, Bryce. That's hardly enough time to get serious."

"Oh, it's more than enough time once you've made up your mind, Teddi. I've seen you in action before. I've just never been on the receiving end."

She shrugged. "You had your chance and you let it pass you by."

"And I survived very nicely."

Teddi chuckled. "Well, I guess that puts me in my place.

And here I thought I was this incredible femme fatale who'd reduced hundreds of hearts to cinders and ashes.''

"Don't flatter yourself," he said. "Your ego is outrageous enough as it is."

"Thanks." She picked up her purse and breezed past him. "Come on, let's go. Dr. Abernathy doesn't know I've arrived yet, and he's been calling for me this morning. I need to let him know I'm here, and I want to get the editing room set up this afternoon. Tomorrow we'll get started on some preliminary interviews."

She moved outside and Bryce followed her. "I wouldn't count on doing any interviews just yet."

She closed the door and looked at him, squinting against the bright sunlight. "Why not?"

"Because I talked to Abernathy this morning, and he's deliriously happy about something called a dry line. He seems pretty positive that we'll chase tomorrow afternoon."

Teddi's heart slammed into her ribs. *So soon?*

It took everything she had to force a bright smile as she fished her sunglasses out of her purse. "Then we'd better get a move on, hadn't we, cowboy? We've got a lot to do to get ready."

"Whatever you say, boss," Bryce answered as he followed her into the parking lot.

THERE WAS NOTHING OMINOUS about the Center for Tornado Research except that it sat squarely in the middle of nowhere—an isolated island of buildings, parking lots and manicured lawns surrounded by flat, cultivated fields that stretched to infinity. The center was a sprawling two-story structure, but it didn't dominate the island. That privilege was left to the huge white geodesic dome that sat on the western edge of the property. Nearly forty feet tall, it rested on a circular, windowless black base.

The dome was fifty yards from the parking lot where Teddi was standing, but she still felt dwarfed by it.

"Looks like a giant whiffle ball, doesn't it?" Griff Vandover said as he climbed out of the van.

Teddi turned and looked at him from across the hood of her Bronco. "Yeah, but I sure wouldn't want to see the bat that goes with it," she replied with a grin for the other member of her crew. Griff was short and stocky, with a weathered face that showed every one of his fifty years. He could be irascible at times, but he was one of the best assistants Teddi had ever had. "I assume that's the Doppler radar station."

"That's right, boss," Bryce said as he appeared from behind the van. "They say it's so sensitive it can detect a swarm of insects a hundred miles away."

"Great. That ought to come in handy when the killer bees arrive."

Bryce chuckled. "I don't think it can get quite that specific." He patted the van. "You want the cameras for this, Teddi?"

"I don't think so," she replied thoughtfully. "I want to get the lay of the land before we start filming. You might want to take some preliminary light readings, though, Griff. We'll have to do a number of setups in the center eventually."

"Right." He disappeared around the van. When he came back he had a bulky equipment bag hanging over one shoulder.

With her crew flanking her like sturdy bookends, Teddi started across the parking lot. She noticed immediately that vehicles with out-of-state license plates outnumbered Oklahoma vehicles almost two to one.

They were still a dozen yards from the glassed-in lobby when a young man bounded out the door, smiling and waving. He was tall and slender, with a shock of corn-silk hair clipped fashionably close over his ears but left long on top so that it bounced on his forehead as he jogged toward them. "Teddi O'Brien?" he called out enthusiastically.

"That's right."

"Hi! I'm Corey Cochran." He approached with his hand outstretched and Teddi accepted the welcome. "I'm one of Dr. Abernathy's interns. Welcome to the center."

"Thanks." She gestured to the men flanking her. "Have you met my crew yet?"

He grinned at both men in turn. "Nope. I wasn't here yesterday when they arrived. I always seem to miss the good stuff."

"This is Bryce Lowell, who does second camera, and this is Griff Vandover who does everything else—lights, sound, third camera, everything."

Corey shook hands with them, then gestured toward the building. "Come on in. Matt's expecting you. He called the Westwind a few minutes ago, and Gus told him you'd already come and gone. He figured you were on your way here."

"Are you the official greeter?" Teddi asked.

He nodded. "Greeter and tour guide, at your service," he replied with a comical bow. "Matt's out back in the maintenance garage. One of the antennae on the chase van is acting up, and he's pretending he knows how to fix it."

Teddi laughed. Obviously there was a healthy camaraderie between Matt and his subordinates. "That I'd like to see."

"Come on, then. I'll take you to him and give you a quick tour of the center on the way."

"Have you been working with Dr. Abernathy long?" Teddi asked as they started for the building again.

"This is only my first year as a grad assistant, but I've known Matt all my life. He's the best tornado researcher in the country."

His glowing assessment sounded highly subjective to Teddi, but she wouldn't have dreamed of disputing it. "Bryce told me Matt plans to chase tomorrow," Teddi said conversationally. "Will this equipment problem force him to cancel?"

"Not likely," Corey replied with a chuckle. "We've got so many hot spots shaping up that Matt will chase even if he has to do it on foot."

"Hot spots?"

"The most likely areas for tornado activity."

"Of course."

Corey held the door open for them, and Teddi stepped into the lobby. It was a small room with a vacant reception desk to one side and a few chairs scattered along the walls. What captured Teddi's attention, though, were the enormous poster-size photographs that dominated the room—photographs of tornadoes.

Reminding herself sternly that they were only pictures, Teddi moved to the center of the room and forced herself to scan the walls with a dispassionate eye. What she saw chilled her to the bone. It was like being surrounded by death.

"Spectacular, aren't they?" Corey asked as he slipped through the door behind Teddi and the others. "Matt took most of them."

"Really?" Teddi said, striving for nonchalance. She must have failed, because Bryce glanced at her curiously. She edged away from him, and forced her attention back to the photographs. "No two...storms are the same."

"That's right. Matt says that every tornado has a personality all its own." Corey gestured toward a remarkably vivid photo that showed a perfectly formed wide black funnel against a brilliant blue-and-white background. "That one is his favorite."

"Photograph?" she asked hopefully.

Corey chuckled and moved to the wall. "No, his favorite tornado. He took this picture just moments after it touched down in a wheat field. And this one..." He pointed to the next poster, which showed a long, lonely stretch of highway framed by telephone poles and power lines. The tornado was a narrow white tube that connected the highway to the dark sky above it. "This one was taken about five minutes later as the tornado crossed the road in front of him. That bright flash you see right there isn't lightning, it's sparks from a power transformer."

He stepped to the next photograph. "And this last one was taken just minutes later as it roped out."

"Roped out?" Griff questioned.

"That's usually the last stage of a really good tornado. It's rotating so fast that it starts collapsing in on itself—tightening up like a spring that's being wound. It starts to lose power and stability, so it ropes out." He traced the curving line of a dark gray coil that snaked from sky to ground like the letter "S" turned backward.

Bryce joined Corey at the wall. "So these three are all of the same tornado?"

"Yes. They're so different because they were taken at three different stages, and from different directions. In the first one, Matt was facing west with the tornado coming toward him. When it started getting close, he drove south about a mile and took the other two, one looking north and the last one east. That's why it's dark in the first one and light in the others."

Teddi suppressed a shudder. "Were you with him when this happened?"

"No, but I wish I had been," he replied with obvious envy. "These were taken nearly ten years ago. But you don't see many storms like this one even when you've been chasing as long as Matt."

Another lunatic, Teddi thought, but kept the observation to herself. "How many…of these things have you seen?"

Corey's smile faded. "Only one, when I was about six."

Teddi frowned. "You're not a storm chaser? But I thought you said…"

"I'm not a member of Chase One," he said tightly. "I'm sorry if I gave you the impression I was."

"No, no," Teddi said hurriedly, wondering what lurked behind Corey's sudden change of mood. "It's my fault. When Dr. Abernathy briefed me in L.A., he said he had a couple of grad students on Chase One, so I just assumed you were one of them."

"I am a grad student from the University of Oklahoma up in Norman, but I'm just a data assistant. I help Matt and the others analyze the information they collect. It's fascinating work."

And I hate every minute of it, his look said, even if his words didn't. Teddi sensed more than just lack of job satisfaction behind Corey's attitude, but probing an obviously sensitive issue wasn't her job. Besides, she would undoubtedly find out eventually. In the next two months she expected to come to know quite a lot about Matt Abernathy and the people he worked with.

"We'd better move on," Corey said, casting a quick glance down a corridor that led deep into the bowels of the building. "Matt will be wondering where you are."

"Lead on." Teddi fell in behind him and found Bryce

at her elbow. She tensed when he leaned toward her solicitously.

"Are you okay?" he whispered.

"Sure. I'm fine," she replied, hoping she sounded as though she meant it. "Why wouldn't I be?"

"I don't know. You were just acting a little...strange."

Teddi managed an impish grin. "And you find that unusual?"

Bryce didn't respond to her attempt at humor. "Frankly, yes. I don't think I've ever seen you this tense. What's going on, Teddi?"

"Nothing," she insisted as she started after Corey and Griff. "Come on. Let's catch up before we get lost."

"Okay," he murmured, falling into step with her.

But he was still darting curious glances at her as they moved down the hall, and Teddi realized she was going to have to do a lot better job of hiding her feelings. If she didn't, it wouldn't be long before everyone learned that Teddi O'Brien had lost her entire family to a tornado—and that just saying the word scared her to death.

CHAPTER SIX

COREY'S TOUR TOOK THEM through a warren of corridors, past offices and rooms filled with equipment Teddi couldn't begin to identify. In the center of the building they passed a huge, glass walled room. In the middle of the room was a modular control panel inset with radar screens and computer monitors. Along one wall computers spewed out information, and on another a gigantic map of North America flashed with rainbow splotches of color.

It looked very high tech to Teddi. "Is this a branch office of NASA?" she asked facetiously, and Corey grinned at her.

"Close, but not quite. Although we do call it Mission Control. This is the Central Information Network, where we collect data from satellites and weather stations around the country. We also monitor the Doppler radar from here. During a storm chase, the teams stay in touch with Mission Control to keep abreast of where a storm is heating up."

Teddi glanced at Griff and he nodded. Years of working together made it unnecessary for her to ask him to assess the lighting in the room. She asked with a look, he answered with a nod. Before the day was over, Griff would know exactly what it would take to film in there.

They left Mission Control and a moment later Corey led them out of the air-conditioned building into a cavernous garage where the air was stifling and the smell of stale oil almost overpowering. Light flooded through the open garage doors behind three CTR vehicles: a station wagon, a pickup truck and a large van. All three were tan-colored, and the closest one to Teddi—the station wagon—had a tornado stenciled on the door. She suspected the other two did, as well.

"Matt?" Corey called out as he moved into the garage.

"Over here."

The familiar voice drew Teddi's gaze up to the roof of the long, snub-nosed van. Matt was nestled precariously in the midst of a network of wires, boxes, antennae and a small satellite dish. He poked his head over the edge of the roof and grinned down at them. "Hi, there." The greeting encompassed them all, but a second later his gaze settled on Teddi and his smile was for her alone. So was the warmth in his voice. "Welcome to Oklahoma."

"Thanks." Teddi returned his smile in full measure, and her pulse accelerated. "Are you practicing to be a hood ornament?"

He nodded. "How am I doing?"

"I can see we're going to be spending a lot of time cleaning the bugs off your teeth."

Matt grimaced. "Yuck."

"What's your problem up there?" she asked as she stepped to the rear end of the van where a ladder led to the roof.

Matt tapped a screwdriver against the base of the satellite dish. "Our communication antennae won't oscillate. The wiring checks out fine, but it still refuses to turn smoothly."

Teddi went up two rungs of the ladder until she could see Matt fully, stretched out across the van with his legs dangling off the other side. Her close-up view made it clear that the roof had been reinforced to withstand the weight of the equipment. "Can you fix it yourself, or would you like some expert assistance?"

"Are you mechanically inclined?"

Griff and Bryce both hooted with laughter, and Teddi shot them a look that didn't bode well for their continued health. "No, but I've got a crew who think they know everything—and one of them actually does. If it's mechanical or electronic, Griff can fix it."

Matt glanced at Griff. "At this point, I'd appreciate anything you can do. Chase One is usually self-sufficient, but the team member who handles equipment maintenance and repair has been called away on a family emergency. I don't expect him back until Monday." He looked at Teddi and explained, "His wife, Mona, picked a lousy time to have her baby."

Teddi chuckled. "Your sentimentality is overwhelming."

Matt grinned at her. "Around here family planning means no deliveries during tornado season."

"Let me take a look at it," Griff offered. He stepped to the end of the van while Teddi climbed down. It took Matt a little longer to extricate himself from the maze on the roof, but a moment later he was standing beside Teddi and Griff was on the ladder.

Matt dropped one hand onto his graduate assistant's shoulder. "Corey, why don't you climb into the van and fire up the scanner," he suggested. "Get Griff anything he needs while I talk to Ms. O'Brien."

"Whatever you say, Matt," he replied as he hopped to obey. The look the young man gave his boss said he would have agreed to jump off the building if Matt had asked him to. Obviously Corey had a first-class case of hero worship.

Bryce shot a quick, speculative glance from Teddi to Matt, then followed the young grad student. "I'll join you, Corey. I want to get a closer look at the equipment." The van jostled back and forth as Griff crawled across the roof, then it jolted again as his erstwhile assistants crawled into the side cargo bay.

"Alone at last," Matt said, turning to Teddi. "How was your trip? Did you find the Westwind with no trouble?"

"The trip was fine and the motel was right where you said it would be."

"I hope the accommodations are satisfactory."

"The room is positively palatial compared to some of the places I've stayed," she assured him.

"Good. I'm really glad you're here, Teddi."

She knew he wasn't speaking in strictly professional terms, but that was something they could explore later. At the moment, it seemed best to concentrate on the business at hand. "I can understand why," she replied lightly. "Bryce told me there's a good chance you'll chase tomorrow."

"That's right." He looked genuinely apologetic. "I hate to throw you into the lion's den before you've even had a chance to catch your breath, but conditions are shaping up perfectly for—"

Teddi held up a hand to stop him. "Please don't apologize. I came here to work, and I'd rather get my feet wet quickly than wade in a little at a time. My only regret is that I haven't had more time to plow through the rest of the briefing materials you left with me."

"Don't worry about it. You'll be getting plenty of on-the-job training. We'll consider tomorrow a dry run."

"Unless it rains." Teddi grinned at him and he grinned back. He had such an incredible smile. But she had too many more important things to think about. She had expected to have a few days at least to get to know Matt's team and how they operated before she actually had to film them in action. Now she had less than twenty-four hours. "All right, let's get down to business."

"What do you need to know?" he asked, understanding her need to fill in the enormous gaps in her knowledge.

Teddi thought back to her briefing in L.A. three days ago and tried to remember what he'd told her. "You chase with four team members in the van and two in the truck, right?"

Matt shook his head. "Normally, yes, but we'll only have three in the van with Tom Patten out. We've cleared an area for you in the back of the van, and I thought we'd put Bryce in the Deploy truck. Ryan Sawyer can ride with Griff. That way, your people will have someone with them who can explain what's happening. Does that sound reasonable?"

She nodded. "How do we keep in touch with the other vehicles while we're on the road? CB radio?"

"That's right. And we have a cellular phone in the van that keeps us in touch with Mission Control, which is—"

"I know. The big glass room inside the center. Corey showed it to us on our way through."

"Okay. What else?"

One by one, Teddi fired off questions until Griff got the antennae operating smoothly. With that minor crisis averted, Teddi's crew joined the makeshift briefing.

"Matt, I heard something yesterday about a deploy team we're supposed to film," Bryce said. "What's that going to entail?"

Matt moved across the garage toward the pickup, and everyone followed him. "The deploy team is in charge of this," he said, indicating a bright yellow barrel with wires and gizmos sticking out of its lid. "This is Toto II—a second-generation Totable Tornado Observatory. Once we've tracked down a storm, we project the most likely path the tornado will follow. We get Toto II as close to the anticipated strike zone as possible, wheel it out of the truck and get the hell out of there. If we're lucky, the tornado will strike close enough to give us data we couldn't hope to obtain otherwise.''

Bryce jumped into the back of the pickup to inspect the device. "How often do you get lucky?''

Matt chuckled. "Not often enough. Toto II has been built to withstand a direct hit, but so far all we've had are a few close swipes.''

"Then how do you justify the risk?'' Teddi asked. She heard Griff suppressing a snort of laughter, and she realized how absurd the question sounded coming from her, but she didn't back down. "I mean, deploying this thing in the path of a tornado has to be very dangerous.'' Teddi was proud of having said the T-word without tripping over it, but of course no one else realized she'd achieved a small victory.

"The deploy maneuver is dangerous,'' Matt conceded. "In fact, everything about tornado chasing has an element of danger about it, but my team members understand the risks involved, and we all believe it's worth it. Nearly everything we know about tornadoes today has come from observations made by storm chasers.''

"That's right,'' Corey said, leaping to Matt's defense. "You see, Doppler radar wasn't much more than a bunch of colors on a screen until meteorologists like Matt and my father were able to compare their on-site observations with the readings taken at the center.''

Teddi appreciated the explanation, but she found the personal tidbit even more interesting. "Your father is a meteorologist, too? He must be very proud to have you following in his footsteps.''

The young man's face fell, and he cast a quick glance at Matt. "My father died when I was seven.''

Without even thinking about it, Matt placed a comforting, protective hand on Corey's shoulder. "Joe was killed during a chase,'' he explained.

Teddi looked from one to the other and realized that what she'd sensed in Corey wasn't hero worship. It went much deeper than that. Suddenly she remembered Matt's confession that he had lost his best friend to a tornado, and the relationship between the young man and his mentor fell into place.

"I'm sorry," she said, her glance encompassing both of them, because it was a grief they shared. And one she understood only too well.

"It's okay," Corey replied. "You had no way of knowing."

Teddi's gaze settled on Matt, and he realized she had pieced together what she'd just learned with what he'd told her in L.A. He acknowledged her assumption with an almost imperceptible nod, then changed the subject. "Well, any more questions?"

Bryce was the first to pick up the invitation. "I want to know how you actually find a tornado to chase."

"That's the trickiest part of all," Matt told him. "As you'll soon discover, this isn't an exact science."

"Yet," Corey said. "That's all going to change this season."

"What's so special about this season?" Teddi asked.

"Matt's going to prove his theory and completely revolutionize tornado research," the young man announced proudly.

Matt had to laugh. "And after that, I'm going to walk on water, find a solution to world hunger and clean up the environment single-handedly."

"What is this theory of yours?" Teddi asked. "I ran across several references to it in Pat Dennison's notes, but I didn't have time to explore it."

"Basically, it's a very complicated mathematical formula that predicts which storms will spin out a tornado." Matt stepped to the van, ducked through the open cargo doors and returned a moment later with a sleek black box about eighteen inches square. He flipped the lid open to reveal a small instrument panel and handed the device to Teddi.

Instantly, Bryce was peering over her shoulder from the bed of the truck and Griff was at her side. "It looks like something out of a science-fiction movie," Teddi commented as she studied the small monitor, keypad and gauges housed inside. "How does it work?"

Matt reached over and flipped a panel on the upright edge of the lid and an umbrella-shaped antennae unfolded. "This is Pandora, a portable Doppler radar scanner with a dedicated computer on board. It's designed to be used in direct contact with a storm to predict a tornado fifteen to twenty minutes before it actually spins out."

"How accurate is it?" Bryce asked.

"I don't know," Matt replied. "That's what I'm hoping to learn this season. We ran some preliminary tests with it at the end of last season, but it failed miserably. Of course, it didn't help any that we had almost no tornadoes to test it on. Last year was a relatively quiet season."

"I don't mean to be dense, Matt, but if the device only works when you're in contact with a storm, what's the point?" Teddi asked, handing Pandora back to him.

Matt took her skepticism in stride. "As our technology stands right now, standard Doppler radar can only tell us if a storm *might* spin out a tornado or let us know if one is actually on the ground somewhere. But if Pandora is accurate, we'll be able to issue warnings far enough in advance to give people plenty of time to seek adequate shelter. That could reduce the number of lives lost from a few hundred a year to only a handful."

Teddi certainly couldn't argue with the importance of that, but Matt still hadn't answered her original question.

"That's wonderful as far as it goes, but my point is that you still have to be in actual contact with a specific storm to use Pandora."

Bryce nodded. "I see what she's getting at. How can you possibly cover every storm that breaks out across the country?"

"It's not as difficult as it might seem," Matt replied. "Nearly every community in the midwestern section of the country has a group of volunteer storm watchers. When a tornado watch is announced, spotters are sent to key locations to observe and report in if a tornado develops. If Pandora works, the first thing we'll do is equip each community with one." Matt disappeared into the van to stow the box, but his voice could still be heard. "Of course, there are other long-range plans in development—if it works— but that's our immediate goal."

He popped out of the van again and smiled. "Any more questions?"

"Just one," Teddi said. "What if it doesn't work?"

Matt's smile faded, and it was a moment before he answered. "If it doesn't work, I lose my research grant and the project gets scrapped. You see, Teddi, it's taken me five years to get this far, and my time has run out. For me, this chase season is all or nothing."

Teddi nodded thoughtfully. "So, in addition to filming your storm chases, we're also going to be recording your success or your failure." That was something he hadn't mentioned in L.A.

"That's right."

The filmmaker in Teddi found that idea very exciting; it added yet another layer to the dimensions of the documentary. Not only would she have to capture the tension inherent in the chase, but she would also have to find a way to convey the stakes involved as they pertained both to the public at large and to Matt Abernathy personally. Executing a film with that many layers was the kind of creative challenge she enjoyed most.

"You're taking a big risk," she warned him. "No one wants to have his failure recorded for posterity."

But Matt shook his head. "I'm not worried about that, Teddi. Even if Pandora fails, this documentary can still save lives. That's all I care about." He shrugged off his serious mood. "And that concludes today's lecture, ladies and gentlemen. Thank you all for your kind attention." He bowed, and they gave him a polite smattering of applause. "Now, shall we get down to work? I've got a room cleared for you, if you want to get your editing equipment unloaded."

Teddi nodded. "Good. I'd like to be set up before we chase tomorrow."

"And I have some equipment that needs to be stowed, too," Griff added.

"Why don't you bring the vehicles around to the garage," Matt suggested. "It'll be closer than carrying it through the lobby."

"Okay." Teddi fished her keys out of her pocket, but Bryce plucked them from her hand. When she looked at him quizzically she found him smiling at her.

"Allow me," he said gallantly. "You go check out the room, boss."

"Thanks."

"Don't let it go to your head."

"Oh, I won't," she retorted. "I know better than to expect subservience from you."

Matt watched their friendly exchange and tried not to frown. His curiosity about Teddi's relationship with Bryce had grown by leaps and bounds yesterday after he'd met the irritatingly handsome cinematographer. Lowell seemed like a really nice guy, but that hadn't alleviated any of

Matt's unwanted feelings toward him. It had been a long time since he'd experienced jealousy, and he didn't like it.

"Corey, why don't you give them a hand," he suggested, and the three of them headed back into the center.

Teddi turned to Matt as the others left, and she was surprised to find the merest hint of a scowl on his face. "What's wrong?"

"Nothing," he said hastily, forcing a smile. "I've just got a lot on my mind. There's a lot to do to get ready for the chase."

Teddi didn't believe him for a minute. "Matt, are you irritated by what I said earlier? I didn't mean to sound like I was questioning the importance of your work."

It took him a moment to figure out what she was referring to. "No, Teddi, not at all. You were just asking questions about safety that any normal, sane individual would ask."

Teddi wasn't positive, but she thought this was the first time anyone had ever applied those adjectives to her. She didn't want to challenge his assessment, though. Instead, she wanted to know where the tension she sensed in him had come from. "Then what's really wrong?"

Matt sighed deeply. "I was just speculating on your relationship with Bryce Lowell," he admitted reluctantly.

"He's my favorite cinematographer," she told him.

"And that's all?"

Teddi frowned. "He's also a good friend, if that's what you're getting at."

"Yeah, I guess it is," he replied, feeling like a total idiot. One passionate, unforgettable kiss gave him no right to question Teddi's relationship with another man. "It's just that you mentioned taking a vacation with him, and I thought..."

Teddi finally caught on and smiled. "We're not a couple,

Matt. I swear. We're just good friends who happen to have quite a bit in common.''

His relief was completely out of proportion to what he should have been feeling. Where Teddi was concerned, though, ''should'' didn't mean much. The feelings were there whether he wanted them or not. ''Actually, it's none of my business. I shouldn't even have asked.''

''Oh, I don't know,'' she replied lightly. ''I think I made it your business when I kissed you in L.A. I wouldn't have done that if I'd been involved with another man.'' She grinned. ''Just to keep the record straight, what about you?''

He feigned shock. ''Am I involved with another man? Certainly not.''

Teddi chuckled. ''I wasn't questioning your sexual preferences. That seemed pretty obvious when we kissed,'' she told him, her eyes darkening at the enticing memory. ''I meant are you dating another *woman*.''

Matt was totally entranced by the memory of the kiss, too—and had an overwhelming desire to recreate the event. ''I am, as the old saying goes, a one-woman man, Teddi. And it's been a while since I exercised that sexual preference you referred to.''

''It's been a while for me, too,'' she said with a slow nod. ''Maybe that's why there seems to be so much chemistry between us.''

''I hope not. I'd like to think there's a lot more to it than that.''

He was such a tantalizing combination of sincere and sexy that Teddi couldn't help but agree with him. Any idea she'd had about resisting a romantic liaison with him seemed like nothing more than wishful thinking. ''I should probably warn you that I have a lousy track record with relationships,'' she said wistfully.

"That can change."

"I wouldn't count on it if I were you," she warned him.

Matt accepted the challenge with a smile. "Let's not buy trouble before it's up for sale, okay?"

She answered his smile with her sparkling eyes. "All right. Instead, why don't you buy me dinner tonight?"

Matt laughed. "Good Lord! Don't you ever let the man do anything?"

"I don't believe in that sexist nonsense." She looked at him speculatively. "What's the matter, can't your masculine ego take the competition?"

"Now who's being sexist?"

"All right," she said, folding her hands demurely in front of her. "You do the asking."

Matt bit back another laugh. A demure Teddi was about as authentic as a three-dollar bill. He wasn't going to deny her request, though. "My dear Miss—pardon me, *Ms.*— O'Brien, would you do me the honor of joining me for dinner this evening?"

"Why, Doc-ta Abernathy, Ah'd be delighted," she drawled. "What time should Ah expect you to call for me?"

"Would seven-thirty be convenient?"

She inclined her head to one side and batted her eyelashes coquettishly. "Why, that would be just lovely. I have a purr-fectly charmin' new dress Ah think will just knock your little ole socks off."

Matt finally cracked the smile that had been building inside him. "All right, I surrender," he said, chuckling. "Why don't you pick me up, open all the doors and pay for dinner?"

Teddi shook her head and dropped the Southern belle impersonation. "Not on your life, fella. You don't get off the hook that easily. I'll expect you at seven-thirty."

"And I'll expect that new dress." He gestured gallantly toward the center. "Now, shall we get some work done in the meantime?"

Teddi's eyes widened. "Work? We're here to work?"

He pointed firmly to the door. "Get in there."

"Yes, sir!" she said with a brisk salute, and they both dissolved into laughter.

CHAPTER SEVEN

MATT PICKED UP Teddi at seven-thirty as promised, but he didn't take her out to dinner. Instead, he ushered her to his home on the outskirts of town, where Teddi found an elegant table setting for two awaiting them on the deck that ran the length of his sprawling ranch-style house. He lit candles in hurricane chimneys to protect the flames from the evening breeze and served a delicious ragout with salad and freshly baked rolls.

It was the perfect romantic setting. His house sat at the end of a lane and was surrounded by sheltering shade trees that gave him absolute privacy. As they made their way through dinner, Teddi learned a lot about her host, and everything she discovered attracted her to him even more. He read science fiction and murder mysteries. He liked camping and river rafting in the summer; in the winter, he always spent a week skiing in Colorado. He was still very close to his brothers and their families in Kansas, but he hadn't spent many holidays there since his parents had passed away. He was obsessed with his work and deeply committed to making it count for something important.

By the time they finished eating, it was fully dark and the sky was twinkling with stars. Teddi found that the candlelight, moonlight and Matt made for a very potent combination, indeed.

"Okay, Teddi. It's your turn," Matt said.

She looked at him questioningly as she sipped her wine. "My turn for what?"

"To talk," he replied. "You've been worming little secrets out of me all night. Now I get to ask some questions."

"Such as?" she asked, trying very hard not to put her guard up. She wanted to share things with Matt. It felt right to let him know her. But there were still a lot of things she just didn't know how to share.

Fortunately he didn't start with anything too difficult. "What made Teddi O'Brien such a daredevil?"

"Oh, I was born that way," she assured him. "I can't remember a time when my parents weren't yelling at me for some crazy stunt I'd pulled."

Matt grinned. "Like what?"

Teddi thought about it. "I once rigged one of my mother's bed sheets and her clothesline into a parachute and jumped off the roof of the house."

Matt laughed. "You're kidding? What happened?"

"I got grounded for a month."

"You didn't break any bones?"

Teddi shook her head. "That's one of the reasons I believe in miracles."

Matt leaned forward, resting his elbows on the table. "What else did you do?"

She shrugged. "You name it. If it was stupid or dangerous, I did it."

"Why?"

"I don't know. I guess I've always had a need to push the limits, just to see how far I can go."

"You must have given your parents a lot of premature gray hairs."

Teddi reached for her glass and took another sip of wine to cover her sudden discomfort. "They didn't know what to think about me, and our neighbors were convinced I was a Martian who'd been dropped in their midst by an alien spaceship.''

"Where are your parents now? Still living in California?''

"No. They died some time ago.''

"I'm sorry.''

Teddi shrugged. "One of the earliest lessons I learned is that there's nothing you can do to keep from losing the people you love.''

"But it's a hard lesson to learn, isn't it?'' Matt asked quietly.

"Yes, it is,'' she said as she folded her napkin and laid it aside. When she looked up at him, she gave him a bright smile. "Matt, that was a wonderful meal, but now I feel guilty.''

He let the subject of her family drop. "Why?''

"You actually cooked a dinner with all the trimmings— great food, tablecloth, candles, fine wine. All you got at my place was beer and a peanut-butter sandwich for lunch.''

"I was just trying to prove to you that I'm not sexist,'' he said with a grin.

"No, you were trying to prove you're a better cook than I am,'' she accused him lightly. "Now I'll have to cook for you just to keep us even.''

Matt chuckled. "I'm not keeping score, Teddi.''

"I am.''

He studied her speculatively, reveling in the delicious exhilaration that was humming through him. Teddi looked absolutely stunning. She wore a bolero jacket over a strapless dress that clung to her like a second skin, outlining every magnificent curve of her body. Her hair hung loose around her shoulders, as silky and rich as the dark burgundy color of her dress, and her eyes sparkled like emeralds in the candlelight. He'd never wanted a woman as much as he wanted her.

"What's wrong?" Teddi asked when he didn't comment. "Have I dribbled wine down my dress?"

"I was just thinking how competitive you are," Matt said because a lie seemed safer than the truth. For the moment.

"Does that surprise you?"

"Not at all."

"Then you accept my right to a rematch?"

Matt chuckled. "Teddi, you can cook for me anytime. I'll even donate my kitchen, just to be fair, because your resources at the Westwind are limited."

Teddi saluted him with her glass. "A true gentleman, through and through. Now, tell me the truth. How did you find time to do all this? We didn't leave the center until after five."

"Actually, the only thing I made myself was the salad. All the rest came out of the freezer courtesy of my good fairy," he confessed.

"You have a good fairy? I'm jealous."

Matt picked up the wine bottle and Teddi held out her glass. He divided the last of the wine between them as he told her, "Laura Cochran runs a small catering business up in Norman, and I get the fallout whenever she tries a new recipe."

"All guinea pigs should be so lucky. I guess it's Laura I should be challenging to a cook-off," she joked. "Is she Corey's mother?"

Matt nodded. "She's an incredible lady. She runs a business, works on the county Disaster Planning Commission and still manages to find the time to stock my freezer with goodies."

"Those are the best kinds of friends to have," Teddi

said lightly, then sobered as she thought about her conversation with Corey this afternoon. "Matt, the friend you mentioned to me in L.A.—the one who was killed?"

He nodded again. "That was Laura's husband, Joe. The three of us were best friends in college."

"You've obviously stayed close to the family."

"Very close." Matt hesitated a moment, because he didn't want to spoil the mood he'd worked so hard to create. At the moment, Teddi was the only thing he wanted to think about. He wanted to get to know her better, to understand who she was and what made her so special. But in order to do that, he knew he was going to have to let her get to know him better, too. That meant talking about things he would rather avoid.

"I'm Corey's godfather," he said finally. "After Joe died, Laura, Corey and I sort of closed ranks. We supported each other through the worst of it."

"They were lucky to have you," Teddi said, thinking about her own loss and the terrible loneliness she'd endured.

"We were lucky to have each other," he corrected her. "Joe's death took a lot out of us all."

Teddi hesitated a moment. "You said he died during a chase."

"That's right."

She took a sip of wine, trying to ignore the chill that settled at the base of her spine. "Were you with him?"

"No. He was alone."

When Matt didn't elaborate, Teddi wanted to question him further, but she quelled the impulse. If he didn't want to talk about it, she was the last person in the world who would push him. There were too many things in her own life she didn't like talking about. "How does Laura feel about Corey becoming a meteorologist?"

"About how you'd expect, considering the circumstances. She doesn't mind him being a meteorologist as long as he doesn't become a storm chaser."

"But that's exactly what Corey wants, isn't it?" Teddi asked, remembering the young man's reaction to her assumption that he was a member of Chase One.

"How did you know that?"

Teddi recounted her brief conversation with Corey in the lobby of the center. "It seemed pretty clear he wasn't entirely satisfied with being a data assistant."

"You're right. He wants to chase, but so far, Laura has managed to keep him off the road. I don't know how much longer that's going to last, though," he said sadly, then drained the last of his wine. "It's created a lot of problems for them."

"I can imagine."

Matt forced a smile and pushed away from the table. "Let me get us another bottle of wine."

"No, none for me," she said hastily. "I'd prefer a cup of coffee, if you have it."

"No problem. I'll be right back."

Teddi watched him go, wishing she hadn't broached the subject of Joe Cochran. The conversation had definitely cast a pall over the evening. Yet she couldn't deny she was intrigued by Corey Cochran's situation. He'd lost his father to a tornado, but that hadn't prevented him from entering the same profession. Teddi, on the other hand, had simply buried her fear and spent twenty years running away. She sympathized with Laura Cochran, but she also felt a lot of admiration for the woman's son.

She wasn't going to press Matt for more information about them, though. The evening had been too delightful to risk spoiling it with depressing conversations.

Determined to keep things light from here on out, Teddi

picked up their dinner plates and took them into the house. She found Matt in the kitchen spooning coffee into a coffeemaker.

"I'm afraid your host has fallen down on the job," he told her sheepishly as she set the dishes beside the sink. "He forgot to put the coffee on before dinner."

Teddi feigned exasperation. "Well, that does it. I'm going home."

He grinned at her. "Oh, no you're not. The night is still young and we haven't even had dessert."

"I couldn't eat another bite," she swore, then paused a moment. "What is it?"

"Chocolate cheesecake."

Teddi groaned. "Chocolate. My greatest weakness."

"Why don't we save it for later?"

"All right." Teddi took the pot from the coffeemaker and filled it with water. "You know, Matt, I've got to tell you I'm really surprised by your house."

He frowned and leaned against the counter. "What's wrong with my house?"

"Not a thing. It's lovely," she said quickly. "It's just not what I expected. Three bedrooms, family room, two-car garage, a picnic table and barbecue pit in the backyard... There's even a basketball hoop out there. This is a family man's home."

She had him there. "That's because I anticipated having a family at the time I bought it," he admitted reluctantly, then added, "A ready-made family, that is."

Teddi thought that over and came to the logical conclusion. Unfortunately it brought her right back to the topic she'd just decided to avoid. "Laura and Corey Cochran?"

Matt was surprised by her insight, but he knew he shouldn't have been. Teddi was amazingly perceptive. "Yes," he said with a nod. "I bought this place about twelve years ago from a doctor who decided he could make a better living in the city. At the time, I was trying to be a father to Corey and a friend to Laura. It just seemed like a foregone conclusion that we would end up together.''

"What happened?"

He shrugged and took the pot of water out of her hands. "There were too many obstacles standing between us."

"Like your career?"

"That was a big one, yes," he admitted, pouring the water into the top of the coffeemaker. "Laura couldn't handle the fear and insecurity."

"That's understandable, I guess," Teddi said, although she had a hard time imagining feeling that way herself. Considering the risks she took with her own life, it would have been hypocritical of her to reject a man because he had a dangerous profession. In fact, she'd made it a point never to become involved with a man who couldn't understand or cope with her own hazardous life-style.

Of course she'd never been involved with a man who chased tornadoes for a living. That was an entirely different matter—one Teddi didn't want to think about because she was on the verge of being very involved with Matt.

"I offered to quit chasing," he told her, pulling Teddi's thoughts away from the irony of her own situation. "I even gave it up for a season."

She winced. "Ooh, big mistake. I hope you learned you can't change who and what you are just to make someone else happy."

Matt smiled at her. "I learned that the hard way—and so did Laura. She's never stopped trying to get me to give up chasing, but she realized that a relationship built totally on sacrifice could never work."

"Smart lady."

"Yeah, she is," he agreed. "I love Laura, but I guess

the real problem was that I've never been *in* love with her. If we'd gotten married, I could have provided stability, love and companionship.''

''But eventually you'd have grown to resent her for what you had to give up.''

''I know. And so did Laura. She deserves better than that.''

''So do you,'' Teddi said.

Matt looked at her. ''Maybe.''

For a fleeting second his eyes were so haunted that Teddi knew she'd touched something Matt usually kept deeply buried. ''Why wouldn't you deserve the kind of relationship that comes with all the trimmings?''

Matt turned the coffeemaker on and cleared his throat. ''This is going to take a few minutes. Why don't we go back to the deck?''

''Only if you'll answer my question,'' she replied tenaciously. ''Why don't you think you deserve to fall in love?''

''That's not what I meant at all,'' he said defensively, hating himself for having spoken without thinking.

''Then what did you mean?''

''Nothing.''

''But you said—''

''Teddi, let it go, okay?''

''No, I won't. You just told me you were willing to marry a woman you didn't love and give up your career for her because you don't deserve anything better.'' She placed one hand on her hip and the other on the counter. ''You even bought a house that's about three times bigger than anything you could possibly need. Why?''

''I told you. I really thought Laura and I would get married someday.''

''Well, I can't say I blame her for refusing you.''

Matt's frown turned to a full-fledged scowl. "What does that mean?"

Teddi knew guilt when she saw it, and at the moment, it was written all over Matt—from the harsh lines of his face to the rigid set of his body. "You sound as though you were offering yourself up as a sacrificial lamb. What is it you thought you had to atone for, Matt?"

He took a step back, wondering angrily how he'd gotten himself into this mess. Teddi was too damned perceptive for her own good—or his.

So much for their quiet, romantic evening.

"I blame myself for Joe's death," he said quietly after a long moment of grappling with the truth.

Teddi's heart instinctively went out to him, but she didn't understand how he could feel guilty about something he couldn't have controlled. "But you weren't even with him."

"That's the point. I should have been there," he replied, sagging against the counter. "You see, back then, storm chasing wasn't as high tech or as well organized as it is now. We did a lot of chasing on our own time, with damned little equipment to guide us to the storms. Joe called me the day he died and asked me to chase with him, but I had something else to do. I don't even remember what now."

"That still doesn't make it your fault, Matt," she said softly as she reached out and touched his arm.

He looked at her, his eyes filled with regrets. "I shouldn't have let him go alone, Teddi."

"What could you have done to save him?"

He shrugged helplessly. "I don't know, because we don't even know for sure exactly how it happened. There were no witnesses. It looked like he was trying to shoot the core and the tornado just blindsided him."

"Shoot the core?"

"That's what we call going through a storm rather than flanking it," he explained. "Tornadoes form on the rainfree back side of a storm cell, and we always try to get below the storm so that if a tornado drops, we're not in its path. Sometimes we misjudge and get caught in the middle of it, particularly if there's more than one storm cell."

"And that's what happened to Joe?"

"I think so," he replied. "They found his body in his mangled car about a hundred feet from the road. My guess is that he was driving through the rain curtain and couldn't see that he was headed straight into the path of the tornado."

Teddi felt sick to her stomach. She had a very vivid memory of another mangled car, her father's pride and joy. He'd kept it washed and waxed, and had constantly cursed the sap that marred the finish because he had to park it under the trees on Oak Street. The last time Teddi saw that car, it had been sitting obscenely half in, half out of her parent's bedroom.

"I'm really sorry, Matt," she managed to choke out, turning away from him so that he wouldn't see the agony in her eyes. It took her a moment to recover. "But that still doesn't make Joe's death your fault."

"If I'd been with him, I might have seen it coming," Matt argued. "He needed a someone riding shotgun."

"Then he shouldn't have gone alone!" she exclaimed, whirling toward him. "It was a stupid thing to do! Tornadoes kill too many people as it is, without some idiot running around in the rain saying, 'Here I am! Come and get me!'"

She wasn't thinking about Joe Cochran anymore, Matt realized. This was personal. Intensely so. "I'm sorry, Teddi. I forgot you lost someone you cared about, too."

"That's right, but they didn't have a choice. Your friend

did, and it's not fair that you should spend the rest of your life feeling guilty for his mistake."

Matt went to her and gently placed his hands on her shoulders. "Who did you lose, Teddi?"

She pulled away from him, shaking her head. "It's not important."

"Yes, it is."

"I don't want to talk about it, okay?" she said defensively.

"Wait a minute," he said, fighting an irrational burst of anger. "Five minutes ago you were pressing me to talk just because you had a burr under your saddle and wanted some answers. Now that the shoe's on the other foot, you're going to clam up. That's not fair, Teddi."

"Who the hell ever said life is fair?"

"No one, but—"

"Then drop it, okay?"

They glared at each other like contestants in a boxing ring, and Matt realized she wasn't going to give in. "When it comes to stubborn, you've got the market cornered," he said grumpily.

Teddi released the breath she'd been holding, and with it went the knot of anger in her stomach. She even managed a smile. "Our first date and our first quarrel on the same night. That doesn't bode well for the future of this relationship."

Matt couldn't keep himself from responding to her smile. "Actually, it's our second quarrel," he said, thinking of their exchange in the desert. "I lost that one, too."

"Get used to it," she advised him.

Matt's smile disappeared. "I don't understand you, Teddi. I think you're funny, beautiful, gutsy and talented, but I don't understand you."

"And you probably never will," she said, warmed by his assessment of her.

He shook his head and closed the distance between them. "No, you're not *that* big a mystery. You'd like to be, but you're not. You just have very good defenses and an in-grained image of yourself as an outrageous, flamboyant woman of intrigue." He placed his hands on her waist and pulled her even closer, enjoying the way her eyes darkened with anticipation. "Underneath it all, though, there's a little girl who just wants attention."

Teddi raised her eyebrows skeptically. "That's your analysis, Dr. Freud?"

"Yes."

"Well, analyze this while you're at it," she said, fitting her body snugly to his. She wound one arm around his neck and stretched upward, intent on kissing him, but Matt surprised her by leaning away from the kiss rather than toward it.

"Nope, not this time," he said, shaking his head. "This time, I'm going to kiss you, Teddi. This is one situation you're not going to control."

Gently cupping her jaw in one hand while the other remained firmly around her waist, Matt lowered his lips to hers. It was only a whisper of a kiss, a tantalizing brush of lips, but it was enough to ignite a slow-burning fire inside both of them. Teddi arched closer, intent on taking more, but Matt retreated again, then returned. This time, his mouth slanted across hers, and she opened to him, eagerly accepting everything he offered. He kissed her deeply, plundering her mouth, then retreating, only to return again and again, taking a little more with each kiss, building the flame a little higher, until every one of Teddi's senses screamed with the need to be sated.

She moaned breathlessly as she struggled to get closer

to him, and when Matt's hand slid beneath her jacket, forcing it off one shoulder, Teddi eagerly slipped out of it. It fell to the floor as Matt brushed her hair aside and pressed his lips to her throat, then lower. Teddi's head fell back and she moaned again as he worked his incredible magic on her, but she wanted more. His lips on her shoulder weren't enough. His hand pressing her against the hard ridge of his manhood was only an infuriatingly vivid torture. When his other hand slipped between them to cup one of her breasts, Teddi thought she might die of the need for more of him.

Impatient with longing, she wove her hands through his hair and brought his mouth back to hers, telling him with the depth of her kiss exactly what she wanted. She plunged her tongue into his mouth and one hand reached eagerly for the buckle of his belt.

Gasping for air, Matt stilled her hand and wrenched his mouth away from hers. When he looked into her eyes, the naked hunger in them nearly robbed him of thought. "Are you sure, Teddi?" he asked, his voice hoarse with the intensity of his own need.

Her hand was trapped between them, and it took very little to move it just enough to splay her fingers across the bulge in his trousers. "I'm every bit as sure as you are, Matt."

He kissed her again, hard, then grabbed her wrist and pulled her toward the door.

TEDDI THOUGHT she'd died and gone to heaven. She hadn't lied today when she'd told Matt it had been a long time since she'd been involved with a man. Four years to be exact, and a lot of sexual frustration had built up in that length of time.

But frustration had nothing to do with what happened in

Matt's bed, unless she counted the infinite ways he had tortured her by bringing her to the edge of fulfillment, then retreating. He controlled their lovemaking skillfully, manipulating and maneuvering, holding the ultimate gratification just out of her reach until she was ready to scream. It was frenzied and frantic, but when he finally sheathed himself in a condom and pressed into her, Teddi experienced a kind of instantaneous, shuddering explosion of sensation, the likes of which she had never felt before.

And it was only the beginning. By the time Matt groaned with the force of his own release, Teddi was somewhere in the clouds, stunned by the intensity of it all. She didn't want to let go. She didn't want to come back to reality. She didn't want to face the world again, because the world in Matt's arms was safe and secure; a place where she felt cherished, and where she was with a man who understood her and accepted her for what she was.

Having found that, how could anything possibly be the same again?

MATT HAD DRIFTED into a drugged, sated sleep with Teddi in his arms, but when he awoke, she was gone. For a fraction of a second, he wondered if he'd dreamed the whole incredible experience, but then he smelled her perfume on the pillow and sighed with relief. It hadn't been a dream. And how could it have been, anyway? No dream could have accounted for the wonderful way he felt—exhausted and exhilarated, ready to conquer the world.

But where was Teddi?

Reluctantly, Matt slid out of bed and groped for his trousers. It took a minute to find them in the tangle of his clothes and Teddi's in the middle of the floor, but he finally located them and went in search of the woman who should still have been in his bed.

"Teddi?" He checked the bathroom, living room and kitchen. Nothing. He stepped onto the deck and found gutted candles in the hurricane lamps, but no Teddi.

He frowned. Her clothes were still in the bedroom, so she couldn't have gone far. Where was she?

"Teddi?" he called out again, and a moment later a voice answered him.

"Out here."

Matt stepped to the deck rail and peered into the darkness. He finally spotted her lying on his picnic table, wearing nothing more than the shirt she'd eagerly helped him remove earlier. "What are you doing?" he asked as he moved down the stairs and across the lawn.

"Stargazing, of course."

"Of course," he said dryly. "Found anything worth reporting?"

"It's what I can't find that's bugging me," Teddi replied. "Pollux and Castor are missing. I think they've been kidnapped."

He chuckled as he sat on the table and looked to the heavens. He took a moment to get his bearings, but it wasn't long before he was able to solve the mystery. "Aha! Don't call in the FBI just yet. There they are." He pointed to a spot high in the western sky.

Teddi sat up and followed the line of his arm. "Now how did they get up there?" she asked, frowning. She'd been looking in the wrong place entirely.

"You want the mythological answer or the scientific one?"

She shot him an exasperated glance. "Neither, smartypants. If you're such a genius, show me where Camelopardalis is."

"I wouldn't have a clue," he said, pulling her into his

arms. She snuggled against him, and Matt gave her a long, slow kiss. "I missed you when I woke up."

"I couldn't sleep, and I didn't want to wake you with my thrashing around."

Matt captured her gaze in the moonlight. "Are you all right?"

Teddi grinned at him and wove one hand into his hair. "You want a report card? Is that it?" she asked lightly. "You were wonderful."

"No, *we* were wonderful together," he told her.

"Yes, we were."

Matt felt himself becoming lost in the sparkling depths of her eyes. "Do you always do everything with such complete abandon?" he asked quietly.

Teddi nodded. "Are you always so thorough and meticulous?"

He grinned. "It's the scientist in me. They train us to do things slowly and methodically."

She brushed her lips against his. "You must have been a straight-A student. I'd certainly give you high marks in foreplay."

"Thank you. Of course, you realize that the hallmark of any scientific endeavor is research. You have to prove your results over and over again, or the experiment becomes invalid."

Teddi's eyes widened at the possibility. "Oh, we wouldn't want that to happen."

Matt nodded gravely. "It's really terrible when a theorum collapses."

"I imagine it could even be painful."

"Yes, it is."

"Then we must make every effort to prevent that from happening."

His grin was nothing short of devilish. "Wanna start now?"

Teddi thought it over for a moment. "Are you sure your theorum can handle it?"

"Come back inside with me and we'll find out," he said, but when he started to slip off the table, Teddi stopped him. Matt looked at her and found a truly wicked gleam in her eyes. "Here?"

Teddi nodded slowly. "What's the matter, Doctor? I thought you believed in experimentation."

"You're crazy."

"So I've been told," she murmured, teasing his lips as she leaned back, bringing him onto the table with her.

CHAPTER EIGHT

"THAT'S IT, THEN," Matt said, hopping off the table he'd been sitting on. His chase team was clustered around him at the front of the briefing room, and it was clear they were as eager to get started as he was. "We'll head southwest and get into position around Altus. If my projections are correct, that should put us right in the thick of the storm, but we can move into Texas if things start heating up down there. Let's go!"

Someone released a bloodcurdling war whoop as the team trooped out, and Matt laughed at the enthusiastic response. It was always like this just before a chase; adrenaline and expectation flowed freely in everyone, including him. Emotions were heightened by the anticipation of finding the elusive storm that was gathering out there somewhere, waiting for them. For Matt, there was no other feeling like it in the world.

No, that wasn't quite true, he realized as he glanced across the room toward Teddi, who was conferring with her own crew. Making love with her last night had been more exciting than any chase he'd ever conducted, and just thinking about it now left him with a feeling of expectation that far outdistanced the excitement he felt about tracking down the storm that was brewing today.

After all these years, he'd finally found a woman worth holding on to, someone who understood who he was and why he took the chances he took...someone who would support his choices and who wouldn't try to smother him with the weight of her own fears. With Teddi, he could have it all. He didn't plan to let her go.

When she finally glanced at him, Matt flashed her a smile, and Teddi returned it in full measure. It was frustrating for both of them to have to limit their contact to smiles and flirting glances, but they were both too professional to give in to their mutual desire to do more. It was obvious, though, that they both remembered what had happened last night in Matt's bedroom—and outside of it.

The chase team began trooping out, and Teddi gave a nod to Bryce and Griff. They left with the others as Matt moved toward the back of the room.

"Did you follow all that?" he asked, referring to the briefing.

"Only about half," she told him as she picked up her bulky camera from the table. "But it really doesn't matter. You just get us into position and Betsy—" she patted the camera "—and I will do the rest."

"It's a deal." They started toward the door together. "Are you nervous?"

"Who, me?" she asked, all wide-eyed innocence. "I don't get nervous, Matt."

She was only teasing, but Matt sensed that under normal circumstances it was true. It would take a great deal to shake a rock like Teddi O'Brien. Given the way she felt about tornadoes, though, he could believe she might be a little apprehensive today.

"Well, just sit back and enjoy the ride," he advised her. "It's very rare we get lucky enough to spot a tornado on our first chase of the season."

Before Teddi could decide how she felt about that pronouncement, Corey, who hadn't yet left the room, called out to Matt. They stopped just short of the door, and as they turned, Teddi saw Matt tense as though he'd been expecting this—and had really hoped to avoid it.

Corey's posture was rigid, and his jaw was set in hard lines, as though he was steeling himself for something unpleasant. "Can I have a minute?" he asked.

"Sure," Matt said after a moment's hesitation. "Excuse us, will you, Teddi?"

She glanced from the young man to his mentor, wondering what in the world was going on. Corey certainly wasn't the same easygoing young man she'd met yesterday. "No problem," she replied, though she was undeniably curious. "I'll just head on out to the van. See you later, Corey."

He nodded as Teddi took off, but he didn't speak until she'd left the briefing room.

"What's up?" Matt asked.

Corey faced him squarely. "I think you probably know. I want to go with you today."

Matt sighed deeply and shook his head. He'd been afraid of something like this for months, and Tom Patten's absence was just the opening Corey needed. "No, Corey. I'm sorry."

"But this may be my only chance this season. Tom will be back next week, and there won't be room for me."

"Corey, we went through all this months ago. You decided—"

"Well, I was wrong! I've changed my mind!"

"It's too late for that. What would Laura say if I let you chase today?"

"I don't care! I'm not a kid anymore."

Matt ran a hand through his hair. "No, you're not," he agreed. "You're twenty-one and fully capable of making your own decisions."

"Well, I've decided I want to chase."

"I'm sorry, but it doesn't work that way. You had a chance for a slot on Chase One, but you passed it up when you and Laura agreed you wouldn't chase this year. Until you two have worked this thing out, it's not fair to put me in the middle."

Corey glanced down as all the fight drained out of him. "I'm sorry. I didn't mean to do that." He looked up again. "It's just so damned frustrating."

Matt placed both hands on Corey's shoulders, feeling every bit of the young man's frustration. "I know it is. But I've talked to her, you've talked to her... Nothing helps." He dropped his hands to his sides. "It'll kill her if you chase. That's the long and short of it."

Corey looked up hopefully. "She wouldn't have to know. I could go with you today—" The disapproval on Matt's face stopped him cold. "Sorry."

"You should be," Matt replied sternly. "I love you, Corey, and I love Laura, too. I'm not going to do something that would cause her pain."

"I don't want to hurt her, either, Matt."

"Then handle this like a responsible adult, not a sneaky kid," Matt advised him.

Corey took a step back, clearly wounded by the indictment. "I'm sorry, Matt. Forget I asked." He turned brusquely away and Matt stood for a long moment, watching him go.

Corey had so much of his father in him it made Matt ache. He had the same enthusiasm, the same daring, the same commitment. But he also had a mother who couldn't let go of the past. Matt had spent fifteen years trying to be a surrogate father to the boy, and sometimes—like now—he was certain he had failed miserably.

At least for today, though, Matt was confident he'd made the right decision. Letting Corey chase without Laura's knowledge was unthinkable. But eventually something was going to have to give in the relationship between mother and son, and Matt had the feeling things were going to get a whole lot worse before they got better.

THE CHASE ONE VAN would have been spacious if it hadn't been loaded with enough high-tech equipment to launch a space shuttle. Nate Dansing, a CTR staff member, drove the vehicle, and grad-student Olivia Eschavera rode in the middle of the van, glued to a monitor that displayed readings being taken back at the center. Matt divided his time between the passenger seat beside Dansing and the chair opposite Olivia, where the panel that controlled the apparatus on top of the van was housed.

Teddi had been given a space she had immediately dubbed "the rumble seat," a comfortable bucket seat anchored sideways by the rear cargo doors. Her equipment was at her feet, and to her right, she could look out the rear window and wave at Gerry Hampton and Bryce in the deploy truck behind them.

Since they were traveling south, Teddi had an excellent view of the western horizon out of the van windows. Towns were few and far between, and the flat farmland, dotted by the occasional oil derrick, afforded her an almost unrestricted view.

The familiar landscape forced a lot of unwelcome memories on Teddi, and she found herself battling emotions she didn't want to deal with. She was hunting for the very thing that haunted her darkest nightmares, and despite the bravado she'd displayed to Matt, she was scared. The last thing she needed on top of the fear was to be assaulted by memories of her parents, of trips they'd taken down the very same roads she was traveling today. She didn't want to hear her father's baritone and her sister's sweet soprano voice harmonizing to "Michael, Row the Boat Ashore." She didn't want to remember her mother chiding her for her own raucus rendition of "Ninety-nine Bottles of Beer on the Wall."

The last thing Teddi needed to feel today was nostalgic. But she couldn't seem to shake the feeling—or her mounting fear. Oddly enough, the only thing that gave her any respite from that fear was Matt. Every time he looked at her, Teddi felt a tingle of excitement and an indefinable but very intimate kind of connection.

That feeling helped relieve a little of the tension that had her stomach tied in knots, but it wasn't quite enough. She'd have given anything to be able to turn back time to last night when she'd been safe in his arms, secure in the knowledge that nothing could harm her.

For the first two hours on the road, the sky was clear, with only a few cumulus clouds scattered loosely from north to south. Teddi watched them suspiciously, waiting for a sign of the phenomenon Matt had described to her in L.A.

Giants gathering for a town meeting, he had said. At three o'clock, she understood exactly what he meant. The clouds grew into billowing leviathans that bumped into each other and merged into a force to be reckoned with. It was like watching a carefully choreographed, macabre dance.

Teddi found it strange she'd been raised in this part of the country where this phenomenon was a common occurrence, yet she'd never noticed it before. As a child, she had accepted big storms as part of her life, but she'd never paid much attention to the events that preceded them. Maybe it was because she'd lived in town, where trees and buildings had blocked her view. Or maybe she'd just had too many other things to preoccupy her young mind.

But she was paying attention now. The sky overhead was still bright blue, but the horizon was filled with threatening clouds, which were lined up so precisely it seemed as though someone had taken a ruler and drawn a straight line from north to south.

"Matt?" Bending at the waist so she wouldn't bump her head, Teddi rose and stepped over her camera. She held on to the instrument bay to keep her balance as she moved to the sturdy soft-drinks cooler that occupied the space opposite her chair.

He swiveled toward her. "Hi. You getting lonely back there?"

"It's the price I pay for having the best seat in the house," she replied with a grin, then gestured to the west. "Is that what's called a squall line?"

He nodded approvingly. "It's developing into one. You're a very good student." He glanced out the window. "Pretty spectacular, isn't it?"

"You could say that. Is this typical of the way your storms begin?"

"Yes. There's an especially strong 'supercell' building in the middle of it. As soon as we can get off this road, we'll be heading toward it."

Teddi looked at the long squall line. "Where's the supercell?"

"You tell me."

She shot him a vexed glance, but didn't back down from the challenge. She stared at what appeared to be one unbroken line of clouds—dark near the bottom, brilliant white at the top. As she studied the line, she finally saw a pillar of white cloud that seemed to be rising higher than the others. It had to be at least ten miles in diameter. She pointed. "There?"

"Exactly," Matt replied. "Keep your eye on it for the

next hour as it continues to grow. If it develops as it should, it will hit the cap of cold air in the mesosphere and build into a mesocyclone. By then, the whole cell should be dark blue and the top will spread into an anvil.''

"And a tornado will form?''

"Hopefully.''

Teddi cleared her throat and gave him an impish grin. "Why don't you just let me out now and I'll record that process from here?''

Matt laughed. "Because in about an hour the leading edge of the squall line would be right on top of you and you wouldn't see a thing. What we want to do is get south of that big cloud so that we can see the back side. That's where the good stuff will be happening.''

It was Teddi's turn to chuckle. "I just love it when you use all that technical jargon.''

She returned to her chair and watched in awe as Matt's predictions became a reality. Within thirty minutes, Mission Control began reporting that thunderstorms were breaking out sporadically along the one-hundred-mile squall line, and in Teddi's immediate vicinity flashes of lightning lit up the clouds around them.

Matt invited her to join him at his console so that she could see how they tracked the storm, and she was grateful for the distraction. She crouched beside him, wedged between equipment and seats, feeling the level of excitement rising in the van as they lost their observer's perspective of the storm. They became a part of the gathering darkness, the lightning, the occasional patches of rain and the howling wind that bent trees and blew spring-green leaves into their path.

Using a much-creased road map, Matt called out instructions to Nate. They zigzagged south and west, encountering very little traffic on the back roads. Massive black clouds pressed down on the van, and it took every bit of determination Teddi possessed to maintain a semblance of calm.

"Okay, Nate! Here! Pull over as quick as you can," Matt called out urgently. "There it is, Teddi. Do you see it?" he asked, pointing out the window to a distant spot west and slightly north.

"See what?" There was nothing out there but low clouds and empty fields, though Teddi felt a sense of danger she couldn't shake.

"Those wispy fragments descending from the cloud ceiling. Watch closely and you'll see that they're rotating. That's the signature of a mesocyclone."

The van was slowing, and Teddi had to grab Matt's arm to maintain her balance as the vehicle bumped off the pavement. But she saw what he was referring to. About a mile away, gossamer wisps of white had torn away from the body of the storm and were slowly spinning into a wide arc. It wasn't a tornado yet, but it was enough to send Teddi's heart into her throat.

"Okay, Teddi, get your camera ready," Matt instructed, grabbing her arm to steady her as he propelled her back toward the rumble seat. "It's time to go to work!"

You can do this, she told herself firmly, willing her pulse to slow. *You can do it. You can do it.* Crouched on the floor, she slipped into her equipment harness, and by the time she had the cumbersome backpack fastened the van had stopped. Matt was already out the side door, and the other team members were scrambling out of their vehicles.

Teddi's palms were sweating and her hands were shaking as she unlatched the rear door. She jumped out, grabbed her camera and turned just as Bryce trotted up to her. He expected instructions, and Teddi let her years of experience take over. "I'm going to stay on the team members," she told him without preamble. "You stay on that cloud."

"What cloud?" he asked with exasperation, his voice raised above the howling wind. "It all looks the same to me—dark and wet. We're going to get soaked any minute."

Teddi pushed his shoulder, turning him toward the northwest so that she could point out the wisps of rotating clouds Matt had shown her. "Don't take your camera off them," she instructed, then turned to Griff as he ran up. "Get a mini-boom out here and stay on Matt. I want everything he says recorded."

"Done."

Griff ran back to his van and Teddi took off for the field. She jumped a ditch and headed south until she could look back and see all three vehicles in her viewfinder. She zoomed in on Matt as he set up Pandora, and then she got footage of Gerry and Nate releasing a yellow weather balloon.

The storm was to Teddi's left, but she tried to forget about it and concentrate on the chase team. It wasn't easy. The wind plastered her shirt to her back and tore at her braided hair. That kind of distraction was hard to ignore, and so was the frantic pounding of her heart.

She was too far away to hear anything that was being said at the van, which made her feel cut off from the others—and very vulnerable. Gradually, though, the sense of urgency that had driven everyone for the last half hour began to abate. Movements slowed and shoulders drooped. When she saw Matt shake his head and close up his black box, Teddi's pulse rate began to slow. Matt was so clearly disappointed it was obvious the tornado he wanted wasn't going to materialize.

She shut off her camera and headed for the vehicles. Bryce was standing on top of Griff's van, patiently waiting for something exciting to happen, but when he looked back and saw Teddi, he started climbing down.

Teddi approached Matt with her camera still on her shoulder. Griff had positioned himself just inside the chase van so that he would be out of sight during the filming, and Teddi motioned for him to stay where he was. They were here to record every aspect of a chase—including the failures. "What happened?" she asked Matt as soon as she was close enough.

"It..." Matt turned and found himself staring into the blinking red light of the camera.

Teddi held up her right hand. "Look where my hand is, not at the lens, and tell me what's going on."

Matt shifted his gaze a few inches and tried to pretend this was a normal situation for him. "The storm disintegrated. It happens more often than not." He launched into a technical description of the internal structure of a storm and explained how easily the delicate balance of features could be disrupted.

"So this storm isn't going to produce a tornado?" Teddi asked.

"Not within the next hour or so," he replied regretfully. "There's a chance it might reorganize itself, but by then it will be thirty or forty miles east of here and it'll be too dark to chase."

"What about Pandora? Did she work?"

Matt tried not to look as disappointed as he felt. "She indicated that there wasn't enough rotation in the storm to produce a tornado. Unfortunately it won't really prove anything until it accurately predicts a tornado that subsequently develops."

Teddi felt the first pelt of rain on her shoulders, and she shut the camera down. "I'm sorry, Matt. I know you're disappointed."

"Oh, we're used to it. By June you will be, too. This is how ninety percent of our chases end."

That was heartening news to Teddi, but she was ashamed of the deep sense of relief she felt. "What do we do now? Pack up and go home?"

"Not yet," he replied. "We'll check with Mission Control first and see if anything else is heating up in this area."

"Hey, Matt! Come here, quick!" Olivia called from her console inside the van.

"What is it?" He jumped in and his team immediately clustered around the side doors. Teddi held back to keep her camera from being jostled, and all she could do was wait to find out the results of the impromptu powwow. She glanced over the heads in front of her and saw that Griff was still in the van recording, but all she could hear were muffled voices.

Bryce was headed toward her with his camera on his shoulder. "Much ado about nothing, huh?" he said quietly, indicating the threatening clouds overhead.

"Yeah, this supercell dissipated."

"What happens next?"

"I don't know. Matt said he was going to look for another hot spot in the area, but I think Olivia has something interesting on her scanner."

Just then, everyone started scrambling out of the van, including Griff, and Teddi jumped out of the way. Matt ducked his head out the cargo doors.

"Come on! Load up! We're moving out!"

"What's going on?"

"Doppler is showing a hook echo in a cell ten miles south of here."

"A hook echo?" Bryce asked. "What's that?"

"A tornado, my friend," Matt replied. "Load up, Teddi, and keep your camera ready! It's show time!"

Bryce dashed toward the truck, and Teddi barely had time to duck into the rumble seat and slam the door before

Nate had the van moving. He left skid marks and the other vehicles behind as he roared onto the pavement.

Matt was in front, pouring over a road map, and Olivia was glued to the Doppler monitor that displayed their modem link with Mission Control. Rain started peppering the van, and by the time they exchanged a southbound two-lane blacktop for a westbound one, the rain had become a torrential downpour.

Nate switched the CB to the local channel reserved for official tornado spotters, and when he turned up the volume, even Teddi in the back had no trouble hearing the excited, staticky shout that announced a tornado had just touched down a mile north of Manitou.

"That's due south of us," Matt said, his voice raised in excitement. He jammed his finger into a spot on the crumpled road map. "Nate, if we can make it two miles down to County Road Five and double back east, we should be below it." He radioed the same instruction to the vehicles that had fallen behind them, then he slipped between the seats and carefully made his way to his console. He was barely able to maintain his balance against the jostling of the van. "Did you hear all that, Teddi?" he called back to her.

Her throat was too dry to allow her to speak, so she nodded.

"Well, hold on and get ready. We're going to have to shoot the core!"

Teddi flashed him a look of disbelief, but Matt didn't notice. He was too busy with the Doppler monitor and too excited by the prospect of cornering his quarry. He didn't seem the least bit concerned that they were about to execute the very maneuver that had killed his best friend.

But Teddi remembered Matt's description of Joe Cochran's death vividly.

The rain intensified and hail began hammering the van like gunfire. Somewhere ahead of them a tornado was chewing up the earth, and it was completely hidden from them by a dark, shimmering curtain of rain.

Out the back window, hail bounced on the slick black pavement. The red taillights turned the ice crystals into sparkling rubies, and in the distance Teddi could barely make out the pinpoint headlights of the deploy truck. Then without warning, the van skidded around a corner, throwing Teddi out of her seat. From habit, she protected the camera with her body, then wedged herself on her knees between the door and the instrument console. It gave her an unrestricted view of the road behind them.

The road became bumpier, but Nate didn't slow down. They raced along and suddenly the rain and hail stopped. The sky turned a chilling shade of orange, and the quiet was almost deafening.

It didn't last long.

Teddi heard the roar first, like a freight train barreling down a rickety railroad track. She knew the sound. It had haunted her for twenty years, invading her dreams, making her terrified of sleep. But she wasn't dreaming now.

Vaguely, somewhere behind her, she could hear Matt shouting at her, telling her to start shooting, because a hundred yards behind the van a ribbon of death had formed, connecting earth and sky.

Some ingrained instinct forced Teddi to raise her camera to her shoulder, but she could do no more than that. She was frozen—as she'd been frozen that night, a lifetime ago, when only the roar had warned her she was about to die.

This time, she could see it, too.

The tornado bore down on them, eating at the meager distance separating them, and Teddi was suddenly fifteen years old again. Everyone called her Theresa, though she hated the name. She had a mother and father who didn't approve of her rock-music albums, and an older sister who could do no wrong. Cathy was leaving for college in a few weeks, and Teddi couldn't wait to have their bedroom all to herself.

She knew exactly how she would arrange the room and where she would hang the David Bowie posters her parents and sister hated. She had worked all winter at the movie theater concession stand to earn enough money to buy a wild new bedspread and curtains to replace the conventional, frilly pink things Cathy had been allowed to pick out.

Teddi was going to make it *her* room. And *her* room would reflect *her* quirky personality, not her sister's sedate one. And if her parents didn't like the changes she was going to make, well, that was just too bad. She was fifteen; old enough to make a few decisions of her own. She was tired of standing in the shadow of her perfect sister. She was fed up with teachers telling her she wasn't living up to her potential the way studious, straight-A Cathy always had. She was sick of everyone ridiculing her dreams of going to Hollywood to be in the movies. Most of all, Teddi was fed up with her parents' constant criticism.

"Why can't you be more like Cathy? She's never given us a minute's trouble," they said over and over again.

"Theresa...turn that music down!"

"Theresa...don't speak until you're spoken to!"

"Theresa...don't cross your legs that way! Be a lady like Cathy!"

Cathy! Cathy! Cathy! Always Cathy. Teddi loved her parents and her sister, but sometimes she hated them, too, because they were always trying to pour her into a mold that already had the name Catherine O'Brien written on it.

Just once, Teddi wanted to know what it would be like

to be her parents' favorite. She wanted to be the one who got the new dress, instead of her sister's hand-me-downs. She wanted to be the one who got to choose how the bedroom was decorated. She wanted to be the one her parents praised and petted.

And then the freight train had awakened her in the middle of the night and taken away everything. There were no more arguments, no more comparisons, no more demands—and no more of the love and security she had taken for granted. Nothing had been left but the roar that haunted her dreams.

It had left her alone—literally and figuratively—twenty years ago, but now it had come back.

For her.

It was right there behind the van, twisting and writhing like a cobra. It skirted from one side of the road to the other, veering occasionally into a field as though it had momentarily forgotten Teddi was there, then returning to its course.

"Hold on, Teddi! Hold on! We're turning!"

Matt's frantic shout broke through the paralysis that numbed Teddi's brain, and she grabbed the seat beside her. The van barely slowed as it whipped onto a dirt road, plunging them into a field of barley. Teddi was thrown back against the console as Nate accelerated, and the van rocked violently as the tornado streaked past them.

It hadn't been coming for Teddi, after all.

Moments later, the vortex lifted off the ground and vanished into the sky. Nate slammed on the brakes, and the van stopped. No one spoke, but the windshield wipers hammered out a syncopated cadence that echoed Teddi's heartbeat.

The silence was overwhelming.

CHAPTER NINE

IT WAS LIKE LISTENING to a bunch of soldiers reliving their favorite war experiences. The restaurant was practically deserted, because the fearsome thunderstorm had kept sane customers at home. A couple of truck drivers were sipping coffee on the other side of the room and flirting with the waitress. A woman with two children was sitting by a window waiting for the rain to let up. All of them had long since stopped eavesdropping on the chase team, who were crowded around a long table, recounting their adventure.

Two hours ago they had all had a brush with death, and now they were anxious to talk about it. Teddi understood what it was like to describe an escapade as an adrenaline rush ebbed and surged, growing a little weaker with each retelling of the story. But she couldn't enjoy the adrenalin high tonight. The experience had been too real, too powerful, too humiliating—and too painful a reminder of the past. Now, she just wanted to go home—not to Turner, which was still a good three hours away—but to California. She desperately wanted to be snug in her Venice bungalow where she could lick her wounds and recover the peace of mind that had been violently ripped away from her tonight.

She wished the others would stop dawdling over their coffee. She wished they'd stop talking about *it*, because if they didn't, she was afraid she'd fly into a million pieces and disappear forever.

"If we hadn't missed that turnoff, it probably would've

come down right on top of us," Gerry Hampton was saying, his eyes still sparkling with the residue of excitement. "As it was, though, by the time we made a quick U-turn, it dropped down about a quarter of a mile in front of us."

Griff picked up his coffee cup. "And he slammed on the brakes so fast, I almost rammed into his tailgate."

Ryan Sawyer, who'd been riding with Griff, crumpled up his napkin and threw it at Gerry. "Yeah, Ger. Next time give us a little notice, would ya? I nearly went through the windshield."

"Next time wear your seat belt," Gerry retorted as he threw the napkin back. "I can't wait to see the pictures Bryce shot. He jumped out of the van quick as greased lightning."

"Fortunately I still had the telephoto lens on," Bryce said with a nod. "I got some dynamite footage, and I think we'll even have a great shot of the tornado with the van in the background. I couldn't see you guys all the time, though, because of the debris the tornado was kicking up."

"Teddi must have some spectacular pictures, too," Nate said. "She had the best seat in the house. I could see it in my rearview mirror—it just kept barreling down on us. It's a good thing that farm access road appeared when it did. I was about ready to plow a new furrow through that barley field."

Teddi knew that Bryce was looking at her, waiting for her to confirm Nate's assumption, but she couldn't meet his gaze. If she did, he'd see too much. And she couldn't look at Matt, either—she hadn't been able to since she'd told him that out-and-out lie right after the crisis.

At first, she'd just been numb. Then a wave of sickening nausea had engulfed her, and then mortification had taken over, as Matt and the others tried to assess what had just happened. It was appalling to realize she hadn't taken a single shot of what could have been the most spectacular footage of her career.

"What about it, Teddi?" Ryan asked. "Did you get a clear shot, or was the van bouncing too much?"

"Actually, Teddi didn't get any footage," Matt said quickly, darting a glance at her. "Her camera jammed or something."

Teddi couldn't tell if he believed the lie she'd told him, or if he was just covering for her because he'd guessed the truth and didn't want her to be embarrassed. She didn't know which was worse: having him think she was a liar, and an incompetent bungler, or a coward.

It really didn't matter, though, because she was determined to bluff her way through. "That's right. When we turned onto the county road I was jolted out of my seat. I must have banged up the camera as I fell."

The looks of disappointment on the team members' faces were more than she could stand. She didn't need their censure compounding her own. Desperate to escape, she pushed her chair back and rose. "If you'll excuse me, I need to hit the ladies' again before we leave."

As she hurried toward the lobby, Matt stood up. "I could use another pit stop, too. Be right back." He was halfway around the table before the words were out, but he practically had to run to catch up with Teddi at the door to the foyer that led to the restrooms.

"Teddi, wait!" he called.

She stopped, but he was at her side before she finally turned. This had the feel of a confrontation, and it made her heartbeat accelerate. "What?"

Matt looked at her, wishing he knew what to say now that he had her alone. If he could have engineered a private moment an hour ago, he would have, but circumstances hadn't allowed it. Besides, Teddi had been so shaken after the tornado that she'd needed some time to recover. She still wasn't herself, though, and it worried him.

"Are you all right?" he asked solicitously.

"I'm fine. I just drank too much coffee," she said shortly.

"No, you didn't. You hardly touched your coffee or your hamburger."

"Then I'll get a doggie bag and take it with me. Believe me, I won't starve."

"Teddi, please. Talk to me."

She raised her chin defiantly. "About what?"

"Look, I know that was a scary situation. Even *I* don't like to get that close."

"Oh, come on, Matt. You loved every minute of it! There was no time for you to test Pandora, but other than that you were having the time of your life," she said too sharply.

Matt couldn't deny he'd found the event exciting, but Teddi didn't seem to want to believe it had terrified him, too. "You had every right—and damned good reason—to be scared," he told her gently.

Teddi hated the kid-glove handling and detested pity even more. Despite all her promises to Matt, she had failed him completely, and that wasn't something she was accustomed to doing—or admitting. "Save your sympathy, Matt. I'm fine."

"So is your camera, isn't it?" he asked.

Teddi stiffened. "I don't know what you mean."

"Yes, you do. Your camera didn't malfunction, did it?"

"Of course it did!" she snapped defensively.

"Teddi, I was watching you. You had the camera on your shoulder, but I never saw the little red light come on."

"That was part of the malfunction."

Matt wasn't sure he believed her, but he didn't press it. "Teddi, I'm just worried about you."

"Well, don't be."

Matt took a deep breath and tried another tack. "Teddi, we've already established that the subject of tornadoes is difficult for you. Until now we were only talking about something abstract. Today it became a very real—"

"Will you shut up and leave me the hell alone!" she shouted, then turned and stormed into the ladies' room. She slammed the door and collapsed against it because she needed something to hold her up. Her legs didn't seem to want to work. Probably because she was shaking so hard. A knot of something that could have been anger or fear was caught in her throat, and she stumbled to the sink, splashing water onto her face.

It didn't help. When she finally looked into the mirror, she barely recognized the wild-eyed woman staring back at her. It was Teddi's hair, her face, her clothes, but the eyes were someone else's. They were the eyes of a frightened animal, not Teddi's at all. There was no courage in them, no daring, no spark, no spirit.

If she could have gouged them out of her head—and the fear along with them—she would have. But she couldn't. All she could do was close them tightly and try to control the sob of anguish gnawing at her throat.

TEDDI'S MOTEL ROOM was too small to comfortably accommodate her frenzied pacing, but she couldn't very well pace up and down the parking lot at midnight wearing nothing but an oversize football jersey. Even in sleepy little Turner, someone was bound to notice, call the police and have her carted away to the nearest mental institution.

Which was exactly where she belonged tonight. It had been hours since she'd looked into the face of death, but she still hadn't stopped shaking. She had managed to avoid another confrontation with Matt by riding back to Turner in Griff's van and having him drop her off at the motel before he went on to the center, but she couldn't hide from Matt forever. She needed to apologize to him and explain. He deserved that much, at least. But she couldn't do either until she got herself under control.

At the moment, she feared that might never happen. She just wanted to curl into a little ball and make herself invisible; retreat to some place safe where there was no roaring in her head, where images of tornadoes and faces and freshly turned graves didn't flash like grisly neon signs.

Emotions whirled around inside her, crashing into each other so violently that she couldn't make sense of them. Fear, anger, grief, guilt, shame—Teddi tried to sort through them one at a time; to grab on to one so that she could examine it, conquer it and thrust it away, but the feelings were too elusive and powerful. She was out of control, and there didn't seem to be a damned thing she could do to stop the spiraling emotions, which were growing stronger, instead of weaker.

When she heard the soft rapping on her door, Teddi nearly jumped out of her skin. Her pulse rate skyrocketed, and she took several deep breaths to quiet it.

God, please don't let it be Matt, she prayed. *Please don't let him see me like this.*

With a visibly trembling hand, she opened the door. She wasn't terribly surprised that her prayer had gone unanswered. God might have been responsible for her escape from the tornado this afternoon, but He seemed to have made Himself scarce ever since. Matt was standing under the eaves, just barely out of reach of the lightly peppering rain.

"What are you doing here?" Teddi demanded. She

didn't want to sound belligerent, but the question came out that way just the same.

Matt had a speech all prepared. He'd been rehearsing it for the past hour, ever since Griff had returned to the center without Teddi. Matt had been furious with her for avoiding him, and he was determined to force her to admit that she'd lied to him. He'd had Griff check her camera just to be certain there was no damage, and now he wanted some answers.

But his speech and his anger vanished the moment Teddi flung open the door, because the wild-eyed woman confronting him wasn't the same strong, capable daredevil he'd met in L.A. She wasn't the woman who had made love with him passionately last night and then snuggled in his arms looking at the stars. She wasn't even the cold, angry woman who'd stood up to him in the restaurant just a few hours ago.

The woman standing in the doorway had been to hell and back—and Matt had been her tour guide.

He suddenly realized that whatever was wrong with Teddi went a lot deeper than embarrassment about being frightened by her first confrontation with a tornado.

"Teddi, what's wrong?" he asked when he finally found his voice.

"Nothing," she said sharply.

"I don't believe that. You're a wreck."

"Thank you for that clinical assessment, *Dr.* Abernathy," she snapped sarcastically. "Now, would you please go away so I can get some sleep? I've had a long day."

Matt shook his head. "No, Teddi. I'm not leaving until you tell me what's going on."

Teddi clenched and unclenched her fists to keep from screaming at him. She couldn't handle a confrontation right now. She was barely hanging on by a thread as it was.

"Tomorrow, all right? I'll come see you tomorrow and I'll explain everything," she promised. "Just leave me alone now, Matt, please."

"I can't do that, Teddi," he said, stepping over the threshold. "We have to talk."

"Fine." She whirled away and snatched up her jeans from the pile of clothes she'd shed by the bathroom door. "You have a nice little chat with yourself, because I'm leaving."

As she struggled into the jeans, Matt closed the door and looked around. The room was a shambles. Teddi's suitcase was on the floor with clothes half in, half out of it, and the sheets on the bed looked like someone had already spent a hard night tossing and turning in them.

Matt felt completely out of his depth. He'd never confronted a hysterical woman before—at least not one he cared deeply about. But there was no denying that Teddi was on the edge, and if he didn't do something, she could very easily plunge over it. "You're not going anywhere, Teddi," he told her as she snatched up her purse.

She glared at him with undisguised venom. "You think you can stop me?"

"Is that what you want? A physical confrontation?"

"I want you to leave me the hell alone!" she shouted, flinging her purse onto the bed.

"Well, I'm not going to do it, because you don't need to be alone right now. My God, Teddi, you're about to explode!"

"Just let me handle this in my own way!"

"Handle what, for God's sake? Teddi, what's going on?"

"Nothing!"

"I don't believe you."

"Well, that's your problem."

Matt was afraid to move away from the door because he sensed that Teddi would bolt the moment he did. She looked like an animal that had been cornered and would fight to the death to keep from being captured. But Matt didn't want to capture her. He just wanted to understand—and to help.

It seemed as if the only way to do that was to confront her with the truth. "I had Griff check your camera, Teddi. He couldn't find anything wrong with it." She just glared at him with undisguised hostility, and so Matt summoned some belligerence of his own. It was the only thing he could think of to breakdown her barriers and get her to talk. "What's the matter? Aren't you going to tell me you fixed it yourself?"

"Why should I do that?" she asked defiantly. "I'm a coward, not a liar."

"But you lied to me this afternoon," he said.

She shrugged. "All right, I admit it. I'm a coward *and* a liar. Sue me."

"You are not a coward, Teddi," he said, taking a step toward her. When she backed away from him, he stopped. "Cut yourself some slack, okay? You don't have to be Superwoman."

"Oh, I don't think there's any danger of that," she muttered. "I froze this afternoon, Matt. Is that what you want to hear? Well, I admit it. I panicked like a pathetic little rabbit, and then I didn't even have the guts to admit I screwed up. That's not exactly what you expected from the great Teddi O'Brien, is it?"

"No," he said quietly.

The disappointment in his eyes was like a knife in Teddi's gut. She turned away from him and moved into the kitchenette where she could grab the counter to hold herself up. Her legs didn't seem to want to do the job alone.

"Please...just leave me alone, Matt," she begged softly. "I promise I'll explain everything tomorrow. I can't handle having you see me like this."

She heard him moving toward her and she stiffened. "This isn't just about you freezing up, is it, Teddi?"

She swallowed hard. "No."

He paused a moment, but when she didn't make an effort to explain, he finally asked, "Who did you lose to a tornado, Teddi?"

She had evaded the question last night, but she couldn't avoid the truth any longer. Struggling against the swirl of her emotions, she clenched the counter until her hands turned white. "Everyone," she admitted as soon as she was certain her voice wouldn't crack. "My parents...my sister...."

Matt was stunned. This was worse than anything he could have imagined. He'd assumed she'd lost a relative or a friend, but to lose an entire family? It was beyond comprehension. "My God, Teddi. I'm sorry."

He reached out to her, placing his hands on her shoulders, but she jerked away, rejecting his comfort. "Spare me your pity, okay?"

Matt pulled back as though he'd been burned. "All right, no pity," he said evenly, but her rejection hurt. "When... when did it happen?"

"Twenty years ago. In Dry Creek, Oklahoma."

"Dry Creek?" Matt knew about the Dry Creek tragedy. He didn't remember the exact figures, but the death toll had been high. But what mystified him was how a family from California had been caught in an Oklahoma tornado. "What was your family doing in Dry Creek?"

Teddi bit her lower lip and wrapped her arms protectively around her midsection. "That's where we lived."

Matt took another step back, recoiling from the shock

and the sickening realization that Teddi had deceived him from the very beginning. "But you told me you were from California," he said incredulously.

Teddi finally found the courage to turn and look at him. "No, that's what I wanted you to assume so that you wouldn't ask too many questions."

Matt stared at her, trying to digest what she was telling him. A wave of sympathy washed through him, but he brushed it aside. Teddi obviously didn't need it or want it. And besides, the sense of betrayal he felt was threatening to overpower his sympathy. "You lived through the Dry Creek tornado?"

"Yes."

"My God." He turned away from her. "Teddi, why did you lie to me? I asked you point-blank if you'd ever seen a tornado, and you said you hadn't."

"That wasn't a lie," she answered defensively. "I didn't *see* it that night, Matt. Honestly. But I did hear it. I *felt* it. I could almost have reached out and touched it—but it didn't touch me," she said, her voice suffused with pain and awe. "It reduced our house to rubble, wiped out my entire family and left me without so much as a scratch." She shrugged helplessly. "Go figure."

Matt dropped onto the bed, trying to decipher his emotions. Part of him was furious with Teddi for deceiving him, and part of him ached for her. He wanted to gather her into his arms and hold her close. He wanted to protect her and comfort her—but it was too late for that. The damage had already been done twenty years ago.

"Why did you come here, Teddi? Why would you want to subject yourself to something like that again?"

Teddi was grateful that Matt wasn't smothering her with the sympathy she hated so much. If he had, she might have run screaming into the night. As it was, though, a blessed numbness had settled over her, making it a little easier to answer.

"I told you why in L.A., Matt. I didn't even realize I was still afraid of tornadoes. After my parents were killed, I moved to Anaheim to live with my aunt. I had nightmares for a while, but when they finally went away I managed to convince myself that everything was fine."

"Until I asked you to do this documentary."

Teddi nodded. "You caught me off guard, and all the old fears came crushing to the surface. They were so overwhelming it took me a while to figure out what I was feeling, but once I did, I realized I had run away from my fear, instead of conquering it."

"So you decided to use my documentary as a test of courage?" he asked, appalled.

He was angry and he had every right to be, Teddi realized. But his anger was a lot easier to cope with than his disappointment. "Yes. I had to face the fear, or I wouldn't have been able to live with myself."

Matt came to his feet again. "Why didn't you tell me all this in L.A.? Why go through all the elaborate pretense?"

"Because I knew you wouldn't hire me if I told you the whole truth."

"Well, you were right about that!" he snapped, unable to keep the sarcasm out of his voice. "My God, didn't you even once stop to consider the stake *I* had in this? And the center? You were willing to risk a million-dollar documentary just to prove you aren't a coward?"

Teddi could handle a personal attack without fighting back, but not a professional one. "I didn't believe there was a risk, Matt. I knew I could do it."

"But you didn't do it, Teddi!" he practically shouted as he advanced on her. "Do you have any idea how rare it is to find even one tornado in a season? This may have been our first, last and only chance to get a tornado on film, and you froze!''

''Don't you think I know that?'' Guilt and anguish engulfed her. ''I failed you! I failed myself! How am I supposed to live with that?''

Matt took a deep breath and backed off. He was being selfish, but he didn't know how else to react. Teddi wouldn't accept comfort from him, and that left only his deepening sense of betrayal to deal with. ''Haven't you ever failed before?'' he asked.

Teddi stiffened her jaw against a flood of emotion. ''Not professionally. I do things other people are afraid to do, and I never fail. That's—'' Her voice broke and she turned away from him so he wouldn't see her tears. ''That's who I am, Matt. That's how I define myself. It's the only thing that makes Teddi O'Brien special.''

Matt couldn't believe what he was hearing. ''Do you really believe that?''

She nodded mutely and Matt went to her. When he put his hands on her shoulders she didn't pull away. ''Teddi, you're special in ways I can't even begin to count. One failure doesn't mean you're worthless. It just means you're human—like everybody else.''

''So I should be prepared to fail like everybody else?''

''It happens.''

She turned to him. ''Not to me.''

''Teddi, I understand what it means to feel that your work is part of who you are, but—''

''No, you don't understand anything, Matt,'' she said, cutting him off. ''I'm…terrified.'' She said it as though it was a hideous, incurable disease.

''After what happened today, that's only natural,'' he countered.

"No, it's not natural! I've never been afraid of anything in my life! Not since my parents died. Not since the nightmares went away. I thought I could do anything, handle any danger, take any risk. It didn't matter, because nothing could touch me! Now—" Her voice broke. "Now I just want to scream and scream until I can't scream anymore. I want to rip this fear out of my head and forget what it feels like to be so scared I can't move or think. I want to be *me* again, but now I don't even know who the hell I am!"

She choked back a sob, and Matt dragged her into his arms. She struggled against him and the tears, but Matt wouldn't let go. He held on with his arms wrapped tightly around her until finally she stopped struggling and sagged against him, letting the tears take over.

Matt stroked her hair, wishing he knew what the hell to do to take her pain away. Teddi's whole perception of herself had been shattered today, and he couldn't imagine what it would take to restore it. All he could do was hold her until the storm passed. He knew it wasn't nearly enough.

Teddi couldn't remember the last time she'd cried, and she didn't want to. It was weak and humiliating, but it felt good to let the emotions out. Matt's arms around her felt good, too. Wonderful, in fact. For just a moment that feeling of being warm and safe came back to her. Nothing could harm her while she was in Matt's arms.

But it was wrong to rely on his strength. She had to find her own again, so she bundled up her scattered emotions, pulled them under control and gently eased away from him.

"I'm sorry," she said as she moved across the room.

Matt felt bereft as he watched her retreat from him. "Sorry for crying? Teddi, after the wringer you went through today, a few tears are acceptable. In fact, they're even necessary."

"I hate crying," she said, wiping her face on a towel she found just inside the bathroom door.

"It's not a sign of weakness, if that's what you're thinking."

"It is to me."

Matt felt as if he was hitting his head against a brick wall. "Don't be so hard on yourself."

Teddi looked at him defiantly. "It's the only way I know how to be, Matt. I lost a lot of myself today. At least leave me that, okay?"

He sighed. "Maybe your expectations are part of the problem, Teddi. Have you thought of that?"

"What do you mean?"

"You buried a lot of emotions twenty years ago, but you came here expecting not to be affected by what happened back then."

"I thought I could handle it," she said defiantly.

"And when you found out you couldn't, you went into a tailspin. That's why you lied about the camera and why you were nearly hysterical when I walked in here. You're so wrapped up in your expectations of yourself that you can't deal with the fear and the painful memories that came back to you today."

"I'm a professional. I should have been able to do my job," she said without any force.

Matt shook his head. "You're just not going to give yourself a break, are you?"

"I don't deserve it."

"Yes, you do!"

"How can you, of all people, say that, Matt? I took this job under false pretenses!"

"That's right," he said, conquering his anger. He'd save it for later, when Teddi wasn't so strung out. "You never should have taken this job, but you did. The question now is what are you going to do about it?''

Teddi closed her eyes, but her emotions were still too jumbled for her to touch. "I don't know."

Matt held his breath, afraid of the answer to the question he had to ask. "Are you going to leave?"

She opened her eyes. "I *should* leave. I know that much. If you were smart, you'd take the decision out of my hands and fire me."

She was right. Matt knew he should fire her, scrap the documentary and cut the center's losses before it got any worse. But he couldn't bring himself to do it. He didn't want to give up the documentary. More importantly, he didn't want to give up Teddi. "I'm not going to do that."

"I know. We made love last night, and now you feel like you have some kind of obligation to me."

"Is that all you think you are to me? An obligation?" he asked incredulously.

Teddi saw a flash of pain in his eyes, and it was more than she could deal with. "I'm sorry, Matt. I don't know what to think right now."

"Then figure it out, Teddi," he said, moving to her. "I'll help if I can. We'll talk about it and—"

"Talking isn't going to help," she insisted.

"You don't have to do this alone!"

"Yes, I do!" she replied, moving across the room to fight the overpowering urge to seek refuge in his arms. "It's *my* fear, *my* failure...*my* memories. You can't make them go away, no matter how much you might want to."

"No, but I can be here for you. I can help you sort through what happened today."

Teddi shook her head. "I have to do that myself, Matt."

He looked into her eyes and realized she wasn't going

to change her mind. "What made you so damned stubborn, Teddi?"

She managed a smile. "I was born that way. It's too late to change now."

He hesitated a moment, dreading her answer because he already knew what it would be. "Do you want me to leave?"

Telling him yes was a lot harder than it should have been, but she did it, anyway. "I think so. I need to be alone. I have a lot of things to sort through—and some important decisions to make. There's got to be a way to salvage your documentary. I have to figure out what that is."

"Teddi, don't worry about the film right now. Take some time for yourself."

"I don't have that luxury," she countered urgently. "The storm season isn't going to wait until I get my act together. Neither will the documentary. There are interviews to be conducted...the party at your house tomorrow night has to be filmed...." And there was undoubtedly another chase looming on the horizon. The thought made her stomach churn, but she forced herself to ignore it. "I have to find a way to deal with all this, and quickly."

He admired her determination, but not her blind stubbornness. "Teddi, you can't ignore your personal trauma and still direct this film. You tried it that way already and it didn't work."

"I know, but if I can pull myself together, there may be a way to salvage everything."

If she had a solution, Matt wanted to hear it. "Such as?"

The idea had been one of the wild, random thoughts running through Teddi's head before Matt's arrival. She hadn't been able to explore it fully to determine if it was practical or even possible. But Matt deserved to know the direction her thoughts were taking. It was the least she owed him. "I could turn all the camera work over to Bryce and Griff, just as Pat Dennison had planned to do. It would eliminate the risk that I might freeze again, but I could do everything else as planned."

It was a practical solution, but there was a major flaw in it. "If you can handle the subject matter," he said.

Teddi nodded and swallowed hard. "That's the big question. Can I bear to edit the film we shoot? Write copy about tornadoes. Talk about them, think about them. Eat, sleep and breathe them every minute of every day." She couldn't suppress the shudder of fear and revulsion that rippled along her spine. "I don't know if I can do it, Matt. That's what I have to figure out."

Matt didn't know what to say. He wanted to believe she could do it, because the only alternative was that she leave Oklahoma and abandon the film. But he didn't have the right to ask her to go through hell again just because he had a piece of paper with her signature on it. People were more important than contracts.

But Teddi had signed that contract because she wanted to stop running from her fear. What would it do to her if she ran away now? How could she retain her self-respect and her intractable image of herself?

Matt suddenly realized exactly what Teddi was up against. She was fighting a battle that would determine who she was in the most basic sense. And he also realized just how much courage it had taken for her to come to Oklahoma at all.

Unable to bear the distance between them, Matt stepped up to her and gently cupped her face in his hands. "You are a remarkable woman, Teddi. Don't lose sight of that while you're making your decision. Just coming here at all took more guts than most people have."

Teddi looked into his eyes and fought the temptation to

lose herself in the warmth she saw there. But she also found something else she desperately needed to see. Matt believed in her. She had lied to him, she had failed him, she had shoved him away with both hands at a time when he'd only wanted to help her—and he still believed in her. That knowledge was oh, so comforting, because at the moment she couldn't believe in herself.

"Don't romanticize this, Matt," she warned him softly, nestling her cheek against his hand. "Don't romanticize *me*. I screwed up. I deceived you and lied to myself. My mistakes are going to cost us both dearly."

Matt didn't want to think about the price he was going to have to pay for what he was feeling. "We'll handle it, Teddi. Somehow."

She slid her arms around his waist and raised her face to his. The kiss Matt pressed to her lips was as soft as a sigh, and so sweet it made Teddi want to cry all over again. She lowered her head to his shoulder and he wrapped his arms around her.

"I'm so sorry," she whispered.

Matt's heart turned over in his chest, and he pulled her closer, trying to make her a part of him. He had the horrible feeling she wasn't apologizing for having deceived him. She was telling him she was sorry she'd led him to expect something between them that could never be. He'd thought that the Teddi O'Brien he had fallen in love with was a woman who could understand his profession and cope with the dangers of it. Now he knew that was just as much an illusion as Teddi's false confidence had been.

The realization wounded Matt on a level he hadn't even known existed, and he mentally turned away from it. He couldn't accept it—*wouldn't* accept it—not without a fight. Teddi was too special and what he felt for her was too real to be ignored. There had to be a way.

Teddi let Matt hold her for a long time, allowing his strength to bolster her own. Finally, though, she had to let him go and start looking for her own strength.

"I really need to be alone, Matt," she told him reluctantly.

Matt wanted to argue, but he didn't. He wanted to hold her, comfort her, reassure her. But the Teddi O'Brien he'd fallen in love with didn't need those things from him. In fact, there probably wasn't anything she needed from a man who chased tornadoes for a living.

"Are you sure?" he asked, praying she would change her mind and ask him to stay. He needed her to prove that he was wrong, to let him know she did need him.

But Teddi didn't answer his prayer. "Yes."

Matt's heart sank. "All right," he said, moving toward the door. "If you need me, I'm just a phone call away."

"I know."

He stopped and turned to her. "You'll be all right, Teddi."

She dredged up a weary smile. "Are you trying to convince yourself or me?"

"Both."

"I hope you're right."

"I know I am." He leaned toward her, pressed another soft kiss to her lips, then turned and opened the door. "Call me tomorrow?"

"I promise."

He hesitated. "Good night."

"Good night."

He moved away from her, merging with the darkness, and Teddi closed the door.

CHAPTER TEN

MATT CARRIED another empty tray of hors d'oeuvres to the kitchen where Laura was replenishing the trays almost as quickly as his guests were emptying them. His beginning-of-season party had been in full swing for about an hour. Music was playing very softly in the background, and Bryce and Griff were using a camera and microphones to eavesdrop on conversations. Everyone seemed to be enjoying the chance to catch up with old friends.

The only person who wasn't having a good time was the host. He was worried because Teddi hadn't arrived yet, and he couldn't concentrate on anything else. She had called him late that morning to assure him she'd have her camera crew at the party, but she'd said very little else. She had sounded calmer, more centered, but Matt knew that might have been nothing but an illusion. She had kept whatever she was thinking and feeling to herself, and Matt had only her promise that she would come to the party tonight ready to tell him what she'd decided to do about the documentary. He'd offered her more time, but she'd rejected the offer.

Tonight, Matt would know one way or the other what was going to happen to his film. As for what was going to happen to his heart, he didn't want to think about it. He'd spent most of the day avoiding the truth as efficiently as Teddi had avoided her fear for the past twenty years.

"Not another one," Laura said as he placed the empty tray on the island in the center of the small kitchen.

It took Matt a second to focus on Laura and muster his affable host smile. "I'm afraid so. Your crab puffs are a big hit, as usual."

Laura checked her watch. "Well, you're going to have to wait about five minutes for the next batch to come out of the oven," she informed him, then went back to rolling thin slices of ham and pepper cheese around her home-baked bread sticks. Matt snatched one off her neatly arranged tray, and she slapped his hand. "Stop that. If you want one, roll your own and stop messing up my presentation."

"All right." Matt accepted the challenge and clumsily fixed his own snack.

"I take it she isn't here yet," Laura commented casually.

Matt froze for a second, then tried to act nonchalant. "She? Oh, you mean Teddi O'Brien."

Laura rolled her eyes. "Who else would I mean? You started looking for her an hour before any of the other guests arrived."

He should have known he couldn't fool his friend. "Have I been that obvious?"

"You were distracted and anxious all afternoon, and every time I mentioned Ms. O'Brien, you changed the subject," she informed him. "What gives?"

"We had a little…misunderstanding yesterday," he replied evasively.

Laura studied him closely. "Personal?"

Matt shook his head. "Professional," he replied, unwilling to accept that it was both.

"Did it have anything to with that near miss during the chase?"

Laura had returned to rolling bread sticks, but Matt thought she was giving them more attention than they warranted. If she knew about the chase, he could understand why. "How did you hear about that?"

She shot him an exasperated glance. "It's the main topic of party conversation, and I haven't spent *all* my time in the kitchen tonight. I heard she broke her camera."

Matt was growing very uncomfortable. "That's right. Are those crab puffs done yet?"

"No. What was your misunderstanding about?"

"I'm really not at liberty to go into it, Laura."

She stopped and looked at him. "Are you sure it was strictly professional?"

"Yes," he said emphatically.

She studied him for a moment, considering his answer. "You're lying, Matt."

He could always count on his friend not to pull any punches, but in this case he wished she'd been a little less astute. Laura would certainly understand and be sympathetic to everything Teddi was going through, but she would also have a very strong opinion on the subject of Matt's relationship with her.

Matt didn't want to hear the words spoken aloud yet because he still couldn't accept it. "I'm sorry. I don't mean to be evasive, but Teddi has some problems I can't discuss."

Laura frowned as she studied him. "Exactly how far has this relationship gone, Matt?"

"Far enough."

"Have you slept with her?"

"Laura, I don't pry into your relationships with other men," he reminded her. "I'd appreciate the same courtesy."

That was all the answer she needed. "You're in love with her, aren't you?"

Matt didn't want to have this discussion, but he couldn't lie to his best friend. He sighed. "Yes, I am."

"Is she in love with you?"

It was a moment before he answered. "I don't know. I think she really cares, but with Teddi it's a little hard to tell."

The bleakness in Matt's eyes told Laura a lot, and she didn't like it one bit. If the hotshot director from California was playing Matt for a fool, she was going to have to answer to Laura personally. "Just take it slow, okay?" she advised him.

"It may be a little late for that, Laura."

Laura was shocked. "Matt, you've known her for under two weeks."

"A lot can happen in less time than that," he replied. "If I remember correctly, you knew you wanted to marry Joe after your first date."

"That's different."

"Why?"

"Because…"

Matt grinned at her. "Gotcha."

The timer on the stove buzzed, and Laura grabbed an oven mitt. "It's not the same thing at all, Matt. Joe wasn't a slick Hollywood movie director."

"Teddi's not slick," he argued. "And I don't see what her being a director has to do with anything."

"Hollywood is the operative word, Matt," Laura said sharply as she removed a cookie sheet from the oven and placed it on the island. "You two come from entirely different worlds. She lives her life in the fast lane, while you—"

Matt's hoot of laughter stopped her. "Laura, you've been watching too many movies. I was in Hollywood for a week and I didn't see one single orgy or get offered a drug of any sort. Teddi is an extraordinary woman, but she doesn't drive a sports car or run around her house wearing sequined blue jeans and feather boas.'' He paused to study his friend. ''It's not like you to be judgmental, Laura. What gives?''

''She just doesn't seem like the right woman for you.''

''How can you say that without even meeting her?''

''I don't have to meet her to know she's already got you tied in knots,'' Laura said tersely.

Matt reached across the island and placed his hand on hers. ''Give her a chance, Laura. Please. She's going through a rough time right now.''

Laura darted an exasperated glance at him. Matt had a lot to learn about women. ''All right. I'll reserve judgment until I've met this paragon.''

''Thank you.''

Laura thought it was probably a good idea to change the subject, and there was something she'd been wanting to say to him all night, anyway. ''Where's Corey?'' she asked.

''Last time I saw him he was on the deck talking to Bryce Lowell,'' he said as he started loading crab puffs onto the empty tray. ''Ouch. They're hot.''

''You can always count on a man for a brilliant observation,'' she said with a shake of her head as she tossed him the oven mitt.

''Why did you ask about Corey?'' he said, ignoring the dig.

Laura sighed deeply. ''I wanted to say something to you, and I didn't want Corey to overhear.''

''Okay.'' Matt frowned slightly and stepped to the door. He stuck his head into the dining room and a moment later returned to the island. ''He's on the far side of the living room. What's wrong?''

She looked up at him. ''I wanted to thank you for not

letting Corey go on the chase yesterday. I'm sure it wasn't easy to say no to him.''

Matt was surprised. "How did you know he asked?''

"We had another big argument after he got home last night, and he let it slip.''

"I'm sorry.''

"Don't be sorry, Matt. It's not your fault.''

Matt wasn't so sure about that, and he was beginning to wonder if Laura really believed it, either. If he hadn't spent all those years playing surrogate father to Corey, the boy might have chosen another line of work. Laura had never pointed that out to him, though, and he was grateful. He had enough trouble dealing with the situation as it was.

"I meant I'm sorry about the argument,'' he told her. "This has been hard on both of you.''

"What am I supposed to do, Matt? I love my son more than anything in the world. How can I just stand by and let him commit suicide?''

"Laura, being a meteorologist isn't suicidal,'' he argued.

"Not if you're a TV weatherman or a forecast specialist in Kansas City, but Corey wants to be a tornado researcher. He's got some cockeyed idea that it's exciting and glamorous.''

"It's not glamorous, but it is exciting,'' Matt countered. "It's also important work. Laura, have you considered that maybe studying tornadoes is Corey's way of making sense of what happened to his father?''

"Then let him go into disaster relief with the Red Cross! Anything but being a storm chaser!''

Matt put down the oven mitt and moved around the island. "He's going to chase, Laura, whether you like it or not,'' he told her, even though it was the last thing she wanted to hear. "It's just a question of when. Right now he's staying out of the game because he doesn't want to hurt you."

"Oh, don't kid yourself, Matt!" she snapped. "The only reason Corey applied to you for a research internship, instead of a spot on Chase One this year, is that he needs my financial help to get through graduate school. Believe me, it has nothing to do with my feelings on the matter."

Matt disagreed. Corey did care about Laura's feelings, but that might not last much longer if she didn't loosen the stranglehold she had on him. Last winter when Corey had told her he wanted to chase with Matt, Laura had begged and pleaded with him to change his mind. When that hadn't worked, she threatened to cut off all financial support.

That was why Corey was having such a hard time forgiving her. His internship at the center took a lot of hours, but it didn't pay enough to cover his tuition, let alone what it would cost to live off campus. It wasn't possible to take a full load of classes and hold down two part-time jobs, and he hadn't been willing to quit grad school just to make a stand about his independence.

Matt would gladly have helped with his tuition, but Laura would never have forgiven him. Either way, he'd have been hurting someone he loved, so he hadn't offered. Instead, he'd tried to talk some sense into Laura and had interceded with Corey on her behalf. He hadn't been particularly effective on either score. Nothing was going to break the stalemate until Laura had a change of heart or Corey decided it was time to assert his independence, regardless of the cost.

This was one fight Laura couldn't win, but so far Matt hadn't been able to make her see that. They'd had variations of tonight's conversation so many times that Matt was relieved when Nate Dansing stuck his head into the kitchen and demanded to know what was holding up the crab puffs.

Matt gave him the tray he'd just filled, and Nate went away, happily munching.

"You'd better get back to your party, Matt," Laura said, handing him the tray of bread sticks.

"Are you sure? If you need to talk, we can duck out of here and go someplace quiet," he offered.

Laura made a valiant attempt at a teasing smile. "What? You want me to leave and miss the entrance of Miss Hollywood? Not on your life. I want to stick around and see if this woman is worthy of my best friend."

"Have it your way," Matt said with a grin. He leaned over and kissed her cheek. "Come on out and join us as soon as you finish up, okay?"

She promised to do that, and Matt left her reluctantly. He put the tray on the dining-room table, then moved through the crowded living room, hoping to find that Teddi had arrived. When he didn't spot her, he went to the deck and scanned the backyard. No luck there, either.

Where the hell is she? he wondered.

It was a test, and Teddi knew that the outcome would determine the course of her life from tonight onward. She pulled into the CTR parking lot, shut off the Bronco and sat for a long moment staring at the building. She had waited until she was certain everyone but a skeleton staff had gone to Matt's party. She didn't want an audience when she took the test.

It had to be just her and the tornado.

Teddi still felt raw around the edges, but the artificial control she'd imposed on herself during the night had finally become real. She no longer felt as though she was about to come apart at the seams. In the wee hours of the morning, she'd slapped a few mental bandages over some of the more painful memories and shoved them aside so that she could deal with the practical decisions that had to be made—like what she was going to do about Matt's documentary.

She'd signed a contract. She'd made a commitment to direct the film, and no matter what her personal problems were, Teddi didn't think she could live with the knowledge that she'd reneged on a deal. She wasn't a quitter or a coward, but if she left now she would be both. That would be the hardest thing of all to live with.

But on the other hand, she couldn't risk sabotaging Matt's documentary. She had to be certain Matt wouldn't suffer from her mistakes again, and that was what had brought her to the center. She had gained some perspective on what had happened yesterday, and if she could pass this test, maybe, just maybe, everything would be all right.

Matt was waiting for her decision. She knew he'd give her as much time as she needed, but long periods of contemplation weren't Teddi's style. She made decisions and lived with the consequences. But before she made this decision, she had to know whether or not she had the guts to face another tornado.

The film Brycc had shot was in the storage vault in the editing room they'd set up yesterday morning. Teddi was going to watch that film. Seeing a tornado secondhand on an impersonal video wasn't the same as confronting one in person, but Teddi knew that if she could remain calm and view the footage analytically, she could direct Matt's documentary.

But if the panic returned, she'd have to leave Oklahoma and try to come to grips with the knowledge that Teddi O'Brien wasn't the person she'd always believed she was.

In many ways, this would be the most important test Teddi had ever taken, and she wasn't going to pass or fail by sitting in the parking lot. Gathering her resolve, she jumped out of the Bronco and marched to the front door.

BY NINE-THIRTY, Matt decided Teddi wasn't coming. He'd called her motel room an hour ago, and when he hadn't gotten an answer he'd continued playing host, but his heart wasn't in it. For some reason, Teddi had decided not to attend the party, and Matt was afraid it was her not-so-subtle way of telling him what her decision was. Though he couldn't believe she'd be so cowardly as to leave Oklahoma without a word, he knew he had to be prepared for the worst.

"No sign of Miss Hollywood yet?" Laura asked when she emerged from the kitchen and found Matt near the buffet table trying not to watch the front door.

He threw her an exasperated glance. "I wish you'd stop calling her that," he said irritably. "It's not fair to Teddi. You haven't even met her yet."

Laura was shocked by his tone. "You're right. I'm sorry. Being fashionably late isn't exclusive to the West Coast."

"She's not trying to be fashionable, Laura. Something's wrong, or she'd be here by now."

"Are you sure this isn't just her way of punishing you for that argument you had yesterday?"

"We did not have an argument!" Matt lowered his voice when several guests glanced at him questioningly. "Sorry," he muttered.

Laura placed her hand on his arm. "Matt, what is going on? I've never seen you like this before. What has this woman done to you?"

"She hasn't done anything to me, Laura," he said softly, but her concern was so palpable that Matt suddenly felt guilty for keeping her in the dark. Knowing he was probably going to regret it, he led her to a quiet corner and reluctantly confessed, "Teddi took this job without telling me that she'd had a very tragic encounter with a tornado. When she was fifteen she survived a storm that killed the rest of her family.''

Laura was stunned. ''Matt, that's horrible.''

''I know.''

Under other circumstances, Laura would have been overwhelmed with sympathy for someone who had endured such a tragedy, but now, concern for her friend took over. ''Why on earth didn't she tell you?''

''Because she knew I probably wouldn't hire her.''

''She deliberately deceived you?''

''Not maliciously. She really believed she could handle the documentary. If anything, she was deceiving herself.''

''Yes, but you're the one who's paying for it.''

''Teddi's paying, too, Laura. Believe me. The emotional trauma of that chase yesterday nearly destroyed her.''

''Then she won't be able to finish the film, will she?''

Matt hesitated. ''She wants to. She just hasn't decided whether she'll be able to handle it or not.''

''Oh, Matt. I know how much this documentary means to you. I'm sorry.''

''I'm not worried about the film, Laura. Teddi's what really matters. I don't know what it will do to her if she can't complete the documentary. Her whole image of herself is wrapped up in meeting challenges and facing down fear. If this gets the better of her, I'm afraid it will destroy her.''

Laura couldn't have cared less about what happened to Teddi O'Brien, but she cared a lot about what Matt was going through. She'd suspected that Teddi might be playing some game with Matt or flirting with him just because she was attracted by his dangerous profession. But this... This opened the door on a whole set of problems that could only have one outcome. Matt was going to get hurt. ''Well, that certainly explains why she reacted so badly when you first offered her the job," she said, remembering Matt's description of his initial meeting with Teddi. "But it doesn't excuse her for lying."

"She wanted to confront her fears," Matt said. "I admire her for that."

Laura rolled her eyes. "You go ahead and admire her all you want, Matt. The fact remains, she's been using you."

"No, she hasn't. She…" He glanced away from Laura, and whatever he'd been about to say flew out of his head. Teddi was standing on the deck talking to Bryce and Griff just outside the sliding doors to the living room.

Laura read the expression of relief that flashed across his face and looked toward the deck, expecting to see a flamboyant Hollywood type dressed in spandex and sequins. What she found, instead, was a reasonably attractive, auburn-haired woman dressed in jeans and a simple white camp shirt. If Laura hadn't been so angry with Teddi for the pain she was causing Matt, she would have been relieved to see a normal-looking person.

"Is that her?" she asked.

Matt nodded. "Yes," he said, not taking his eyes off Teddi. "Excuse me, Laura. I'll introduce you two later."

"I'm looking forward to it," she replied, but Matt didn't hear her. He was already moving across the crowded living room, unable to control the erratic beating of his heart. He'd thought that Teddi's arrival would be a relief, but it was too soon for that. He couldn't muster anything but dread until he knew what she had decided.

He slipped through the door and heard Teddi say to Bryce and Griff, "We'll get together tomorrow afternoon and I'll explain everything."

"Teddi?"

She turned to him, and Matt felt the knot of apprehension in his stomach unwind when he saw something in her eyes that hadn't been there last night. It was a spark of the old Teddi, the fearless, outrageous, eccentric Teddi O'Brien who didn't back down from anything.

If her being late to the party had anything to do with that spark, it was well worth the wait.

"Matt, I'm so sorry I'm late. I lost track of time," she told him, then glanced back at her camera crew. "We'll meet at one tomorrow, okay? In the meantime, get set up for a crowd shot in the living room. I've got a surprise for everyone."

"Whatever you say, boss," Bryce said, casting a curious glance from Teddi to Matt as he and Griff moved toward the door with their cumbersome equipment.

Teddi watched them go, shaking her head. "Poor guys. They don't have a clue what's going on."

"What *is* going on, Teddi?" Matt asked, leading her toward a shadowed end of the deck where they could have a modicum of privacy. "Are you all right?"

"I'm fine," she assured him. "I'm sorry if I worried you, but there was something I had to do at the center, and it took longer than I thought."

"What on earth did you have to do there?"

Teddi fished a videocassette out of her purse and handed it to him. "This."

Matt turned it over in his hand, looking for a label. "What is it?"

"It's a videotape, of course," she said innocently.

Matt looked at her, and the impish gleam in her eyes made him smile. She really was going to be all right. "Thanks for that useful nugget of information," he said. "What's *on* the tape?"

"It's an edited rough cut of the footage Bryce shot yesterday. I went to the center intending to transfer his tornado sequence to a regular videocassette so you could play it for your guests, but it was also a good test for me. I wanted to see if I could actually watch the thing, and once I got started, I couldn't stop.''

Matt was stunned. He knew what it must have cost her to make the tape. "You are incredible," he murmured. "You didn't have to do this."

"Yes, I did," she replied seriously. "I had to know if I could deal with this subject on an impersonal, analytical level."

"Did you?"

She grinned sheepishly. "No. But I didn't run screaming into the night, either. Considering my behavior last night, I'd say that was a good sign."

The old Teddi was back. She had confronted her worst enemy today and was justifiably proud of herself. So was Matt. "I'd say so, too," he said, caressing her with his eyes because he was afraid to do more. "Does this mean you're staying to finish the film?"

"If you still want me."

She studied his face, waiting for his answer, and Matt couldn't tell if she realized that her comment had a dangerous double edge. His answer certainly did. "Yes. I still want you."

The warmth of his gaze reached all the way into Teddi's heart, and she gathered it in, cherishing it. "I'm glad. You won't regret giving me a second chance."

Matt didn't want to think about regrets at the moment. Teddi was staying. Nothing else mattered. There would be plenty of time for regrets later once he forced himself to face the truth: Teddi was staying to finish the film, and that was all. "I know you can do this, Teddi," he told her. "I've always believed that."

"Even after what happened yesterday?"

He nodded.

She gave him a rueful smile. "Then you're a bona fide cockeyed optimist."

"No, I'm just in—" Matt swallowed the words and quickly substituted "—incredibly confident in your ability."

Teddi wasn't fooled for a moment. She knew what he'd been about to say. It was there in his eyes, as clear as crystal, as warm as the sun, as gentle as a spring shower. Matt was in love with her.

That certainty should have frightened her, but it didn't. There were so many things she had to learn about herself in the coming months; there were challenges to face, fears to confront, memories to battle. It was like being in a dark, lonely tunnel and not knowing which way led to safety. But Matt's love was suddenly like a light at the end of that tunnel. He couldn't show her the way out; Teddi had to find that on her own, but now she knew there was something rare and wonderful awaiting her at the end of the journey.

"Thank you, Matt," she said, reaching up to touch his face. "I am incredibly confident in you, too."

Matt was afraid to read too much into her tender gesture or the strange soft look in her eyes. He cleared his throat. "Should we discuss the practicalities of how you're going to complete the film?"

Teddi withdrew her hand and smiled at him. "Let's save that for later, okay? In case you hadn't noticed, there's a party going on." She tapped a fingernail on the tape he was holding. "Why don't you play this for your guests? I guarantee it'll be a big hit with this crowd."

"All right." He moved down the deck and called out to his friends in the backyard, inviting them to come inside.

"What's up?" Corey asked, bounding onto the deck with Olivia Eschavera in tow.

"Big surprise, courtesy of Teddi O'Brien," he said, flashing her a big smile. "Come on, folks! It's show time."

CHAPTER ELEVEN

TEDDI SLIPPED into the house just ahead of a dozen or so guests who began pouring into the already crowded room. Smiling and murmuring greetings, she retreated into the dining area at the end of the living room. Matt gathered everyone around his big-screen TV set, popped in the tape and paused a moment to look for Teddi. When he spotted her at the back of the room, he introduced her with a flourish of compliments as he motioned for her to join him.

There was no way she could make it back through the sea of people, and she really didn't want every eye on her at the moment. "Just roll the tape," she called back good-naturedly. "I'll meet everyone after it's over."

"As you wish, Your Highness." He picked up a remote control, and the silence in the room became absolute as the ten minutes' worth of tape began to play.

Teddi couldn't see the screen from her vantage point, but she didn't mind. She'd watched the film dozens of times as she'd spliced the sections together. It had been hard at first. The early footage of the storm clouds Bryce had shot had taken Teddi back through the whole ordeal, moment by moment. All the fear had rushed back to her, and when the tornado suddenly appeared Teddi's heart began to hammer wildly. She'd watched, horrified, as the tornado chased the van, turning the hunters into the hunted. But she hadn't looked away.

She hadn't shied away from the memories, either. She'd

let them wash over her until the film ended, then she rewound the tape and forced herself to experience it again and again, until finally it was nothing more than a piece of magnetic tape with wonderfully composed pictures on it. At that point, her training took over, and she calmly made a digital master of Bryce's original and began the job of editing the images.

By the time she'd finished, she'd reclaimed some of the self-respect she'd lost. Completing Matt's film wouldn't be easy, but it didn't have to be. She just had to do it.

And now she knew she could. The fact that Matt believed in her made this first small victory all the sweeter.

But that still didn't mean she wanted to sit through another viewing of the clip she'd brought. Instead, she glanced around and saw a pretty blond-haired woman standing near the open kitchen door watching the TV. Teddi thought her profile looked vaguely familiar, and when the woman abruptly turned and slipped into the kitchen, closing the swinging door behind her, Teddi realized who she was.

Unable to resist the impulse to spend a few minutes alone with Laura Cochran, Teddi followed her. She stopped to collect some empty trays from the table, and by the time she poked her head through the door, Laura was stacking dishes at the sink.

"Hi. Could you use some help?"

Laura turned, ready with the standard refusal she used at the parties she catered, but when she saw who was offering, she changed her mind. She had a few choice words she wanted to share with Matt's new lady friend. "Are you sure you want to miss the big premiere?"

Teddi moved to the sink and set the dishes on the counter. "I'm sure. I don't care what Matt says, when you've seen one tornado, you've seen them all.'' She held out her hand. "I'm Teddi O'Brien."

"I know." She accepted Teddi's hand cautiously. "Laura Cochran."

"I thought so," Teddi replied as she began searching the drawers for a dish towel. "Your son favors you quite a lot."

Laura nodded. "He got lucky and inherited the best features of both his parents. If you're looking for a towel, try the last drawer on the end."

"Thanks. I'm pretty inept in my own kitchen and absolutely hopeless in anyone else's."

"That's understandable. I don't imagine that your line of work requires a lot of domesticity."

"No, I think I was just born without that particular gene," she joked, wondering if she'd imagined the edge in Laura's voice. Surely she had, because there was no reason for Laura to be catty toward her.

Laura didn't smile at Teddi's joke. "I know Matt's relieved you finally arrived," she said mildly as she started running water into the sink. "He was worried about you."

"I went by the center to prepare that tape and it took a little longer than I expected," Teddi explained. "I really wanted Matt to have it tonight."

"As a peace offering?" She darted a quick glance at Teddi and explained, "Matt told me what happened yesterday."

Teddi wasn't surprised that he'd confided in Laura, and she didn't resent it. He'd undoubtedly needed someone to talk to, and Laura was the logical choice. Everyone would know about it soon enough, anyway. Teddi had learned a valuable lesson about keeping secrets, and she didn't plan to let it go to waste. "Did he tell you everything? Even about my parents?"

Laura nodded. "It was a terrible tragedy."

Teddi didn't detect a lot of sympathy in her comment, which was good. "Yes, it was. But I survived."

"No one survives that kind of ordeal without scars," Laura said pointedly.

Teddi tried to smile. "I'm learning that the hard way."

Laura shut off the water and faced Teddi. "It's unfortunate that Matt's having to learn the hard way, too."

The sudden, overt hostility took Teddi by surprise. "I don't know what you mean."

"Oh, come on, Ms. O'Brien," Laura said coldly. "You lied to Matt so that you could use his documentary to confront your fears. Do you really think that was fair?"

Teddi wasn't accustomed to justifying herself to anyone, but these circumstances weren't normal. She had brought this on herself and she was going to have to face the consequences. "No, it wasn't fair. I can see that now. But when I took this job all I knew was that I couldn't run away from something that frightened me and still live with myself."

"Am I supposed to applaud you for that?"

Her sarcasm was so blatant that Teddi had to bite back a sharp retort. "No, I suppose not."

Laura turned to her. "Ms. O'Brien, may I speak frankly?"

Teddi stiffened. "I thought you already had."

"No, I have a lot more to say. My best friend is going through hell because of you, and I care too much about him to stand by while someone callously destroys him."

Teddi couldn't believe what she was hearing. Facing consequences was one thing, but standing still for an all-out attack was something else. "I don't know where you got the impression that Matt was about to be destroyed."

"I got it from him," Laura said hotly. "I can see what you're doing to him, and I don't like it."

Teddi took a deep breath and tried to remain calm. "Look, Laura, you're probably completely justified in being angry with me for deceiving Matt. I know how close you two are and how much your friendship means to Matt. But the only person *I* have to justify myself to is Matt." She carefully folded her towel and placed it on the counter. "Why don't I just leave and we'll pretend this conversation never happened."

"The way you pretended you could direct Matt's documentary? You're very good at pretending, aren't you?"

"Why on earth have you decided to dislike me before you even get to know me?"

"Because Matt is very important to me. We've been through a lot together, and I don't want to see him get hurt."

"Why do you assume I'm going to hurt him?"

"You already have," Laura replied. "Your lies have hurt him deeply."

"Matt understands why I had to come here."

"Does he also understand why you led him on?"

Teddi frowned, confused. "What do you mean?"

"Oh, I think you know exactly what I mean. Your actions might be excusable if you'd kept your relationship with Matt strictly business, but you didn't do that, did you? You seduced a man you couldn't possibly love—"

"Wait just a minute," Teddi said, unwilling to take any more abuse, even from Matt's best friend. "My personal relationship with Matt is none of your business."

"Oh, but it is. I'm the one who's going to be here picking up the pieces after you're gone. He's falling in love with you, for God's sake."

"What's wrong with that?" Teddi demanded.

"How selfish can you be?" Laura said harshly. "Matt's falling in love with you because you let him believe you could understand and cope with his dangerous profession. But that was a total lie! You're the last person in the world who could ever cope with his profession! You'll never be able to have a relationship with someone who chases tornadoes for a living."

"No," Teddi countered, finally fighting back. "*You* couldn't have a relationship with Matt because of that."

Laura took a step back, surprised by the realization that Matt had told Teddi so much about their relationship. But that didn't stop her from asking, "But you think you can? A woman who lost her entire family to a tornado is going to fall in love with a man like Matt?"

Her question had the ring of a dare. Teddi had never refused a dare in her life, but she wasn't foolish or selfish enough to accept this one. Loving Matt or accepting his love was too important to be based on a challenge.

One thing was sure, though. In a few short minutes, Laura had very neatly ripped away a big chunk of the peace of mind Teddi had worked so hard to find. "That's something Matt and I will have to explore," she said finally.

"Even if it destroys him in the process?"

"I wouldn't let that happen."

"You weren't going to be affected by tornadoes, either, despite what happened to your family," Laura reminded her.

"Good shot," Teddi said sarcastically. "Cheap, but good."

There was a burst of applause from the living room, and Laura glanced at the door. "Apparently the show's over. You should go out and take a bow. That sounds like a very appreciative audience."

Teddi's head was spinning from Laura's verbal thrashing

and she needed time to sort through her suddenly confused and conflicting emotions. She didn't think she could face Matt at the moment, let alone a whole room full of people.

"Look, Laura, I don't understand why you despise me so much, but I'm not out to hurt Matt. You have to believe that."

"Then leave him alone and let him get over you. Go back to where you came from and stop using him as a test of bravery."

"Teddi! It was wonderful!" Matt came bursting into the kitchen, all smiles and boyish enthusiasm, and the two women abruptly turned away from each other. "You did an incredible job."

Teddi tried to collect herself, but it wasn't easy. She needed time to think. "Bryce did the hard part—he got the footage. I just spliced it together."

Matt shook his head. "I know better than that," he said warmly, but when he looked into her eyes and saw doubts that hadn't been there a few minutes ago, he frowned. "What's wrong?"

Teddi resisted the urge to glance over her shoulder at Laura. "Nothing. I just..." She pointed toward the door. "I need to check with Bryce and Griff to see what kind of footage they've shot tonight. We'll talk later, okay?"

Before Matt could respond, she slipped away from him and was gone. Matt turned to Laura. "What were you and Teddi talking about?"

Laura had returned to the sink. She didn't look up from the pan she was scouring. "We were just getting to know each other."

Matt didn't think it was that simple. "Did you say something to upset her?"

"I just told her the plain truth—which is more than she did with you."

"Laura…" He took hold of her arm and forced her to look at him. "What did you say to her?"

She lifted her chin defiantly. "I told her she never should have come here to face her fears at your expense. She's using you, and I thought it was high time somebody stood up to her. You're too lovestruck to see her for what she is."

Matt couldn't believe what he was hearing. "Laura, how could you? I thought you of all people would sympathize with Teddi."

"I do, I suppose, in a way," she admitted. "But she's just a selfish Hollywood big shot who blew into town and swept you off your feet. You're my friend, and I'm not going to stand by while someone uses you."

"How did you come to that conclusion?" Matt demanded.

"Isn't it obvious? She tricked you into giving her this job just so she could prove something to herself. That's not fair to you."

"Let me decide what's fair, okay?" he said angrily. "You stay out of it. Teddi's got enough to handle without you dumping on her for no reason."

"I'm sorry," Laura said. "But I don't want to see you get hurt. That woman is just plain crazy, and you're too far gone to see her for what she is. How could anyone who lost her entire family to a tornado be so stupid as to get involved with someone who chases them for a living?"

Matt couldn't believe what he was hearing. "Did you say that to her?"

Laura shrugged. "More or less."

"Damn it!" He snatched up the dish towel and threw it across the room.

"Matt! She's using you. Can't you see that? She used the documentary as a test of courage, and she got involved with you for the same reason. What better way is there for a woman who's afraid of tornadoes to prove how brave she is than to seduce a tornado chaser?''

Matt didn't want to hear that. He didn't even want to think it, because it was the one thing he'd been trying hardest to deny ever since Teddi had told him the truth. Hearing Laura say it made it real somehow, and he wasn't ready to face that yet. ''You stay out of this, Laura. Teddi isn't you, okay? She's got enough guts to face her fears and conquer them.''

''And I don't?'' Laura asked indignantly. ''Is that what you're saying?''

Under other circumstances, Matt would have recanted. He would have soothed her, or assured her he hadn't meant it. At the moment, though, he was too angry to do either. Instead, he leaned toward her and lowered his voice. ''Just butt out, Laura. Okay? Stay away from Teddi. She's got enough problems without taking on yours, as well.''

''Fine!'' she said furiously as Matt whirled away from her and stormed out. ''That's just fine,'' she repeated to the empty room as tears welled in her eyes.

TEDDI BECAME the center of attention the moment she stepped out of the kitchen. Nate took her under his wing, introducing her to everyone, and it quickly became obvious that the Chase One team was no longer disappointed in her performance yesterday. In their eyes, the video footage more than made up for her failure, and they accepted her into the fold without question. No one asked about the condition of her camera, so she didn't have to tell them the truth, and she was grateful for that. Her ugly little scene with Laura Cochran had given her more than enough to handle for one night. As it was, she had to shelve her anger and save it for another time.

Since everyone was clamoring for her attention, it was easy to avoid Matt when he came charging out of the kitchen, obviously looking for her. Teddi could only guess what had happened after she left, and she really didn't want to know.

For the next hour, as the crowd gradually thinned out, she deflected compliments and did her best to understand what made this unusual breed of men and women tick. Once she shoved her own prejudice aside, it wasn't too hard for her to comprehend. Teddi knew what it was like to court danger. Something in her craved that kind of challenge, and she found the same attitude in most of the people she talked to.

On the other hand, she found it difficult to listen impassively to the storm chasers' recitations of "Tornadoes I Have Known." They were eager to share their experiences with her, and Teddi did her best to put her own memories aside.

By the time the last guests drifted away, Laura's tables had been loaded into her catering truck, but the caterer herself was nowhere to be seen. It seemed she had exchanged vehicles with her son, leaving Corey to drive the truck home. Matt appeared as relieved about that as Teddi, and he was also relieved when Teddi sent Bryce and Griff on their way.

"You're not going, too, are you?" Matt asked as they stood on the porch watching the van's taillights disappear down the lane. Everyone else was gone and they were finally alone.

She smiled up at him. "Of course not. We've got a lot to talk about."

Matt escorted her back into the house, and while she settled on the sofa he ejected the cassette. He moved to her and held it out. "Here. You should keep this."

Teddi shook her head. "No, you keep it. I don't collect souvenirs until after I've completed a job."

"Does that mean you really are staying?" Matt asked as he sat on the sofa with his body angled so that he was facing her.

"Yes. I realized that if I could edit that tape effectively, I could handle the rest of the film. With Bryce and Griff doing the camera work we won't have to worry if I freak out during the next chase."

"I think you'll find it gets a little easier each time," he told her, then smiled. "At least, I hope so."

She tried to return his smile. "Me, too. I'm not sure I could survive a repeat of yesterday."

"You will survive, Teddi," he said encouragingly.

"Oh, I know I will, Matt," she said with a wave of her hand. "I'm just being melodramatic. I like playing the long-suffering martyr."

She was trying to make a joke of it, but Matt knew her fear was real. If she needed to minimize it with humor, though, he wouldn't challenge her. She'd been through enough—in fact, too much, thanks to his well-meaning friend. "Teddi, I'm sorry for the things Laura said to you earlier."

She didn't want to think about it right now. "It wasn't your fault, Matt."

"Yes, it was. I never should have told her what you're going through."

Teddi shrugged. "You thought she'd understand. Frankly, so did I. I guess she proved us both wrong."

"Are you upset about it?"

"I'll get over it."

Matt shook his head. "I really thought you two would be friends, Teddi. I hadn't counted on her protective instincts outweighing her compassion and sense of fair play."

Teddi sensed the tension in his voice. "Did you two quarrel about it after I left the kitchen?"

He nodded. "I don't think I've ever been so angry with her."

Teddi took his hand and squeezed it. "Matt, I'm sorry. I didn't mean to come between you and your best friend. Patch it up with her, please. She was just trying to protect you." Suddenly annoyed with herself, Teddi stood up and moved to the windows overlooking the deck. "God, I have made a mess of everything!"

Matt stood and came up behind her. "It'll be all right, Teddi."

He put his arms around her, and Teddi leaned back against the comforting wall of security he offered. "Keep telling me that and maybe I'll believe it."

"Believe it," he said, burying his lips in her hair.

Teddi turned in his arms and reached up to touch his face. "Matt, I would give anything to be able to do this all over again—and do it *right* this time. I never should have asked you to hire me."

"You had to confront your fear, Teddi. I understand that."

"But I shouldn't have used your documentary as a test. I should have come here as a civilian like some of these people I met tonight and faced this on my own."

"It's done, Teddi. Now we just have to live with it."

She slipped her arms around him and leaned her head on his shoulder. "Thank you for understanding. You have no idea how much it means to me."

"Anytime," he murmured, resting his head against hers, letting the wonderful feel of her silken hair and her shapely body soothe away the doubts he didn't want to face yet.

"I don't want to go back to the motel tonight, Matt," she said softly, raising her head to look into his eyes.

"Then don't." He pressed a kiss to her lips, then deepened it into a long, slow expression of what he felt in his heart. Teddi responded, and when the kiss finally ended, Matt smiled at her. "There's a picnic table out there just waiting for us."

Teddi shook her head. "I thought we could try the shower or back seat of your car this time," she said with a teasing smile. In the end they settled for the bed.

CHAPTER TWELVE

THE NEXT MORNING, Teddi and Matt put his house back in order and in general pretended they were just two ordinary people spending a quiet Sunday together. The feeling of normalcy was good for them both. It kept Teddi from worrying about when they might chase their next tornado, and it kept Matt from thinking about the accusations Laura had made last night.

But after lunch, when Teddi left for her meeting with Bryce and Griff, the house became too quiet and Matt had too much time to think. Every time he walked into the kitchen Laura's words and his own doubts came back to haunt him, and finally he couldn't avoid the subject any longer.

How could he and Teddi possibly hope to build a relationship? The question had nagged at him for two days now. Teddi O'Brien, who'd survived a nightmare by some miracle, was subjecting herself to the horror all over again. Why on earth had she so blithely complicated the ordeal by getting involved with a man who was surely the embodiment of all her fears?

It was ironic. Matt had avoided emotional commitment for so long because he knew it wasn't fair to ask any woman to cope with his dangerous profession. Then up popped Teddi O'Brien giving every appearance of being the perfect woman. He'd let himself fall hard for her, and now...

What? Laura certainly hadn't been able to cope with his profession. How could he expect more from Teddi, who had lost her whole family? If nothing else, he would be a constant reminder of the way her family had died.

But if she didn't want a relationship with him, why had she gotten involved with him in the first place? And why on earth had she stayed last night? She'd made love with him and cuddled in his arms until sleep had claimed her. She'd seemed perfectly content—happy, even. But how could she be so at ease with him after what she'd been through?

What kind of comfort could Matt, of all people, really offer her? She hadn't been willing to accept his comfort the night before when she'd been nearly hysterical with panic and shame. She hadn't needed him then, so why had she wanted to be with him last night? Why be with him at all?

The questions went round and round in Matt's head, and the one answer he always returned to was the one he didn't want to believe. To Teddi, everything in life was a test. She defined her existence by the challenges she overcame. Was Matt just the ultimate challenge as Laura had claimed?

He thought he might go crazy just thinking about it, and he knew that eventually he had to confront Teddi with his doubts. He'd have to hear her deny it with her own lips, and maybe then he could put the matter to rest.

In the middle of the afternoon Corey appeared unexpectedly at his door, and Matt was inordinately grateful for the intrusion. Anything to distract him from the emotional circles he was running in was welcome.

"Corey! Come on in," he said. "What brings you down here on your day off? I thought you and Olivia had plans."

"We have to talk, Matt."

The young man marched into the living room, and the

serious set of his face made Matt realize he'd been wrong. This wasn't going to be the kind of distraction he needed at all. "All right. What's up?" he asked guardedly.

"Olivia and I went out to the hospital in Norman this afternoon because she wanted to see Tom Patten's new baby."

"Uh-oh," Matt said with a teasing grin. "Let me give you a little piece of man-to-man advice. When the woman you're dating starts cooing over babies, you'd better watch out."

Corey didn't respond to the joke. "We didn't see the baby, Matt. The hospital transferred him to a neonatal unit up in Oklahoma City last night because he was having trouble breathing on his own."

"I'm really sorry to hear that," Matt said, feeling like a heel. He'd heard at the party last night that Mona had suffered through a difficult twenty-five hour labor on Friday, but he hadn't realized there was a problem with the baby. Tom had worked at the center for only two years after having transferred from a storm-research facility in Colorado. He was a good researcher, but he hadn't been an easy man to get to know. Now Matt felt badly about not having gone out of his way to check on the newborn. "Is the baby going to be okay?"

"The doctors don't think he's going to die, but apparently he's going to need some special care over the next few months," Corey told him. "I don't really know all the details."

"I'll give Tom a call at home later tonight and see if there's anything we can do for him," Matt promised.

"I already know what you can do for him," Corey replied. "He told me he's going to come to the center tomorrow and apply for a short leave of absence—" he paused a moment "—and he's resigning from Chase One, for this season, at least. He doesn't think it would be fair to Mona for him to be out of the area and out of touch so often.''

Matt's stomach tightened as he realized what was coming next. ''Of course I'll give him a leave and accept his resignation. But that leaves me with a big hole in the chase team.''

Corey nodded. ''And I want to fill it,'' he said firmly.

Matt sighed and dropped into a chair. ''Corey, have you talked this over with Laura?''

The young man sat on the sofa across from Matt. ''Not yet.''

''Don't you think you should?''

He shook his head. ''No. This is none of her business. I let her bulldoze me into accepting a position as a data assistant when what I really wanted was to chase. I'm not going to give her the chance to do that again. It's my life and my career. She doesn't have any right to dictate what I do with either.''

Corey was deadly serious and very determined. Matt saw that in his eyes, and he respected him for it. But that didn't solve any of his problems—or Matt's. ''Corey, as long as your mother is helping pay your way through college, she has a lot of rights.''

''I talked to Gerry Hampton before I came here. He shares an apartment off campus with two other guys, and he says there's room for one more. With four of us splitting the rent, I can manage it for the rest of the school year.''

''What about next year?''

''I'm already working for the center this summer, and I can find another part-time job,'' he said with a determination Matt found admirable. ''I'll save what I can and start working now on grants and loans.''

''You make it sound simple.''

"I'm not stupid, Matt. I know it won't be easy, but I've been thinking about this for a long time. I'd decided to chase next year, anyway. I'll be facing the same problems whether you assign me to Chase One this season or not. And you don't really have a choice about that, do you?"

Obviously Corey had figured out every angle. "Tom does have to be replaced," Matt admitted. "We can't do chase-and-deploy maneuvers with only five team members."

"And you don't have any room in your budget to hire another grad student," he reminded him. "Since you're already paying me, I'm the only logical choice."

He was absolutely right, but for Laura's sake Matt felt obligated to protest. "I'm paying you as a data assistant."

"Then I'll work whatever extra hours are necessary to keep up with my other duties."

Matt had run out of arguments. Laura was never going to forgive him, but Corey had a right to make his own decisions. The confrontation that was coming between mother and son had been inevitable, and Matt had always known he'd get caught in the middle. Considering the argument he'd had with Laura last night, though, the timing couldn't have been worse.

"All right," he said finally, knowing he had no other options available. "If Tom resigns, you'll take his place on Chase One."

"Thanks, Matt," Corey said, but whatever relief or enthusiasm he'd expected to feel apparently didn't materialize. Matt knew he had to be thinking about Laura.

"Don't thank me," he said with a shake of his head. "You still have to tell your mother. Moving out is going to be a lot harder than you imagine."

"I don't think anything could be harder than what I'm

imagining," Corey said bleakly. "I don't want to hurt her, Matt. I just want to live my own life."

"Then go easy on her and give her some time to adjust to your decision." Matt gave him an encouraging smile. "When you make it through this chase season without getting hurt, maybe she'll come around."

"I hope so."

Corey left a short time later looking like a man marching off to the electric chair. He promised to call with a report later, and Matt settled in to wait for Laura's reaction. He had a feeling he'd be able to hear the explosion thirty miles away.

When his doorbell rang at five o'clock, Matt prepared himself for the worst. He opened the door and felt guilty for being so relieved that his visitor was Teddi.

"Hi! I'm back," she said as she breezed past him carrying an armload of groceries. "And I come bearing dinner. As I recall, I owe you one home-cooked meal."

Matt followed her into the kitchen, only too happy to let her lightheartedness soothe his worries. "Is this going to be the Great Teddi O'Brien Cook-Off Grudge Match?"

"Yep." She dumped the sacks onto the counter and began rummaging through them. "What'll it be? Omelets at thirty paces, or would you prefer that we toss a little Caesar salad at each other?"

Matt peeked into the sacks and discovered she wasn't joking. "I was thinking more along the lines of beef Wellington."

"Dream on, handsome. Betty Crocker, I ain't."

Matt laughed. "Your meeting with Bryce and Griff must have gone well."

Teddi popped a head of lettuce into the refrigerator. "They were great. I explained the whole situation and they accepted it without question. No recriminations, no hassles. Just a lot of friendly support and professionalism."

"They're your friends. What else did you expect?"

Teddi stopped and looked at him. "Matt, I haven't told anyone about what happened to my family since before I entered film school. I convinced myself that I just wanted to leave the pity behind, but what I was really avoiding was the impact it had on my life. I was trying to redefine Teddi O'Brien and make her into a person whose parents hadn't disapproved of her right up to the day they died. Telling anyone about that seemed a lot harder than climbing Everest." She took a jar of mayonnaise from the sack. "Frankly, I didn't know what to expect from Bryce and Griff. At the very least, I thought they'd condemn me for taking this job under false pretenses."

"But they didn't, did they?"

"No. Like you said, they're friends."

"They also know what you can do once you set your mind to it," he reminded her. "That counts for a lot."

"Yes, it does. So, what did you do while I was gone?"

Matt took a deep breath. "I gave Corey Tom Patten's position on Chase One."

Teddi stopped trying to figure out which cabinet the mayonnaise went in and turned to him. "You what?"

He explained what had happened during Corey's visit, and when he was finished, Teddi gave a low whistle. "Whew. This is going to be tough."

Matt sagged against the counter. "You're telling me. Laura will never understand that I didn't have any other choice."

"Maybe she'll come around eventually," Teddi said hopefully.

"I'm not counting on it," Matt replied. "It's been fifteen years since Joe died. Laura accepted his death and even turned the tragedy into something constructive by working on the Disaster Planning Commission. But she still blames his death on his profession. I don't think that's ever going to change."

"Maybe you should remind her that even innocent by-standers get killed by tornadoes," Teddi said softly.

Matt understood the haunting sadness in her eyes. "I'm sorry. This is all very difficult for you, isn't it?" He moved to her, intending to take her into his arms, but apparently Teddi only accepted comfort on her own terms, because she went back to unpacking groceries. Matt backed off, stung by her unspoken rejection.

"I suppose you haven't heard from Laura yet," she said.

"No, but I will," he replied. "I told Corey he had to be the one to break the news to her, but I've had to fight myself all afternoon to keep from calling her. Maybe it would have been easier on her coming from me."

"You know better than that. This is between Laura and Corey."

"Yes, but I'm caught in the middle. Corey is like a son to me. Laura is my best friend. I can't bear the thought of either of them being hurt."

Teddi gave him a sympathetic look. "I know."

"But there's nothing I can do for the time being," he said, then began digging into the grocery sacks. "So what do you say we—"

The doorbell cut him off. Matt and Teddi both froze, looking at each other. "The moment of truth?" Teddi asked.

Matt nodded. "I'd stake my life on it." He moved toward the kitchen door. "Why don't you stay here out of the firing line?"

"Don't mind if I do," Teddi said. "Matt..."

He stopped and looked at her questioningly.

"It'll be okay," she told him. "No matter how angry or hurt she is, Laura still loves you very much."

The doorbell rang again and Matt went to answer it. He was expecting the worst, and he got it. Laura was there, her face blotchy from the crying. But her eyes were dry now. They were also blazing with a rage that chilled Matt to the bone.

"Come on in, Laura." He stepped back to let her enter and was amazed by the tight rein of control she had on herself as she moved into his living room. She dropped her purse onto a chair and turned to face him.

Matt had expected screaming and shouting, but what he saw was far worse. He hadn't imagined Laura was capable of hatred.

"Why?" she said softly. Just the one word.

"He asked for the job, and he's earned it. He's met every criteria of academic standards—"

"Don't feed me any bull about academic standards!" she shouted. "This has nothing to do with grades. My son just moved out of his home!"

"I'm sorry about that, Laura, but he's a grown man. He has a right to make his own decisions."

"He's a child! He thinks he's immortal. He doesn't understand that this is going to kill him!"

"Laura, he is not going to die!"

In her mother's heart, Laura knew he was wrong. "Why are you doing this to me, Matt? Are you just trying to punish me?"

Matt frowned, thoroughly confused. "For what?"

"For the things I said to your girlfriend last night!"

The accusation caught him completely by surprise. This was the last thing he'd expected. "Of course not, Laura. This has nothing to do with Teddi."

"I don't believe you. She's got you so screwed up that

you can't see straight anymore!" Laura put one hand on her forehead, as though that would contain her anger. But it didn't work. "I can't believe that you would turn your back on our friendship because of her."

Matt struggled to remain calm. Laura wasn't being rational, or she wouldn't be looking to place blame where none existed. "This has nothing to do with Teddi," he repeated patiently but firmly. "If Corey had applied for a chase slot last December, we'd have been having this conversation back then, long before I even met her."

"Then why are you doing this to me?" she asked as tears sprang into her eyes.

Matt couldn't bear to see her in so much pain, but when he moved toward her, looking for a way to comfort her, she backed away from him as though he had the plague. "I'm doing it *for* Corey," he insisted.

Laura laughed harshly. "You're killing him for his own good?"

"He is not going to die!" Matt practically shouted as frustration overwhelmed patience. "He just wants to be his own man, Laura. And for Corey, that means following in his father's footsteps."

"Damn it, he's not following in Joe's footsteps! He's trying to follow in yours, and it's going to get him killed!"

"Laura, look at me. I'm alive. I've been chasing tornadoes since before I graduated from high school, and it hasn't killed me yet. In fact, no one at CTR has died or even been hurt since I established the Chase One program."

"Oh, really? What about Nate Dansing?"

Matt frowned, unable to imagine what she meant, then it hit him. "Oh, for crying out loud. A drunk driver plowed into the van as we were coming home from a chase, and Nate wasn't wearing his seat belt. He got a bump on the head and a cracked rib. It could have happened anytime, anywhere!''

"But it happened!"

"Good Lord, Laura, it was a traffic accident." Matt wiped his hand over his face. "If you're really this paranoid, why don't you just have Corey stuffed into a glass bubble and keep him on display in your living room?''

Laura drew her shoulders back indignantly. "That's not fair. I've never been overprotective of my son."

"You've always been overprotective," Matt countered heatedly. "But you've managed to keep it in some kind of perspective until now. Let him live his life the way he sees fit, or he's going to cut you out of it."

"You'd like that, wouldn't you?"

Matt felt as though he was beating his head against a brick wall. "Why are you blaming me for this, Laura? It was Corey's decision to chase. If I had refused him, he would have applied for one of the teams in Norman. You can't keep him from chasing if it's what he really wants."

"I can try," she argued.

"Yes, you can. But if you succeed, he'll always resent you."

"I don't care if he resents me, as long as he's alive to do it!"

They weren't getting anywhere. Nothing he could say was going to make her understand. "I'm sorry, Laura," he said gently.

"If you're really sorry, you'll tell Corey you've changed your mind."

"I can't do that."

"Then we don't have anything else to say to each other." She snatched up her purse and swept past him, then turned as she reached the door, her chin raised in defiance and indignation. "This is on your head now, Matt. When he dies, I hope to God you'll be able to forgive yourself, because I sure as hell won't.''

She slammed out, leaving Matt standing shell-shocked in the middle of the living room, feeling as though he'd just lost his best friend. Which, of course, he had.

"Matt?"

He turned and found Teddi beside him, but it took a second to focus on her. "You heard?"

She nodded. "It was kinda hard not to." She took his hand. "I'm sorry."

"Don't be. It's not your fault."

"Laura doesn't agree with you."

"Teddi, I did not give Corey this job just to punish her for what she said to you. I was furious with her last night, but I would never be vindictive about it." He looked at her. "You believe that, don't you, Teddi? This has nothing to do with you."

"I know you weren't being vindictive, Matt," she assured him. "But you do have to admit that Laura might not have been quite so irrational today if you two hadn't had a fight about me last night."

"Our argument has nothing to do with this," he insisted. "Laura had no right to say those things to you."

"Don't be angry with her for that. She was only stating the obvious, based on what she'd just learned about me. I mean, from her point of view we're not exactly the most logical couple in the world, are we?"

Matt stiffened, inside and out, because Teddi had struck too close to the heart of his doubts. "Are you saying you're sorry you got involved with me?"

Teddi was surprised. "No, of course not. I'm just trying to see this from Laura's point of view. When you look at our relationship honestly—"

"Teddi, I've always been honest with you," he said sharply.

Matt was upset, and Teddi realized he was transferring some of his anxiety about Laura to their situation. Still, she couldn't blame him for being angry with her for the way she'd misled him when she took this job. She certainly deserved it. "I know you've been honest with me. My deception, on the other hand, has caused nothing but trouble. But I had to come here, Matt. I had to face this. My only regret is that I wasn't fair to you. Laura was right about that."

"What else was she right about, Teddi?" Matt asked, knowing he was going to regret it, but he couldn't stop himself. The fight with Laura had brought too many painful emotions to the surface, and his doubts about Teddi were a very powerful ingredient in that emotional stew.

Teddi frowned. "I don't understand what you're asking me, Matt."

"I'm asking why you became involved with me."

"Because you're wonderful," she said as though it should be perfectly obvious.

"I'm a tornado chaser," he countered. "Didn't you just say we're an unlikely couple?"

"Yes, but—"

"Don't you think I was entitled to know that? Why did you let us become so involved? Couldn't you have warned me about your past instead of letting me walk into this blindly? I thought we were two people admirably suited to have a relationship. But what Laura said last night was true."

"Don't spout Laura's words at me, Matt," Teddi said defensively. "I didn't 'warn' you because I didn't think it was necessary. Just because she couldn't handle your profession doesn't mean that I can't."

Matt glared at her. "How can you say that? You couldn't possibly hope to have a relationship with me—not with your background." There. He'd said it. God, how it hurt, but it was time he faced the truth.

"Matt, what kind of person do you think I am? Your career doesn't matter to me!"

"How can it not matter, Teddi? You lost your family to a tornado. I chase tornadoes for a living. That makes us about as compatible as fire and rain."

"There's a lot to be said for that combination, Matt. Ask anyone who's ever fought a forest fire."

Matt looked at her in astonishment. "You're honestly going to stand there and tell me you think we've got a chance of making a relationship work?"

Teddi wanted to give him an emphatic yes, but she couldn't. She'd lost too much trust in herself to be firmly convinced of anything. She didn't believe that Laura was right, but Teddi couldn't risk hurting Matt any more by making promises she wasn't certain she could keep.

"I don't know what's going to happen to us, Matt," she said, trying to be as honest as she knew how. "That tornado chase stripped me of everything I believed about myself, and I'm not foolish enough to think I'll be able to pick up the pieces overnight. When all this is over, maybe we will discover we don't have a prayer of making a relationship work. I just don't know. But that doesn't mean we can't have something very special while I'm here."

"Damn it, Teddi, I want more than that!"

"Well, I can't promise you more!"

"So I'm just supposed to sit around like a love-starved puppy waiting for you to throw crumbs at me while you decide whether or not we have a future? Is that it? I'm supposed to wear my heart on my sleeve and moon over you until you make up your mind?"

Teddi felt a sudden rush of tears pressing against her eyes, but she fought them back. "I had thought you might be my friend—and my lover. To help me cope," she said softly. "But I guess that's asking too much."

"Oh, come on, Teddi. You don't need my help. You made that clear the other night when you asked me to leave your motel room. If ever you needed someone, it was then. It's a little late to start playing the damsel in distress."

Nothing he could have said would have made Teddi any angrier. She wasn't in the habit of asking for help from anyone, and getting slapped in the face this time was too much. "I am not a damsel in distress, Matt. I can take care of myself and I'm proud of it. I thought you knew that about me and appreciated it, but I guess I was wrong. You've let Laura Cochran lean on your strong manly shoulder for so long that you want all women to be as dependent on you as she is."

"I don't want you to be dependent on me, Teddi, but I don't want to be used, either," he said harshly. "I was just another test for you, wasn't I? Another challenge to be met and conquered. Making love with a tornado chaser gave you a real thrill, didn't it? It was one more way to prove how brave you are!"

"That's not true!"

He advanced on her, so angry he could barely think. "Yes, it is. Your life has been one long test of courage. You got involved with me for the same reason you jumped off a roof with a sheet for a parachute. You wanted to see if you could do it and survive." He bowed to her. "Well, congratulations, Ms. O'Brien. You did it. You can pat yourself on the back and go on to the next challenge."

"Matt, I don't believe I'm hearing this."

"Believe it, Teddi, because I'm not going to let myself be used anymore. You've got my documentary to use as a test of courage. That's going to have to be enough for your ego."

Teddi felt as though something precious was slipping away from her, but didn't know how to call it back. "This isn't about ego! I care about you, Matt. Very, very much."

He wanted to believe that, but he had learned better than to trust anything Teddi said. "Why? Because I chase tornadoes for a living?"

"Yes, damn it! That's part of who you are. The risks you take helped you understand and accept me. At least, I *thought* you understood me. But if you can really believe that I was just using our relationship, then you don't know me at all."

"What I do know is that I don't want to be another notch on the belt of the fearless Teddi O'Brien."

Teddi took a deep breath, trying to calm herself, but it didn't work. Finally she backed away from him with her hands raised, as though the gesture could make this whole nightmare go away. "I'm sorry, Matt, but I can't deal with this right now. You're being as irrational as your friend, Laura, and I'm just not equipped to handle it." She started for the kitchen where she'd left her purse. "Obviously it was a mistake for me to come here this afternoon."

"I think it was a mistake for you to come to Oklahoma at all," Matt said quietly.

Teddi stopped and turned to him, feeling as though he'd just slapped her. "Well, that's just too damned bad," she said, her voice filled with quiet fury. "Because I'm here whether you like it or not. I've got a contract that I intend to fulfill."

"Of course you will. Teddi O'Brien never fails, does she?"

She glared at him defiantly. "No, she doesn't." Teddi whirled away from him and stalked into the kitchen. Matt was still standing in the same spot when she returned and headed straight for the door. ''I'll see you at the center tomorrow,'' she said tersely as she threw it open.

She didn't look back as she stormed out, and Matt didn't try to stop her, because there was nothing left to say. It was over.

CHAPTER THIRTEEN

TEDDI SPENT THE NIGHT pacing the floor of her motel room, not knowing whether she should be angry with Matt or with herself. As much as his accusations had hurt, she couldn't really blame him for feeling used. She'd walked into their relationship with her eyes wide open, but that was a privilege she'd denied Matt. He had a right to be hurt.

But to accuse her of making love with him as a test of courage? That was unfair. She had become involved with him *despite* his profession, not because of it, and as a result she had found a place that had made her feel truly safe and secure for the first time in her life. She didn't know why that was true, but it was.

But that safe place was gone now. Even if she could convince Matt she hadn't been using him, she still couldn't guarantee that their relationship would become something permanent. She had too many demons to face before she could look clearly into the future and see what was there. Letting Matt believe there was hope for them and then having to snatch it away would be far crueler than anything she'd ever done.

Besides, he wouldn't believe her, anyway. Laura Cochran had seen to that. She had done such a number on him he was completely convinced no woman could cope with his profession—especially not a woman who'd been through the kind of ordeal Teddi had. It might take a lifetime to prove to Matt that Laura was wrong—and Teddi didn't have a lifetime. She had less than two months until the storm season ended and she had to return to L.A.

In the end, she decided that the best thing she could do was take Laura's advice and leave Matt alone so that he could get over her, but on Monday morning she realized how hard that was going to be. Just being in the same room with him and not being able to touch him or laugh with him was torture, but seeing the anger and hurt in his eyes and hearing coldness in his voice drove a stake into her heart.

"Kick me if this is none of my business, but what the hell is wrong with Matt?" Bryce said to her as they left Matt's office where they'd been discussing the new shooting schedule. "If looks could kill, you'd be pushing up daisies."

Teddi was reeling from her first encounter with Matt since their argument, and she didn't really want to get into it with Bryce. He could be as overprotective as Laura Cochran if he thought Teddi was being threatened. Having him become involved in this whole mess was the last thing she needed. "We had a disagreement last night."

"About what?"

"My motives for coming here." It was only one step away from the truth, but Bryce didn't need to know anymore.

He frowned. "You told Griff and me that Matt understood."

She glanced at him as they moved into the editing room. "It's complicated."

"Ah," he said with a nod. "You mean the bloom has fallen off your budding romance."

"That's about the size of it," Teddi said lightly, trying to cover her pain. She pulled a chair up to her desk and began sorting her notes, but Bryce wasn't finished with her.

"Are you okay?" he asked as he sat on the edge of the desk.

"Sure."

"Funny, you don't look okay."

Teddi forced a smile in his direction. "What does 'okay' look like?"

"On you, it's a smile that makes your eyes sparkle and everyone around you feel on top of the world."

"Sorry," Teddi said, "but that chase the other day threw a bucket of water on my sparkler."

"I think Matt Abernathy has as much to do with it as the chase," Bryce said, clearly unhappy with this turn of events.

Teddi covered his hand with hers. "Stay out of it, Bryce. Please," she begged, unwittingly letting some of her pain bleed through. "I screwed up. I didn't tell Matt the whole truth when he hired me. Professionally speaking, he forgave me for that when I decided to turn my camera duties over to Griff, but personally, it's a lot more complicated. He's hurt and angry. I can't blame him for that, and you shouldn't, either."

Bryce studied her closely. "You fell for him pretty hard, didn't you?"

Teddi went back to shuffling papers. "Yes."

"Let's-have-fun-during-the-shoot hard, or happily-ever-after hard?"

Teddi fought back a sudden rush of tears as all the emotion she wanted so desperately to suppress caught up with her. "It should have been the happily-ever-after kind, Bryce," she said quietly, wondering what it would take to stop the ache in her heart. "But I screwed up. Now we'll never have a chance to find out."

Bryce leaned over and kissed her cheek. "You'll work it out, Teddi."

She looked at him bleakly. "Not this time. It's over. Matt doesn't want anything to do with me and I can't really blame him."

Bryce started to respond, but Griff's arrival stopped him. "Somebody want to give me a hand?" he barked as he came in juggling two armloads of videotapes he'd culled from the center's archives of amateur tornado- and storm-chase footage. They would have to review it all to see if any of it could be used in the documentary. Bryce jumped up to help him with the tapes, and Teddi began giving orders, laying out the day's work for them.

With so much to do, it was easy for Teddi to avoid Matt for the next few days. Except for the routine Chase One weather briefing every morning, there was really no reason for her to see him, and he certainly didn't make any effort to seek her out. When he did, their conversations were terse and professional. Teddi tried twice to talk to him, hoping somehow to disarm his anger and ease the hurt she'd caused him, but Matt wouldn't listen to her. He seemed determined to hold on to his anger, and Teddi finally stopped butting her head against a brick wall.

Though she missed Matt and the easy camaraderie they'd once shared, Teddi's time was easy to fill. She set up personal interviews with the team members and made appointments with all those on the long list of area officials who had agreed to discuss tornado precautions. There were so many people to interview on camera it would take every bit of the two months she had to get everything done.

Her first interview outside the center was scheduled for Thursday at the local elementary school, where students and staff were going to perform a tornado drill. Unfortunately, the weather didn't cooperate. When Teddi arrived at the morning briefing, she learned that a promising storm system had developed overnight, and Matt expected that by afternoon it would be ripe for the chasing.

If the Turner elementary school excused classes for a tornado today, it wouldn't be a drill. Teddi canceled the interview and got her crew ready for the chase.

"Are you okay?" Bryce asked her that afternoon as they loaded their equipment into the van. Matt's team was just a few yards away inside the garage doing the same thing.

"I'm fine," Teddi told him, despite the rapid pounding of her heart. "Just don't expect any sparkle."

"You'll get through it, Teddi."

She held her sweaty palms up for his inspection. "When was the last time you saw me break out in a cold sweat?"

Bryce threw his arm around her shoulder. "As I recall, you were hanging by an ice pick and a fraying rope from the face of the Asapeka Glacier. You wanna go back there?"

"No."

His expression grew serious. "You wanna go home to L.A.?"

Teddi met his gaze evenly. "Not on your life."

He grinned. "That's my girl," he said, giving her a swift peck on the cheek.

Teddi glanced at the garage and found Matt standing there, watching them. She couldn't tell whether he was scowling because the sun was in his eyes or because Bryce had his arm around her. "Are your people ready to go?" he asked.

Teddi nodded and eased away from Bryce. "We're ready. Bryce will be in the chase van with you, and Griff will ride in the deploy truck." That left Teddi bringing up the rear, driving the equipment van where she could do the least amount of damage. "Did Griff get all your people wired for sound?"

Matt nodded as he self-consciously fingered the tiny microphone clipped inside his shirt pocket. "He's just finishing up with Corey."

"Then we're ready to go when you are," Teddi said.

"All right. Let's do it." He looked as though he wanted to say something else, but apparently the urge passed, because he turned on his heel and disappeared into the garage.

"Good luck to you, too," Teddi murmured, as she climbed behind the wheel of the van.

For the next three hours, the three vehicles moved along a circuitous intercept route with the storm. Ryan Sawyer rode in the van with Teddi, and she was surprised to learn that he had picked up quite a bit of technical knowledge from Griff during their first chase. He knew all about the two remote channels Griff had programed into his equipment, so the young man spent a lot of the trip in the back with a headset on, eavesdropping on the conversations taking place in the other vehicles.

Teddi had her own headset on and was doing much the same thing. Periodically Nate would radio back a change in course, though there really wasn't any need; thanks to the microphones, Teddi knew everything they did about the storm brewing in the west. It wasn't as big as the first squall line had been, but it was just as terrifying.

When they finally got into position below the storm, the procedure was exactly the same as before, only this time Bryce was the one standing alone in a field recording the release of the weather balloon and Matt's careful study of Pandora.

Teddi stayed in the van at first, recording the conversations, but once she was sure the equipment was running smoothly, she got out and forced herself to watch the storm. The smaller squall had given them the luxury of being farther away this time, but Teddi still felt the thunderclaps all the way to her bones. Every streak of lightning made her jump, and every stray wisp of cloud that tore away from the main body of the supercell caused her heart to skip a beat. But the tornado she dreaded never appeared.

They waited nearly an hour as the storm moved ponderously toward the east, and finally Teddi heard Matt tell his team to pack it in. Relief flooded through her, but Matt's disappointment was so obvious she couldn't help feeling sorry for him. He didn't have a lot of time to prove his theory.

Without really understanding why or stopping to think, Teddi moved toward the lead van where Matt was folding Pandora's antennae. The frigid look he gave her when he glanced up made her regret her impulsive gesture, but she didn't back down. "I'm sorry. I know that was disappointing. Maybe next time."

"Don't worry, Teddi," he said. "I'll find you a storm before the season is out so you can prove to us all how brave you are."

She stepped back, stung, but when she realized that Bryce and Griff were right behind her and at least three other team members were listening, too, the hurt turned to anger. "I didn't make that storm collapse, Matt. Don't take your disappointment out on me," she said tersely. "Are we finished here?"

"Oh, yes." he said. "We're finished."

Teddi refused to acknowledge the double entendre. "Then if there are no other cells developing, I'll meet you back at the center." She turned to her crewmen. "Come on, Griff. Let's collect the body mikes and get out of here." She threw one last venomous glance at Matt and stalked off.

ALL THE WAY BACK to Turner, Matt berated himself for snapping at Teddi. She was right. It wasn't her fault the storm dissipated. But everything she did these days put him on edge. He'd spent a week trying to conquer his anger and he was failing miserably, because every time he saw her he was reminded of what had been and what was never going to be.

It infuriated him, that she was doing such a good job of keeping their relationship professional. While he was struggling with his anger, Teddi was charming the pants off his team members and the CTR staff. She laughed and joked with Bryce and Griff as though she didn't have a care in the world. Everyone adored her, and it made Matt furious to think that whatever Teddi wanted, she got...

A sky-sail certificate? No problem.

A film she never should have agreed to direct? Piece of cake.

The love of a man she couldn't possibly have any lasting feelings for? Easy as pie.

That knowledge made Matt feel like a fool and pointed up how easy it had been for Teddi to deceive him. She had made him want things he'd never believed he could have, and then she'd snatched them away. Their relationship had been built on deceit, and Matt just couldn't forgive her for that.

All in all, this had been one of the most miserable weeks of his life.

It hadn't helped his state of mind that Laura still wasn't speaking to him. She refused to take his calls at work, and she hadn't returned any of the messages he'd left on her answering machine at home. Corey was now living with Gerry Hampton, and Laura wasn't speaking to her son, either.

Matt felt as though the breach between them was his fault. That, at least, was one thing he couldn't blame on

Teddi. But he did blame her for his sleepless nights and the ache in his gut that wouldn't go away.

When he got back to the center, Griff's van was parked outside the garage, but there was no sign of Teddi or her crew. It was just as well. He felt as though he owed Teddi an apology, but he didn't think he could stomach saying the words. He just wanted to go home, even though he knew he wouldn't find any comfort there. Everything in the house reminded him of Teddi.

Once all their gear was secured, he dismissed his team and went to his office to stow the Doppler tapes they'd made during the chase. They wouldn't be any help in proving his theory, but they still had to be analyzed.

Matt was behind his desk with his back to the door as he put the tapes in the storage cabinet, and he nearly jumped out of his skin when he heard his door slam. When he whirled around he found Teddi standing there, her eyes spitting fire.

"You will never, ever, speak to me like that in front of my crew. Do you understand?" she said angrily as she came to his desk. "If you've got something to say to me, say it in private, *not* in front of an audience."

Matt slammed the cabinet shut, making the tapes inside rattle. "Sorry. I didn't know you were so sensitive."

"This has nothing to do with sensitivity. I am trying very hard not to let our problems affect the job that has to be done. I expect the same from you. We have to be able to work with each other professionally, and that's not going to happen if you take a swipe at me every time you get an opening."

She was right, of course. "I'm sorry," he said.

Teddi tried to put a lid on her anger, because a display of it wasn't going to do either of them any good. "Matt, like it or not, we're in this together until the season ends. We're going to have to learn to live with it."

He nodded. "I'll see what I can do."

"Damn it," she muttered, turning away from him in frustration. She clenched and unclenched her fists, and when she finally turned back to him, she was closer to begging than she'd ever been in her life. "Matt, what's it going to take to get you to forgive me?"

He could see she was sincere, but he was afraid to trust his own eyes. "How about a little honesty?"

"I *have* been honest with you!"

"How can I believe that when our entire relationship was based on deception?"

"I made a mistake. I'm sorry."

"And that's supposed to make it all better?" he asked bitterly. "Teddi, there are times when 'I'm sorry' just doesn't cut it."

"Well, that's all I've got, Matt."

"That's too bad, because it's not enough."

The pain in his eyes was all her doing. She had put it there, and obviously there was nothing she could do to soothe it away. "You have every right to despise me, Matt. I did deceive you. But if you don't believe anything else I say to you, believe this..." She placed her hands on the desk and leaned toward him. "I did not make love with you just to prove I could do it. I was falling in love. Whether it was because you chase tornadoes or in spite of it, I really don't know, and I don't see that it makes a helluva lot of difference. It's a part of who you are, and I accepted it. If you can't at least accept that I'm human enough to make mistakes, we're not going to make it through the next six weeks."

Matt wanted to believe her, but he was afraid to. He thought he'd been conquering his anger, but he saw now that wasn't true. He'd been holding on to it, because without it he'd have nothing left to protect himself against his love for her. He'd start wanting her all over again, he'd start to hope...and he couldn't let that happen, because it didn't matter whether she'd really been falling in love with him or not. Matt wanted forever, and Teddi wasn't able to give him that.

But hard as he tried, he found he couldn't hang on to his anger. It crumbled into dust, and he quickly shored up his heart with something less violent—and much less effective. "All right, Teddi. I'll agree to a cease-fire."

That was something, at least. It was not nearly as much as she wanted, but she didn't have the right to ask for more. "Thank you." She backed away from the desk, edging toward the door. "I'll see you tomorrow, then?"

He nodded, and she turned for the door. When she reached it, she stopped and looked back at him. "Just for the record, Matt, I wasn't out there today to impress anyone. That storm scared me to death."

Without waiting for a response, she slipped out the door, leaving Matt amazed by her admission. When Teddi set out to do something she did it all the way. Only a week ago, she'd done everything in her power to deny her fear. It had taken a major confrontation to get her to admit it existed at all.

Now, she'd brought it out into the open for anyone to see. Not only was she trying to conquer her fear, she was dealing with all the complicated emotions that had nearly destroyed her image of herself. She was finally being honest with herself and everyone else.

No matter how hard he tried, Matt couldn't stop himself from loving her all the more for that courage.

Before he realized what he was doing, he started around the desk after her, but he stopped himself when he reached the door. Going after her wouldn't change anything. Taking her into his arms as he ached to do would only make it harder to let her go.

Instead, he went back to his desk and tried to figure out how he was going to survive until Teddi left. He didn't know what he'd do when she was gone, but he had the horrible feeling that the pain wouldn't stop even then.

CHAPTER FOURTEEN

THE TRUCE HELD. Matt stopped snapping at Teddi. He kept their relationship professional, but he also kept his distance. That made Teddi's job easier, but it didn't do anything to assuage her guilt or curb the tender, aching emotions that engulfed her every time she looked at him.

Teddi had never felt such regret or remorse. She was accustomed to charging through life making as few mistakes as possible, trying not to hurt anyone and accepting the consequences of the mistakes she did make. But this time she had hurt Matt, and in the process destroyed something rare and precious. As the weeks passed, she found she wasn't able to accept that. Somewhere along the line, she'd fallen in love with the man, and now she had to deal with the consequences of her folly.

On the other hand, she discovered that each storm chase they conducted was a little easier for her than the one before it. That was some comfort, at least. Of course, it helped that there had been no more chases like the first one. In fact, in the six chases they conducted in the first month of the season, not one tornado materialized. Winds howled, rain poured and lightning slashed through dark, ominous clouds, but that was all.

Matt was clearly concerned about his inability to prove his theory, and Teddi began to worry that if they didn't get more chase footage she wouldn't be able to piece together an effective documentary. A tornado film without tornadoes wasn't too exciting. She found a few usable clips from the center archives, but they all looked like the amateur home videos they were.

Hoping for better luck from the professionals, Teddi began scouring television stations in Oklahoma City for news footage of tornadoes. What she found mostly, though, was film of the destructive aftermath—towns that had been decimated, buildings that had been smashed to kindling, people weeping as they sorted through the rubble of their lives.

In a way, those old films were harder on Teddi than the chases, and the one she'd discovered today had been devastating. A knot of pain stayed with her as she left TV station KOAK, and it was still there when she pulled into the center parking lot late in the afternoon.

Feeling vaguely nauseated, she picked up the videocassette from the seat beside her and hurried into the building. She had given Bryce and Griff the day off because they'd forfeited their weekend on back-to-back chases, so the editing room was dark when she entered it. She turned on lights and equipment, then settled down at the editing console and cued up the tape.

The tape case was labeled "Dry Creek Tornado," with the date Teddi's life had changed marked in bold ink. The general manager of the TV station had very generously granted permission for her to use the footage and even had one of his technicians transfer the twenty-year-old celluloid film to videotape. He hadn't known what Teddi really wanted the tape for, though.

This wasn't for Matt's documentary—it was for her. One more test in a long string of probes into her psyche.

So far, Teddi had passed every test, but this one was a real killer. She hit the play button and was transported back in time. The wooden-voiced announcer began describing the devastation of her hometown as the images rolled, one after another.

Teddi recognized all of them: the caved-in roof of Riley's Five and Dime where her mother had purchased her first Barbie doll. The gaping hole in the high school gymnasium where she'd watched dozens of basketball games while her cheerleader sister urged the Wildcats on to victory. A street filled with rubble where she and Jessica Novak used to ride their bicycles. A pickup truck sitting placidly in the vegetable garden where she had once swiped the gardener's prize-winning tomatoes.

The images were fleeting, but Teddi's entire childhood was on that video. The pain of so many memories was almost more than she could bear.

When the last image flashed, showing the car that had been hurled through the wall of her own home, tears were streaming down her face. She brushed at them and rewound the tape, then forced herself to watch it again.

The idea came to her during the third viewing. She was a little surprised by it because it was something the old objective Teddi would have thought of, not this new one who most of the time seemed to be holding on by a thread.

She sat back and considered the idea for a moment. She could do it. Or at least, she could *force* herself to do it. She could take her crew to Dry Creek and film the town as it was now, twenty years later, then use the old footage as contrast. Surely there were still survivors there she could interview. It could be a powerful segment of the documentary....

If Matt approved.

Knowing she had to ask, Teddi rolled her chair across the floor to the phone on her desk. As she reached for it, though, she hesitated. Every time she saw him it became harder to contain her feelings, so she had been avoiding him as assiduously as he avoided her. Except for their morning briefings or the on-camera interviews he had given her in the first two weeks, they spoke very little.

But this had to be done. Shoring up her defenses, she reached for the phone and dialed his extension.

He picked it up after two rings. "Matt Abernathy."

"Matt, this is Teddi," she said.

There was a short pause, as though he was making a mental adjustment to her voice. "Hello, Teddi. I didn't realize you were back from the city."

"I just arrived a few minutes ago."

"Did you have any luck at KOAK?"

A grim smile worked its way to the surface. "I'm not sure you'd call it luck, but I did find something I'd like you to see. Have you got a minute to come down to the editing room?"

Another pause. "Sure. I'll be right there."

Teddi barely had time to rewind the tape before he arrived.

"What's up?" he asked as he came around the console.

"I have an idea for a segment of the documentary. It's an idea we haven't explored before, and I need your approval before I proceed."

"Teddi, if you think it's a good idea, I'm sure I'll agree, whatever it is."

"Thanks. Take a look at this before you decide, though."

She gestured for him to pull up a chair, and he took the one from behind her desk. He rolled it toward the console, but every muscle in his body ached from the tight rein he'd been keeping on his emotions for the last month. Without his anger to use as a shield, he didn't have many defenses. Being this close to Teddi was the last thing he wanted.

No, being close to Teddi was *exactly* what he wanted.

That was what made it so torturous to sit beside her. He could smell the clean, sexy scent that always drove him crazy. When he edged his chair up to the monitor, he could see her out of the corner of his eye, composed and beautiful, intense and vibrant, everything he wanted in a woman and couldn't have.

She cued the tape, then flipped a switch to eliminate the sound, and Matt tried to direct his attention to the film. When the images had played through, she swiveled her chair toward him.

He steeled himself and faced her. "That's a fairly old film, isn't it?"

"Yes."

"From what I could tell, the damage patterns were severe, but pretty typical overall," he said, trying to sound casual. "Why did this one in particular catch your attention?"

The sudden flash of pain in her eyes answered him before she got the words out. "This is the aftermath of the Dry Creek tornado."

Matt went very still, and it was everything he could do to keep from reaching out to her. Teddi had done such a good job in the past few weeks that he sometimes forgot she had a lot of painful memories to deal with. "I'm sorry, Teddi. That must have been hard to watch."

"It was," she admitted, then she shoved away the pain and summoned up some enthusiasm for her plan. "But it gave me the idea I mentioned. I want to go back to Dry Creek and do a 'twenty years later' bit. You know, how they rebuilt the town, what they still remember from that night—things like that. It wouldn't be a long segment, but it could be very effective."

"Are you sure you want to put yourself through something like that? It's above and beyond the call of duty."

She appreciated his concern. "I want to do it, Matt. I think I probably need to do it."

"Another test?"

There was no rancor in the question, and Teddi realized they had passed a major hurdle. "No, I just need to put a few ghosts to rest. I've been thinking about driving down to Dry Creek for weeks, but I've kept putting it off. This will make it impossible for me to avoid."

He looked at her, wishing he could gauge how deeply this was affecting her, but Teddi had an invisible wall erected and he couldn't see through it. It was maddeningly frustrating, and it only compounded the emotions he was working so hard to keep bottled up. Despite that, though, he couldn't keep himself from asking, "Are you doing all right, Teddi? I mean, I've seen for myself how well you're handling the chases, but I don't have any idea what it's costing you in other ways."

Teddi was touched that he could still be concerned about her after what she'd put him through. "I'm doing fine, Matt. In fact, I'm even getting a little impatient to start doing my own camera work again," she told him, striving for a cheerful tone.

"Would that be wise?"

"Probably not," she admitted. "But I take it as a very positive sign. And I don't quake in my boots anymore whenever you announce a chase," she said brightly. "In fact, I've even started looking forward to them in a way."

That surprised Matt. "Why?"

"Because I've always preferred activity to indoor entertainments like this," she said, gesturing to the editing console. Her smile faded. "And I know you're running out of time to validate your theory. The season's half over, and you're no closer to proving that Pandora works than you were a month ago."

"Don't remind me," he said with a little shake of his head, rolling his chair a few feet away from hers. "The center's director, Ed Parker called me into his office yesterday to tell me that it was almost time to apply for a grant renewal. If Pandora fails, there's no way they'll even consider appropriating any more funds."

"The season isn't turning out as you expected is it?" she asked, then instantly regretted her words. She'd only meant there'd been less tornado activity than he'd predicted, but the pain that flashed in his eyes told her he was thinking of something else entirely.

"No, it hasn't," he admitted softly.

"I'm sorry."

Matt knew what she was apologizing for. "Maybe it would be better if we didn't get into that," he said, trying to shut the door on all the sadness and regrets he felt. Nothing she could say would make his feelings for her go away.

He stood up. "Teddi, if you want to do a segment on Dry Creek, you have my approval. It will take some time to set up, but we should be able to do it. Lem Bridger, the head of the Logan County Disaster Planning Commission, is a friend of Laura's. I'm sure she'd pave the—"

Matt stopped in midsentence. He'd forgotten for a moment that he could no longer ask anything from his former friend. Laura wouldn't see him, wouldn't take his calls. She was mourning a son who was still alive, and she blamed Matt for her loss.

"On second thought, I'll call down to Logan County myself," he said.

Teddi knew exactly what he was thinking. Though they hadn't discussed Laura again, everyone at the center now knew she was furious with Matt. Corey was miserable and he blamed himself for the rift between Laura and Matt, but he wasn't willing to back down from the stand he'd taken to win his independence.

It was a situation with no winners.

"Matt, aren't things any better between you and Laura?" Teddi asked, hoping there'd been some new development she hadn't heard about.

"No. She still believes I'm going to get her son killed," he said wearily. "She's never going to forgive me."

"Give her time," she suggested, wishing she could offer him some comfort. He looked as though the weight of the world was about to crush him into the ground.

"I don't think time will help anything," he replied.

He rolled the chair back to Teddi's desk, and she took it as a sign that he wanted to drop the discussion. "Look, Matt, you have a great deal to do already," she said. "Why don't you let me set up the Dry Creek shoot? I'm sure Mr. Bridger will be willing to cooperate with me."

"If that's the way you want to handle it," he said with a nod.

"I do." Teddi rose. "This documentary has disrupted your routine too much already. It's my job to keep it from affecting you any more than necessary."

"Teddi, everything you do has an effect on me." The words were out before he thought, and there was no way he could call them back.

They looked at each other, trapped by the invisible thread of longing that still bound them together, then Matt moved quickly toward the door. "I'll see you later," he said and disappeared before Teddi could stop him.

And there really wasn't a reason to stop him anyway. Nothing she could say would ease the pain she'd caused him. And nothing would ease her own.

She couldn't wait for the storm season to end.

TEDDI SCHEDULED the shoot in Dry Creek a week later. Lem Bridger had helped set up interviews, and the mayor—who had moved to Dry Creek a few years after the tornado—had been glad to provide Teddi with facts and statistics about the town. She was going to interview six survivors of varying ages in a group session, and if necessary, she'd return another day to do individual interviews.

All the participants knew there was a chance the interviews might have to be rescheduled, but as it turned out the day Teddi had selected was perfect. The weather had been depressingly clear all week long and Matt expected fair skies to last at least through the weekend.

The four of them—Bryce, Griff, Teddi and Matt—drove down to Dry Creek early. She'd tried to tell Matt he didn't need to take the time off to make the trip, but when she had, a look of pain flashed into his eyes and Teddi realized she'd hurt him all over again. She'd only been concerned about his busy schedule, but he thought she meant she didn't need him, and Teddi hadn't been able to tell him just how wrong he was. She needed him desperately, but she didn't have the right to ask him for anything when she didn't know what she could give him in return.

So she had accepted his decision to join them without telling him she was glad he'd be there.

The drive took three hours, and with every mile that passed, Teddi tried to brace herself for what was to come. How would it feel to see her hometown again after all these years? Nothing stayed the same; it would be an entirely different place. Would she find the changes encouraging or depressing?

Had anyone bothered to rebuild her family's house on Oak Street? she wondered. Had the school built a new gymnasium or simply replaced the wall of the old one? Was

Dry Creek thriving, or had the tornado destroyed more than just buildings? Had it taken away the town's will to go on?

What Teddi discovered as they left the freeway and approached Dry Creek was that her home had almost become a ghost town. The first thing she saw was the old drive-in movie theater. The huge white screen was gone now, a victim of the tornado, and no one had bothered to replace it. The rolling mounds of the parking area were still there, though, covered with weeds instead of gravel. A few of the speaker posts were still there, too, looking for all the world like empty-handed sentries. The concession stand was missing, but the little ticket booth still sat near the highway, its windows boarded and its walls overgrown with ivy and weeds.

The rest of the town was almost as bad. On Main Street, many of the stores were eerily vacant. The Five and Dime was now a karate studio. The marquee of the old movie theater advertised gospel singing every Saturday night. There was evidence that at one time an effort had been made to renovate the street, give it a face-lift as a gesture of hope, but it hadn't worked.

There were lots of places Teddi remembered and some things she'd never imagined—like a fast-food restaurant where a locksmith's stand used to sit. The old soda fountain was now a video-rental store, and the factory where her father used to work had been converted into a flea market.

Out of courtesy, Teddi checked in with the mayor, even though it was still several hours before their scheduled appointment. In the meantime, she wanted to recreate the shots from the KOAK footage if she could. Naturally the presence of a small movie crew didn't go unnoticed, but no one seemed to recognize Teddi. The police chief stopped traffic for her and store owners cooperated, grateful for the publicity.

Through it all, Teddi maintained a stoicism Matt found disturbing. He hated the way she seemed able to shut her emotions off like water from a faucet. She had to be feeling *something,* but he didn't have any idea what it was. All he saw was an occasional crack in the facade, as though the faucet had sprung a temporary leak.

That changed early in the afternoon when they went into a small restaurant Teddi remembered from the old days. Its facade had been changed and its interior modernized, but the barbecue sandwiches it served were exactly the same as she remembered. Something about the place triggered an avalanche of happy memories, and as they ate lunch in a crowded booth, she regaled them with stories.

"This was *the* place to hang out on weekends," she told them as they finished their sandwiches. "Jessica Novak and I would ride our bikes out here to spy on my sister. Of course, we pretended it was purely an accident that we'd run into her, but she always knew. She had to. It happened every Saturday."

"Maybe she should have taken the hint and gone elsewhere," Griff said.

"Oh, Cathy tried, but we found her wherever she went," Teddi replied, her eyes sparkling mischievously. "I can't tell you how many times Jessica and I snuck into the drive-in to spy on Cathy and her date. Then I'd go home like the bratty little sister I was and report to Mom that I'd seen her necking."

Bryce chuckled. "That must have made you real popular with your sister."

Teddi shook her head. "No, Cathy didn't care, because Mom never believed me." She raised the pitch of her voice in a joking imitation of a disbelieving mother. "What? My daughter behaving like a normal teenager? That's unthinkable." She chuckled and dropped the impersonation. "So

I was the one who always got in trouble for sneaking into the drive-in and for telling tales.''

Matt was entranced. The light in Teddi's eyes was back, shining just as brightly as it had the day he met her, and he prayed it would stay there. "Were you a rebellious teenager?" he asked.

Teddi laughed. "I was an absolute hellion. My parents were convinced I was destined to be the worst juvenile delinquent Dry Creek had ever seen. And Jessie's parents were terrified I'd drag their daughter down with me. Where I went, she followed, no matter what. We were outrageous."

"What happened to Jessica?" Griff asked. "Did you keep in touch with her after you went to L.A?"

The light in Teddi's eyes died. "No. Jessie's house collapsed during the tornado. She died two days later without ever regaining consciousness." Teddi reached for her soft drink and took a sip.

Griff could have kicked himself, and the other two men very nearly did. "I'm sorry."

"Yeah. Me, too." She glanced at her watch. "We'd better get moving. It will take a while to get set up for the interviews."

The pleasant interlude was over. Teddi had turned off the tap, closing down her emotions. It was time to go back to work.

The mayor had generously donated the use of his spacious living room for the filming. He and his wife watched in fascination as the crew set up lighting stanchions and mounted cameras.

The survivors began arriving, and every one of them remembered Teddi. And she remembered them. Myra Brick, now nearing ninety, was as stern and crotchety as ever. Toby Daniels had been two grades ahead of Teddi in school. She'd had a terrible crush on him, but he'd been equally smitten with Cathy. Bob Hennessey had been a cop until the tornado had turned over his cruiser with him in it; now he was confined to a wheelchair and worked as a dispatcher for the county ambulance service.

All six of them had touched Teddi's life in some way, and seeing them now gave her a solid connection with her childhood. While Bryce and Griff filmed, Teddi encouraged them to talk, drew out their memories of the storm and gently prodded them into telling how it had changed their lives and the town as a whole.

As they talked, Teddi realized that their memories weren't so different from her own. Everyone in Dry Creek had lost someone that night; everyone had struggled for years to make sense of the tragedy. Intellectually Teddi had known that must have been the case, but discovering it firsthand eased a bit of the isolation she'd always felt.

"Okay, guys. Cut. I think we've got everything we need," she said after nearly two hours of reminiscences. The cameras were instantly shut down, and the dismantling process began.

Teddi looked at the survivors. "Thank you all for sharing this with me. I know it wasn't easy."

"You're right," Lois Esterhaus said as she rose from the couch, drying her eyes with a damp tissue. "There are some things even time can't cure."

Without even thinking about it, Teddi moved to the woman whose son had been one of the twenty-seven victims the town had buried. She put her arms around her, and they clung to each other for what seemed like an eternity. "Thank you for coming, Mrs. Esterhaus," she said when they finally stepped apart.

The others rose, too, and prepared to leave. Teddi touched them all as they departed, either with a handshake or a hug, until finally only Myra Brick was left. Teddi took her arm as the old lady shuffled along with her cane toward the door.

"I must say, you turned out rather nicely, after all, Theresa," Myra told her.

Teddi laughed. "Well, if anyone had a right to doubt it, you did. Have you forgiven me for stealing the beefsteak tomatoes you were planning to enter in the county fair?"

Myra looked up at her through pale blue eyes. "No, and I never will. That was the first year I ever lost the blue ribbon."

"I'm so sorry," Teddi said, trying to sound sincere.

Myra wasn't fooled. She patted Teddi's arm. "It's all right, dear. You were young, and Dry Creek just wasn't big enough to contain you. I always knew you were one of the young people who wouldn't stick around. It's just a shame you had to leave the way you did."

"Yes, it is," she replied.

"Have you been out to the cemetery yet?" Myra asked.

Teddi stiffened a little. "No, I haven't."

Myra wagged an arthritic finger at her. "You really should, dear. Every year on Memorial Day the Baptist church puts fresh flowers on the victims' graves, but that's not enough. Your family plot shouldn't be neglected."

Teddi dug her fingernails into her palms to fight back a sudden urge to cry. "I'll do that," she promised.

The old lady gave her an impish smile. "I don't have any tomatoes for you to steal, but you're welcome to drop by and pilfer some roses."

Teddi laughed as her eyes misted over. "Thank you." She walked Myra out to the street where her great-grandson was waiting impatiently in a beat-up old Chevy. "Goodbye, Mrs. Brick. I'm glad I got to see you again," she said as she helped her into the car.

"So am I, dear. None of us lasts forever. Come back and see me again sometime."

Teddi shut the door, and it was everything she could do to keep from crying as the car pulled away.

"Teddi?"

When she realized Matt was behind her, she wanted desperately to throw herself into his arms, but she fought the impulse. She didn't have the right to turn to Matt for anything. Instead, she carefully gathered her emotions into a neat bundle and put them away before she faced him.

"That was a beautiful interview in there," he told her, his face filled with a tenderness and concern that threatened to unravel the neat bundle. "You were incredibly good at getting them to talk."

"That's my job."

"But it hurt, didn't it?"

She nodded. "I'll be all right."

He looked as though he wanted to say more, but the chasm between them was too wide to be bridged. "Are we done here?"

She shook her head. "No. There's one more shot we have to get."

Matt thought they had covered everything. "What is it?"

Teddi tied another piece of string around the bundle. "Oak Street," she said, then turned away and started for the van.

CHAPTER FIFTEEN

TEDDI HAD TWO DISTINCT mental images of Oak Street. One was of a tree-lined avenue with modest, well-kept houses, green lawns and lovingly tended flower beds. The other was like a war zone. The houses were reduced to kindling; only an occasional wall stood in the midst of the rubble. Bits and pieces of people's lives littered the street and lawns: shingles, pieces of china, appliances, clothing, a mangled bicycle, a broken doll…

Neither of those images applied to the street Teddi found twenty years later. Not one of the homes had been rebuilt. A rundown government housing project now occupied the blocks that had sustained the worst damage. It could have been a street in any town in America: shabby and fraying around the edges, featuring long rows of identical duplexed houses.

The change broke Teddi's heart. She'd wanted to see something familiar here. Not the same houses necessarily, but similar ones at least, with a hint of the old neighborhood.

"I don't recognize any of this from the KOAK film," Bryce said as they climbed out of the van.

"Here," Teddi replied, handing him a series of still photographs she'd made from the news footage. They had been using the pictures all day to help them re-create before-and-after shots of the town.

Bryce flipped through the photos, shaking his head. "There's nothing even vaguely similar."

"I know."

He handed the pictures to Griff and looked at Teddi. "What do you want us to shoot?"

Teddi looked around, trying to remember the job she had come here to do, instead of the memories. "Start on the other side of the street and walk down the sidewalk, the way they did in the original film. I want you to circle these two blocks completely."

"Done." He and Griff began unloading equipment, but Teddi didn't pitch in this time. Instead, she began her own walk back through time.

"May I join you?" Matt asked as she stepped onto the sidewalk.

Teddi felt a flush of relief. Matt couldn't have any idea what this particular street meant to her or that she didn't want to face it alone. But she'd never have asked Matt to join her, and so was glad he'd offered.

"Please do," she said.

Matt had the pictures now, and he leafed through them as they strolled. "Bryce is right. There's nothing left, but considering the extent of the damage, that's not surprising. In fact, it's hard to tell from the photographs what this street looked like originally."

"It was beautiful," Teddi told him wistfully. She pointed to one of the duplexes across the street. "That used to be the Morgan house. It was one of the oldest in town, but it had been lovingly maintained by four generations of the same family. It had this wonderful round turret on one corner."

Matt looked through the photographs until he found the house. He recognized it by the two-story turret—the only part of the house that had been left standing. As they strolled, Teddi went on with her description of the old neighborhood—not just of the houses, but of the people who lived in them. Her voice was strained, but she seemed composed, as though she was narrating a folksy travelogue. Matt knew the reaction was much more personal than that, though, and when they crossed the street into the next block, he realized just how personal.

"Oh, look!" Teddi said, kneeling on one knee on the sidewalk. "It's still here."

Matt squatted beside her and looked at the stick-letter scrawl, frozen in time and concrete, where Teddi had written her name with a big five-pointed star underneath it. This was *your* neighborhood," he said quietly.

"Yes." Teddi reached out and traced the lines of the star. "I was going to go to Hollywood and become the world's greatest actress. I used to pretend this was my star in front of the Chinese Theater." She gestured to the next block in the sidewalk. "See, I put myself right next to John Wayne."

Matt moved along the sidewalk and laughed. Sure enough, there was the Duke's name and star, and beyond that were stars for Katherine Hepburn and Sean Connery. Teddi had created her own Walk of Fame in Dry Creek, Oklahoma.

She followed him down the sidewalk. "I snuck out of the house at night to do this, and by morning the concrete was completely set," she told him. "The town council was absolutely furious and wanted to make my parents pay for having the sidewalk repaved, but since it wasn't obscene or anything, Daddy refused. They argued about it for weeks, and finally everyone just dropped the whole thing."

"I'm glad," Matt told her. "It's nice to know that Teddi O'Brien's dreams are still here."

"Yes, it is."

Tears were misting her eyes when she looked up at him, and Matt fought the urge to touch her. "Where was your house, Teddi?"

She looked toward the end of the block. "See that big oak tree between the sidewalk and the street?"

Matt saw the sprawling, misshapen oak. It looked oddly out of balance, fuller on one side than the other, and he recognized the signature of the tornado. The tree had survived and grown, but even after all this time, the evidence was still there. "I see it," he told her.

"That's where I lived."

"In the tree?"

Teddi glanced up at him and returned his smile. "Sometimes. It was my favorite hiding place—which made it totally ineffective, of course."

They moved on until they were standing under the sheltering limbs that dipped and twisted just over their heads. Then Teddi turned and looked at the spot where her house had sat. The emotion that hit her was entirely unexpected. "I'm glad it's gone," she murmured.

"What?"

"I'm glad no one rebuilt it. I don't think I could bear to see it if they had." She took the photographs from Matt and shuffled them. A chill rippled along her arms as she handed them back. "That's it."

Matt looked at the picture and felt sick. At one end of the house, a car had been thrown through a wall. At the other end, the corner had been ripped away, leaving a gaping hole in what had once been a bedroom. He could see an old brass twin bed standing against the remaining interior wall. A closet without a door had clothing hanging in it. There were even a few pictures still on the wall.

Matt knew that wasn't unusual. Tornadoes were unbelievably freakish. He'd once surveyed the damage done by a rare winter storm and found a Christmas tree with its ornaments undisturbed standing in a room with only two walls.

But that hadn't been the home of the woman he loved. "Where were you when it happened, Teddi?" he couldn't prevent himself from asking.

Teddi's hand moved toward the picture and Matt saw that it was trembling ever so slightly. "Right there." She pointed to the bed. "Cathy's bed is...there." She indicated a blurry spot on the edge of the photograph. Matt studied the spot closely and realized he was seeing a mangled version of the twin bed that had been left in the house.

The impact of that hit Matt in the chest. "You and your sister were sleeping in the same room?"

Teddi nodded, but she was looking at the duplex, not Matt. What she was seeing, though, was twenty years in the past. Her face was pale, and her jaw was clenched from the effort to hold in the pain.

Matt couldn't stop himself this time. He reached out and touched her. When she didn't pull away, he gently ran his hand down her arm until his palm touched hers. Her fingers convulsed around his hand, and she held on tight, as though he were a lifeline between the past and the present.

"You don't have to do this, Teddi," he whispered.

"Yes, I do. I came to Oklahoma because I wanted to stop running away from what happened." She looked up at him, her eyes glazed with tears. "There's no point in stopping if I can't look around and see what I've been running from."

She looked so vulnerable, so fragile, that it nearly broke Matt's heart. But she also had the strength to face the past, and he could only admire her for that. The wall Matt had erected to shield himself from Teddi crumbled like a sand castle in a windstorm.

In the next block, a car without a muffler came around the corner, and the roar made Teddi jump. Matt's hand squeezed hers, but it didn't help. Before she knew what was happening, the words came tumbling out. "I remember the sound most of all. That horrible freight train barreling down on us. It woke me up, and I couldn't figure out what was happening." Her voice was filled with a kind of horrified awe.

"Flashes of lightning lit up the room, and I remember thinking how odd it was that I couldn't hear the thunder. Just the roar. I looked over at Cathy and she sat up, looking at me with this sleepy, confused expression, and then the lightning faded and everything went dark again. I heard a terrible crash and the house just...shuddered, like it was falling apart. The roof groaned and for a minute I couldn't breathe."

She stopped, gulping in a deep breath of air just to prove that she could, to reassure herself that this feeling of suffocation was only a memory, because it felt real. It felt as though it was happening again right now. The images played out in her head like a film in stark black and white, and all she had to hold her in the present was Matt's hand. Everything else was a blur of intense pain that knotted in her chest.

It was a moment before she could tell him. "When the lightning lit up the room again, Cathy was gone. The bed, the walls, the dresser, the stereo—everything, everyone, gone. Hours later, when the rescue crews started looking for survivors, they found me still in bed, my hands clinging to the brass rails of the bed so tightly they had to pry them loose."

Her voice broke and she had to stop for a moment. "Everybody else was dead. My parents never even woke up. The car—"

"It's okay, Teddi," Matt whispered.

She nodded and looked down at their hands. Matt's skin was white from the pressure she had applied. "I'm sorry," she muttered, and let go of him abruptly, but Matt grabbed her hand again.

"Teddi, it's okay to hold on to someone."

When she looked up at him, the tenderness and understanding in his eyes was her undoing. The knot in her chest exploded, shattering into a hundred painful pieces, spreading out and engulfing her. "Why?" she whispered as tears began flooding down her cheeks. "Why did they die, Matt? Why didn't they take me with them?"

Matt dragged her into his arms, and Teddi clung to him, sobbing out the anguish. "They didn't choose to die, Teddi," he said as he stroked her hair. "It just happened."

"But they took Cathy," she choked out. "Why didn't they want me, too?"

Matt recognized the depths of her pain, but he didn't have an answer for her. Instead of giving her platitudes she didn't need, he held her, sheltering her from the past as best he could, keeping her in his arms where she belonged—but would not be able to stay.

She cried until there were no more tears, and when she finally let go of Matt, he felt as though he'd lost her all over again.

TEDDI WAS QUIET during the long ride back to Turner, and she was grateful that no one pressed her to talk. The country-music station Griff had found filled what would otherwise have been silence, but Teddi paid little attention to it. She had too much pain and too many memories to deal with.

She had fully intended to take Myra Brick's advice and visit the cemetery before she left town, but she hadn't been able to do that. What had happened so long ago seemed too real to her now—not just the tragedy that had taken her family, but other things repressed or long forgotten: moments around the dinner table, fights over curfews and laughter over silly accidents around the house, picnics and family trips to the zoo...

Teddi had always rejected those memories because they reminded her of the pain. Now she saw what a mistake that had been. She had shut out the bad, but in doing so, she had shut out the good, too. Now, she was going to have to do what she should have done twenty years ago: deal with the bad memories so that she could cling to the good ones. It was the only way she'd ever be whole again.

The sun was already down by the time they made it back to the center. They stored their gear in the editing room, and Teddi dismissed her crew. Bryce seemed hesitant to go—Teddi knew he'd seen her crying in Matt's arms as he and Griff had completed their filming—but he cast a quick glance at Matt, then left.

"Are you all right?" Matt asked her when they were finally alone.

Teddi nodded. "I will be. Today wasn't exactly a cakewalk, but it was good for me. This may sound silly, but I feel like I found a piece of myself. Something I didn't even know was missing."

"That's not silly. We all leave parts of ourselves behind as we grow and mature. Sometimes we leave too much."

Teddi leaned against the storage vault. "I guess that's what I did when I got on that plane for L.A. twenty years ago. I didn't want to remember the pain, so I shoved it away too soon."

"Will you go back to Dry Creek before you leave Oklahoma?" he asked.

An image of a cemetery with fresh mounds of earth

smothered in flowers flashed through her mind. "No. Once was enough. There's nothing left for me there." She turned away and locked the film vault.

Matt hesitated, wondering if that was her way of subtly telling him to leave her alone. She had turned to him in Dry Creek, but that didn't mean she needed him now.

Still, he had to ask. He was risking a rejection he didn't think he could bear, but he did it, anyway. "Teddi..." He waited until she looked at him. "Would you like to catch a bite of supper with me? If you don't want to talk about what happened today, we don't have to. We could talk about sports or current events or..."

"The weather?" she asked, flashing him a grin he was only too happy to return.

"I would have thought you'd be sick of that subject by now."

"I'd like to have dinner with you, Matt, but..." Her smile faded.

"But what?" Matt tensed for her rejection.

"I don't have the right to use you just because I don't want to be alone."

Relief washed through him. "I offered, remember? You didn't ask."

Teddi wanted to talk to him. She had missed him desperately, but it was more than that. Matt was one of the few people in the world who would truly understand what she had been through and how it had changed her life. She'd always known that about him, even when she'd been hiding the truth. If she'd told him sooner, maybe...

She didn't finish the thought. She couldn't undo her history with him any more than she could bring her family back to life. She could only try to cope with the results of nature's whims and her mistakes.

She couldn't have refused his offer if her life had depended on it. "I'd love to have dinner with you, Matt."

HE TOOK HER to the Chat 'n Chew, where they found a booth in the back that gave them a little privacy without affording any real intimacy. Matt was amazed that Teddi wanted to talk about what had happened in Dry Creek. She took him on a rambling tour of her childhood, much as she had done during lunch. The picture that emerged was that of an energetic child whose dreams were too big for the small town of Dry Creek.

Her parents had wanted her to be like her conventional older sister, and when Teddi had rebelled against those restrictions, her parents hadn't understood that being different wasn't necessarily bad. They had tried repeatedly to clip her wings, and when that hadn't worked they had labeled her incorrigible.

As she talked, Matt kept remembering the agonized questions that had been ripped out of her this afternoon, and finally he asked, "Teddi, do you really believe your parents left you behind deliberately?"

She looked at him, surprised. "Of course not. I didn't even know that feeling was there until I blurted it out. Frankly, I've always thought it was just the opposite. If they could have chosen which daughter would live, they'd have picked Cathy," she said matter-of-factly.

"You can't really believe that."

"Yes, I do." They had finished dinner and Teddi was sitting with her back against the wall and her legs drawn up to her chest. "You know, there were times when I was a child that I actually hated them."

"All children go through phases like that, Teddi," he said. "I hated my parents because they wouldn't let me play Little League baseball with the town kids."

"Do you still resent them for that?"

"Of course not. We grow out of those feelings as we grow up."

Teddi toyed with her beer mug, drawing circles in the condensation on the sides. "I didn't," she said in a very small voice. "I've been angry at them for twenty years."

"Because they wanted you to be like your sister?"

She met his eyes, wondering how he would judge her for what she was about to say. "No. For dying before I had a chance to prove to them that I wasn't all bad." Teddi felt the anger welling up all over again, and with it came the persistent, nagging emptiness she had never understood but couldn't shake. "They probably wouldn't have approved of what I've done with my life, but I'll never know that."

"Why wouldn't they approve?" Matt asked, wishing he could take away some of the pain he saw in her eyes.

"Because I don't do things the way so-called normal people do things," she replied with a touch of sarcasm. "I didn't settle down, get married and have kids, like good little girls are supposed to do."

"Come on, Teddi. If that's what your parents wanted for you, it's only because they were a product of the times they lived in. They would have eventually accepted you and been very proud of all you've accomplished."

"I'd like to think so," she said, but she didn't really believe it. She took another sip of her drink. "Maybe we'd better change the subject."

Matt didn't agree. "Why? Are we getting too close to something you'd rather not deal with?"

An automatic denial sprang to Teddi's lips, but she bit it back. She'd always been good at challenging herself physically, and she was getting better at doing the same thing emotionally. If she'd learned nothing else about herself in the past month, it was that she was much too adept at avoiding anything that had the power to hurt her. "You'd have made a good psychologist, Matt," she told him wryly.

"I once said the same thing about you," he reminded her, thinking of the day they'd spent together in L.A.

Teddi laughed. "Physician, heal thyself? For what it's worth, I'm trying."

"It seems to me that you've come a long way already."

Teddi was glad to hear him say that. "I certainly hope so. After that first chase, there was no place to go but up."

"No, you could have gone back," he argued mildly. "Back to burying your fears and your feelings. But you didn't, and in the long run, it's going to make you much stronger."

"I always thought I *was* strong." She shook her head. "It's not easy, having a lifetime of beliefs about yourself destroyed in one fell swoop."

"Are you having any luck rebuilding those beliefs?"

"Some," she admitted. "I think talking to the other Dry Creek survivors helped a lot. It proved to me I'm not alone."

"Teddi, being alone isn't like a disease that can't be cured. It's a *choice* people make, like your decision to come out with me tonight."

She looked at him sharply. "I meant emotionally alone, Matt. Alienated. Different from other people."

He shook his head. "You're no different from anyone else, Teddi. You've made being different your calling card, but you have all the same needs and the same aches as the rest of us. Everyone has a secret pain that has to be dealt with in one way or another."

"Sometimes it's hard to know that in your heart," she said quietly.

Matt paused for a moment, regarding her thoughtfully. "Teddi, why haven't you ever gotten married?"

The question took her by surprise. "I've never found a man who could accept me as I am. Most men are intimidated by my career, and the ones who understood my work couldn't cope with my independence."

She almost added, "I thought you were different," but she didn't. There was no point. That door was closed and couldn't be opened again. It seemed that she and Matt had forged a tentative bond of friendship, but they couldn't go back to anything more.

Instead, she asked, "What about you? Laura Cochran isn't the only woman in the world, you know."

"No, but she made me see that no woman would want to live with the fear and insecurity my job creates," he said. "And when I watched her suffering through her grief and trying to raise her son alone, I knew I couldn't take the chance of inflicting that kind of pain on anyone else. I made the choice to be alone because I didn't believe that a woman who could understand my profession really existed."

Teddi read the look that said, "Until I met you," as clearly as if he'd spoken the words aloud. It made her ache all the more, because she did understand him. And she loved him. She wanted the life that Laura hadn't been able to share with him. That realization surprised her. Teddi had never really thought about lifetime commitments until she met Matt. The relationships in her life had been brief and sometimes intense, but they had all burned out quickly. Matt had made her want things she'd never wanted before.

Just for an instant, Teddi was tempted to tell him that, but she couldn't. She had reclaimed a lot of pieces of herself that had been scattered by that first disastrous tornado chase, but she still had a long way to go on her quest of rediscovery. Until she could see what was at the end of the journey, she wouldn't be able to give him a commitment, and she knew Matt wouldn't accept anything less than all of her.

And the awful truth was, even if she could give him a commitment, he wouldn't believe her. Her deceit had shaken his trust in her, and Laura Cochran had done the rest. Trying to convince Matt that Laura was wrong would be nothing short of cruel as long as Teddi wasn't completely certain herself.

Because they had done more talking than eating, there wasn't much time to linger over drinks. The restaurant closed at nine on weeknights. When the busboy began mopping up the floor, they took it as their cue to leave.

They had driven separate vehicles, and theirs were the only ones on the lot as Matt walked Teddi to her Bronco.

"Thanks for letting me bend your ear," Teddi said as she dug out her keys. "And for all the rest."

Matt just nodded. He was glad she'd reached out to him. "We did this backwards, didn't we, Teddi."

She stopped by the door and looked up at him. "What?"

"Us. Our relationship. We became lovers before we gave ourselves a chance to be friends."

"Yeah, I guess we did," she said sadly. "That's my fault. Impetuous Teddi O'Brien strikes again."

He shook his head. "You didn't exactly drag me into bed kicking and screaming, Teddi."

"No, but I let you believe I was something I'm not. I'm sorry for that, Matt. If I could make it right, I would."

"Let's just say we both made mistakes and forget it, okay?"

Teddi had to smile. "Yes, but my mistakes were bigger than yours."

Matt chuckled. "That's my Teddi. Competitive to the

last." His smile faded when he realized what he'd said. She wasn't his Teddi, and she never would be.

Teddi read his thoughts as clearly as if he'd spoken them aloud. A fresh wave of guilt washed through her. "I'm sorry I hurt you, Matt. I never wanted that to happen."

"I expected too much, Teddi. That's my fault, not yours. I was thinking 'happily ever after' and you were thinking 'let's enjoy our short time together.'"

Teddi remembered what Bryce had asked her a month ago, and how she'd answered him. She wanted to tell Matt, too, but she couldn't. He wanted guarantees, and Teddi didn't have any to give.

"And instead, we ended up with neither," she said softly.

Matt shook his head. "We can't undo the past, Teddi."

"No, we can't." She reached out and took his hand. "Thank you for what you did today, Matt. For being there and understanding."

His eyes darkened at her touch, and he slipped his hand out of hers. "No problem," he said dismissively, and Teddi realized she'd made a big mistake. Their talk had opened a door between them, but her need to be connected to him physically had closed it.

And it was probably just as well, she realized. She didn't really have anything to offer him except apologies for the pain she'd caused.

It wasn't nearly enough for either of them.

A moment later, Matt murmured a good-night and they went their separate ways.

CHAPTER SIXTEEN

TIME WAS SLIPPING AWAY. One failed chase followed another over the next two weeks, and Teddi's chance of capturing another dynamic tornado chase on film was becoming as remote as Matt's proving that Pandora worked. Teddi worked feverishly to pull the documentary together, spending long hours with the editing equipment, as though creating a dynamic film could somehow make up to Matt for all the hurt she'd caused him. But she knew that unless they got more dramatic tornado footage during a chase, the final film would be flat and lifeless.

That wasn't what she'd promised Matt in the beginning, and she couldn't bear the thought of failing him yet again.

Things hadn't gotten any better between them since their conversation at the restaurant. If anything, they were worse. Every time Teddi looked at Matt she saw the pain in his eyes and a growing resignation to her impending departure. They talked more now and avoided each other less, but the problems that stood between them created a barrier neither of them could cross.

Teddi knew that the weight of those problems was adding to Matt's burden. He was under tremendous pressure to prove that his formula worked, but she didn't realize just how much pressure until she walked into his office one afternoon and found him opening and slamming one file-cabinet drawer after another.

"Matt, what's wrong?" she asked, stopping just inside

his door. When he turned to her, his handsome face was as dark and turbulent as the storms he loved so much.

"I can't find the damned statistical ratio charts!" he snapped, then resumed his search.

Teddi didn't have a clue what those were, but it was obvious they were important. "Have you asked Corey? He does most of your filing, doesn't he?"

"I can't ask Corey. He has a special lab course at the university this afternoon."

"Is there anything I can do to help?" she offered.

"No!"

Teddi took a deep breath and another step into the room. "Matt..."

He jerked around toward her again. "What?"

"What's really wrong?" she asked, keeping her voice quiet and soothing. She knew Matt too well to believe that a missing file was responsible for the waves of frustration pouring out of him.

Matt slammed another door shut, letting the cabinet absorb some of his anger. When he finally answered Teddi, he was a lot calmer. "Ed Parker called me into his office this morning to ask for a final report on Pandora so that they can close the book on the project."

"What?" Teddi said, experiencing a flash of anger at Ed for being so callous. "Did you remind him the season isn't over yet?"

Matt moved to his desk and sat. "As far as he's concerned, it might as well be," he replied sarcastically. "He's never been a big supporter of the project, and he doesn't believe I can confirm my theories in just a week. To him, it's all been a waste of time and money."

"The season's not over, Matt," she said, trying to be optimistic. "You could pull it out of the fire yet."

"In a week?" he asked skeptically. "Ed's right. It's not very likely."

"The storm season doesn't end as predictably as the baseball season or a football game," she reminded him. "You had to put a time limit on our filming schedule, but there will still be storms to chase after I leave."

A shadow passed over his face, but he quickly brought the emotion that had caused it under control. He didn't want to think about Teddi's departure. "The season may not have a time limit, but my grant does. It's due in ten days."

"Don't give up yet. This is too important."

Her words took on a second meaning as they looked at each other. All their emotions were resting just beneath the surface of that glance, and Teddi knew it wouldn't take much to bring them into the light. She would have given anything to touch him, to make a connection, but she had learned the hard way what a mistake that would be. Besides, it was a poor substitute for what she really wanted.

Then the moment ended. The fragile web of longing that had been woven between them broke. Matt cleared his throat and tried to smile. "Did you have a reason for coming in here, or were you just looking for a little verbal abuse?"

Teddi got back down to business. "I hate to bring this up right now, but I need to ask you about the interview."

She didn't have to explain which one she meant. Matt leaned heavily back in his chair and shook his head. "I'm sorry, Teddi, but it's no go. I've tried three times to get Laura to reconsider, but she won't. I'm afraid we're going to have to settle for the interview you did with John Hogan last month."

Teddi was disappointed, not just for her sake, but for Matt's, too. In the past two months, Teddi had learned that Laura's ground-breaking work for the Disaster Planning

Commission had made their Tornado Rescue and Recovery operation the best in the state. When Laura reneged on her promise to grant an interview, Teddi had been forced to replace the segment with an interview with John Hogan, the other commissioner.

"I'm really sorry to hear that, Matt. Mr. Hogan was a nice man, but he was tongue-tied through the entire interview. Nothing I did put him at ease. And frankly, his knowledge of the R and R plan isn't as good as Laura's."

"I know that, Teddi. Don't you think I'd get Laura in front of your camera if I could?" he said testily, then recanted. "Sorry. It's not your fault."

"Yes, it is. What I said sounded callous. I know how hard this has been for you." And for Corey, she added silently. Laura still wasn't speaking to her son, either. In Teddi's opinion, she was making the men in her life miserable for no good reason. But of course, Teddi didn't have the right to condemn the other woman too much. Teddi hadn't exactly made Matt's life a bundle of joy, either.

"Don't worry about it, Matt. I'll make do with what I've got," she promised him, but when she left his office a few minutes later, Teddi realized she couldn't let the matter drop. An interview with Laura Cochran wasn't going to make the difference between the success or failure of the documentary, but it would certainly be a big plus. Teddi owed it to Matt to give him the best film possible. If that meant convincing Laura to give an interview, that's what Teddi would do.

Or at least she'd try.

And besides, Laura had said some very frank things to her two months ago. It was time Teddi returned the favor.

FINDING LITTLE GREEN Martians on her doorstep wouldn't have surprised Laura as much as seeing Teddi there that evening. She opened the inner door reluctantly, but didn't unlatch the screen. "I'm very busy, Ms. O'Brien," she said without any kind of greeting.

"Then I'm sorry to disturb you, but I'd really like to talk to you for a minute," Teddi replied pleasantly.

"I can't imagine what we could have to say to each other."

"Why don't you let me in and find out," she suggested.

Laura hesitated a moment, but curiosity finally got the better of her. She unlocked the screen door and stepped back to allow Teddi to enter. "Have a seat," she said, gesturing toward the sofa.

Teddi moved into the living room and discovered that, though Laura's house was small, it was beautifully decorated. In fact, she saw a lot of similarities between the decor of Matt's home and this one. Apparently Laura had done more for her friend than stock his freezer with food. "You have a lovely home," she commented as she sat on the floral-print sofa.

"I'm sure you didn't come here just to tell me that," Laura replied. "Why don't you get down to it, Ms. O'Brien. As I said before, I'm very busy preparing for a wedding reception."

So much for pleasantries, Teddi thought. Laura wasn't going to make this easy for either of them. "All right. I want to talk to you about the documentary. You had agreed to do an interview, and I'd like to set something up."

Laura perched on the edge of a chair and regarded Teddi frostily. "You're wasting your time, Ms. O'Brien. I've told Matt repeatedly that I won't do the interview. I'm sure John Hogan gave you everything you could possibly need."

"Actually, he didn't," Teddi replied. "You created the R and R plan. You know it better than anyone. Frankly, it surprises me that after all the hard work you've done on tornado safety you'd pass up a perfect opportunity to share a plan that could save hundreds of lives."

Laura laughed harshly. "You're good, I'll grant you that. But it won't work. I'm not going to let you use my commitment to the public to manipulate me into doing this interview. No matter what you or Matt say to the contrary, this film is nothing more than a glorification of tornado chasers."

"Apparently you didn't feel that way when Matt first asked you to do the interview," Teddi said.

"Things change."

"What's changed is your relationship with Matt."

"That's none of your business," Laura replied sharply.

"And my relationship with him was none of yours," Teddi countered. "But as I recall, that didn't stop you from expressing some pretty harsh opinions at our first meeting."

Laura had to concede that point to Teddi. "I was only trying to keep Matt from getting hurt."

"Then why are you working so hard at hurting him now?"

Another point for Teddi. "I don't know what Matt's told you, but you couldn't possibly understand what's going on between us," Laura said stiffly. "He betrayed our friendship, and I can't forgive him for that."

Teddi felt sorry for her. Despite her defensive posture, Laura looked like a brittle piece of paper that might crumble at any moment. "Friends can forgive anything," she told her gently.

"Not this," Laura said, shaking her head vehemently. "If you were a parent, Ms. O'Brien, you might have some inkling of what I'm going through, but since I don't think that's the case, you should just butt out. It's none of your business."

"Laura, I see two good friends in pain for no reason, and I can't stand—"

"Saving my son's life is all the reason I need," she said hotly.

Teddi nodded. "If your strategy was working, I might agree with you, but it's not, is it?" She paused, then said, "I've gotten to know Corey pretty well. He's miserable because you've cut him off so completely, but that hasn't stopped him from chasing. Matt is miserable, but he can't fire your son without a good reason. And you're miserable because you've convinced yourself that Matt's betrayal is going to get your son killed." Teddi raised her brows questioningly. "Tell me, Laura, have you already started planning Corey's funeral?"

Laura was on her feet in an instant. "That's a horrible thing to say! I want you out of here. Now!"

Teddi stayed where she was. "Not until I'm finished."

"You *are* finished. I'm not going to listen to any more vindictive garbage. I know that you and Matt stopped seeing each other right after the party. If you blame me for that, fine. I accept the blame, but I don't have to let you dump on me like this."

"Matt isn't trying to punish you, Laura. He's doing what he thinks is best for Corey."

"But he has no right to interfere."

"He doesn't? Laura, you gave him that right when you allowed him to help you raise Corey," Teddi argued. "You wanted a father figure for your son and someone to help you make the tough decisions that go hand in hand with bringing up a child."

"What's wrong with that?" Laura asked defensively. "I was alone and Matt wanted to help."

"There's nothing wrong with it," Teddi replied. "But you can't have it both ways. You've used Matt—"

"Don't talk to me about using Matt after what you did to him. You seduced him as a test of courage! What could be worse than that?"

Teddi didn't waste time with a denial. "Expecting him to be a father to your child, then all of a sudden saying, 'Oops, sorry. That's enough.'"

"That's not what I've done!"

"Isn't it? You encouraged Corey to think of Matt as a father, and you let Matt regard Corey as a son. Don't expect either of them to shut off those feelings now, just because you can't handle your own fears."

"This isn't about feelings. I lost my husband to Matt's precious profession. I have a right to be afraid of losing my son, too."

"Yes, you do," Teddi agreed. "But do you have the right to control his life?"

Laura's eyes were as hard and cold as glass. "Why don't you come back and give me this lecture when you become a mother? You've lived your life as some kind of free-spirited daredevil who loves to pull death-defying stunts. It's no wonder you think chasing tornadoes is an acceptable profession. Well, I don't have a death wish like you do, and I don't want my son to have one, either."

"Corey doesn't have a death wish, and neither do I."

"Oh, no? Then why did you come here to do this film? A woman who lost her whole family to a tornado, then comes back to chase them? If that's not a death wish, I don't know what is."

Teddi wasn't sure how she'd allowed herself to be placed on the defensive, but she couldn't back down now. "I came here to confront my fears—*old* fears that I'd buried and tried to forget. I don't like running away from the past, Laura. I'm trying to learn how to make peace with it, and you should, too."

Laura wanted to tell her she didn't understand what it was like to lose someone she loved, to be left alone and terrified of the future. But Teddi did know. She had lost everything when she was just a girl. Laura, at least, had been grown when she lost her husband, and she'd had a son to cling to and a dear friend to rely on. But that didn't change the fact that Teddi had no right to criticize the way Laura had raised her son.

"Are you finished?" she asked coldly.

Teddi could see that she hadn't even made a dent. Laura wasn't going to do the interview, and she wasn't going to forgive Matt. Coming here hadn't solved a thing. "Yes. I'm finished," she said as she rose and moved to the door, with Laura close behind her. "Thanks for hearing me out."

"You didn't give me much choice," Laura replied as they paused by the door. "You didn't really come here about the documentary, did you?"

Teddi was surprised by the question. "Yes. But it wasn't the only reason."

"Why did you even think you had to come?" she asked with genuine curiosity. "You're not dating Matt anymore, so my relationship with him is really none of your business."

"I told you a month ago that I really do care about him, Laura. It hurts me to see him in pain."

"Then you should have thought of that before you got involved with him."

It was a worthy parting shot. "Everyone makes mistakes, Laura," Teddi told her sadly. "We think we're doing the right thing, but it can backfire and turn out all wrong."

Laura studied her intently. "You really do love him, don't you?"

Teddi nodded. "Yes, I do."

"Then I feel sorry for both of you."

"I feel sorry for all of us, Laura. We're all bound together by a common thread, trying to do the best we can to make sense of the tragedies in our lives."

"Have you made sense of yours yet?"

"No, but I'm getting there. I may never understand it all, but I'm trying to accept it so that I can get on with the challenge of living."

"I'm just doing the same," Laura said.

"But you're trying to live your son's life, too. I may not be a mother, but I do know that's a losing proposition anyway you look at it." She opened the screen door and stepped onto the porch. "Goodbye, Laura."

"Goodbye."

Laura closed the door and leaned her forehead against it, trying to shut out the logic of Teddi's arguments, which were suddenly warring with her need to protect her son...

MATT TOOK ANOTHER SIP from the bottle of beer, then set it on the deck railing as he looked into the darkness.

One week. No, less. Six days. Teddi was leaving in—he stopped to calculate—132 hours. The torture would be over and Matt could get on with his life—what there was of it.

Two months ago he had been perfectly content with things the way they were. He'd had his work to occupy his time and the hope of proving his theory to brighten his future. The blank spaces in between had been filled by Laura and Corey. Then Teddi O'Brien had swept into his life with all her vivacious charm and made him believe there could be more to his life than work, theories and a family that wasn't really his.

And then she'd snatched it away.

Now he just wanted her to be gone, but the bitter irony was that he dreaded her departure more than he craved her absence. The past two months had been torture. Seeing

Teddi without being able to touch her, watching her struggle to reinvent herself and conquer her fear, listening to her laughter and wanting more than anything to have the sparkle in his eyes directed at him and only him... Every day had become a kind of hell on earth.

Their day in Dry Creek had been the worst. He'd finally understood the depth of her trauma, and he'd known even as he held her while she sobbed out her anguish that he couldn't allow himself even a fragment of hope. Not even fearless Teddi O'Brien could walk away from that kind of devastating tragedy into the arms of a tornado chaser. A moment or two was fine, but a lifetime? Not a chance. So he'd pulled away from the fragile bonds of friendship that had been forming between them and tried to shut out the hope.

Maybe it would be easier once she was gone, but he really didn't think so. She'd be leaving too big a hole in his life and in his heart.

Matt drained the beer and thought about going for another one, or maybe even something stronger, but a little alcohol-induced forgetfulness wasn't going to help any.

When the doorbell rang he was grateful for the chance to escape his depressing thoughts. He had never approved of self-pity, and he didn't like the fact that he had been wallowing in it too often lately. That was something else he'd change as soon as Teddi left.

"Just a minute," he called out when the bell rang again as he crossed the living room.

Because he hadn't been expecting Teddi, he wasn't prepared for the emotional jolt he felt when he opened the door and saw her. There wasn't enough time for him to erect his protective barrier.

"I'm sorry to disturb you, Matt, but I need to talk to you for a minute."

"Sure. Come in." He stepped back to let her pass and closed his eyes for a second to ward off the sudden assault on his senses. "I was out on the deck enjoying the night air. Would you like something to drink?" He lifted the empty bottle in his hand. "A beer? Wine?"

"A beer would be nice," she said.

"Be right back." He slipped into the kitchen, and when he came back carrying two bottles, Teddi was waiting for him on the deck. The moonlight filtering through the trees cast delicate patterns on her face, and Matt almost groaned with the need that coursed through him. Whatever it took, he knew he had to find a way to stop loving her.

But that wasn't going to happen tonight.

He moved onto the deck, extended the bottle, then leaned back against the rail. "What's up?"

Teddi mirrored his position, keeping a discreet distance between them. "I may have done something very stupid tonight."

"Don't tell me. Let me guess," he said. "You erased the rough cut of the documentary."

Teddi smiled. "Uh, no."

"You overloaded the circuits in the editing room and blew out the power in Mission Control."

"Not that, either," Teddi said, giving him a curious look. "How much have you had to drink tonight?"

Matt held up the beer. "Second bottle. Don't worry, I'm sober."

"That's good. I guess."

Matt frowned. "Why do you think I'm going to need some liquid fortification for this news of yours?"

"Because," she replied, growing serious. "I just came from seeing Laura."

"Then you're probably the one who needs a stiff drink."

Teddi chuckled. "I'm glad you can joke about it."

"Oh, I don't think it's funny, Teddi. This situation with Laura makes me sick," he said, taking another sip of beer. "I feel as if a very important piece of my anatomy has been surgically removed, and it wasn't something innocuous like an appendix or gall bladder. It was a major organ." He turned and looked into the darkness. "Why did you go see her, and what did she have to say? As if I didn't already know."

"I asked her to reconsider doing the interview," Teddi told him. "I tried to play on her civic-mindedness, and when that didn't work, I lost it and gave her the piece of my mind I've been saving up since she blasted me at the party. I wanted you to know, because I'm afraid I might have made things worse between you two."

Matt knew that wasn't possible, and he certainly didn't blame her for needing to clear the air with Laura. Teddi wasn't the kind of person to leave behind unfinished business. "Having seen you when you're angry, I'm forced to ask whether Laura was still standing when you left."

Teddi smiled, relieved he was taking it so well. "Oh, yes. She got her licks in. She accused me of using you again, and I threw the same charge back in her face." Teddi gave him a condensed version of her conversation with Laura.

"You're right, in a way," Matt said when she was finished. "But Laura didn't really ask me for help. It just sort of happened. I volunteered."

"The way you volunteered to take me out to dinner a few weeks ago?"

That was a memory better left untouched as far as Matt was concerned. "Something like that."

Teddi turned to him, leaning her hip against the rail as she studied his face for a long time. "You're a nice man, Matt," she said finally, her voice as soft as a caress. "You have a kind heart and a sense of fair play. You feel things deeply, and once you commit yourself to something—or someone—you don't back off. That's a lot to say about any man."

Matt discovered a knot of emotion suddenly clogging his throat. He swallowed hard as he looked at her, but it didn't go away. "I'm...glad to know you feel that way. Thank you."

"It's just the simple truth."

Matt had to grip the rail to keep himself from reaching for her. He glanced back at the yard, because he knew he couldn't look at her without touching her. "Why does this feel suspiciously like two people saying goodbye?" he asked.

Teddi was having a hard time with the distance between them, but she didn't dare cross the invisible line. "I guess it's because we both know I'll be leaving soon. We do such a good job of avoiding each other that I wasn't sure I'd get another chance to say the things I need to say to you."

"Such as?" he asked, wondering if he could bear to hear whatever she wanted to say, particularly if it was goodbye.

"I wanted to tell you that you were right," she replied.

He had to look at her then. "About what?"

Teddi found she couldn't meet his gaze while she made her confession. "I've been doing a lot of soul searching since that day in Dry Creek. I went to Oak Street because I had to prove to myself I could face the memories. And I think..." She hesitated, because she knew this was going to hurt him. "I think you were a test, too. In the beginning."

Matt had known it all along, despite her denials, but hearing her say it made it hurt that much more. "Well. Thanks for being honest."

"Do you remember when I kissed you at the door of my apartment?" she asked.

Matt's hands tightened on the rail. "I seem to have a vague recollection of it."

"That was the test, Matt. That, and only that. I was so drawn to you, so incredibly attracted, but I spent that whole day fighting it because I was a little afraid of what you represented. When we said good-night, I knew you wouldn't cross the line between professionalism and a personal relationship without some encouragement, and I didn't want to run from what I was feeling, so I kissed you." She shrugged a little. "If you want to call that a test of bravery, I won't argue with you."

Matt looked at her and felt an ache so powerful it threatened to drive him to his knees. "And the night we made love?" he forced himself to ask, because he had to know. "Was that another test?"

Teddi smiled at the memory that had become a bittersweet ache in her heart. "That was Teddi O'Brien at her most impulsive, Matt. I wanted you, and it didn't make a damned bit of difference what you did for a living. I think deep down I believed you were the one man who could understand me—not just the public daredevil Teddi, but the private one who was running from the past. That wasn't a test, Matt. What we felt that night was real. At least, it was for me."

Matt looked into the depths of her emerald eyes and knew she was telling him the truth. He could barely breathe, because all the barriers came crashing down, leaving nothing but love and longing. "It was real for me, too, Teddi. More real than anything I've ever known."

He extended his arm and touched her cheek with his fingertips. Before he realized it, his palm was cupping her jaw and Teddi was leaning toward him. She took a step, and the dam broke. Matt pulled her into his arms and kissed her with all the fury of the hundred sweet, bitter, powerful, painful emotions that he'd been bottling up for so long.

And Teddi kissed him back, her emotions mingling, clashing and finally blending with his as she poured her need and her love into the embrace. This was what she wanted, what she had waited so long for, and she couldn't bear to let the moment go.

Matt's mouth slanted across hers, and he pulled her tighter against him. One hand moved over her body, touching and caressing her, creating sensations more intense than any she'd ever known. She groaned as an exquisite agony blossomed inside her, and she clutched at him, begging for more. The kiss was like a fire raging out of control, and Teddi never wanted it to end. She wanted to make love with Matt, and this time, when it was over, she wanted to tell him that she loved him. She wanted to give him all of herself tonight, and in the morning promise that she would keep on giving as long as he wanted her.

But somewhere beyond all the passion and need, Teddi heard a voice telling her she couldn't make that promise. She did love him, and exploring all the facets of that love could be the greatest adventure of her life. It could be the ultimate challenge in a lifetime of challenges. But in order to give him all of herself, she had to be whole. Matt deserved nothing less. He would *settle* for nothing less.

And the painful truth was that for all her searching, for all the tests she'd passed and the agony she'd forced on herself, Teddi still hadn't found all the pieces of her soul she had lost or hidden away. Until she did, the most she could give Matt was a night of passion that wouldn't change anything in the morning.

Matt knew it, too. He sensed the moment her desperation turned to regret, because the kiss softened, even as their need grew. He wanted more than Teddi could give him. He always had.

The pain of that certainty turned his hunger into a bitterness that was too overpowering to be ignored. He drew a ragged breath, and the hands that had been clutching her shoulders were suddenly pushing her away. Matt held her at arm's length, hating her more than he'd ever thought it was possible to hate—until he looked into her eyes and saw a pain as deep as his own.

The flash of hatred vanished, leaving nothing but emptiness in its wake.

"I think you'd better go," he said quietly. He released her and turned toward the house. "You know the way out."

CHAPTER SEVENTEEN

AT THE THINGS REMEMBERED flower shop, Teddi ordered three bouquets of bright spring flowers and took them to the cemetery. An early-morning shower had drizzled on her all the way to Dry Creek, but the sky was clear now, just as Matt had predicted it would be in their morning briefing. He hadn't even glanced at her once when he announced to the team that it didn't seem likely they would chase today.

Teddi had known then exactly what she had to do. She had made up her mind in the sleepless hours before dawn, and she knew that this might be her only chance. Last night when Matt walked away from her, she had almost called him back. For just an instant, she would have said anything, given him any guarantee he wanted just to stay in his arms for one night.

But she didn't want one night. She wanted a lifetime, and she knew she couldn't promise him that until she'd opened the one door she'd been too much of a coward to walk through a month ago. She had to cross the threshold, turn on all the lights in the dimly lit room, chase away every swirling shadow and take a good hard look at what was inside. Until she did that, she wouldn't have reclaimed herself; and if she didn't have all of herself, she wasn't too worthy of a man like Matt.

That was why she was kneeling now beside three graves that had been neglected for too long. She carefully weeded the three small plots and forced herself to remember—and feel.

It was hard to let the emotions surface, to willingly open herself to pain that was easier to ignore if she left it hidden, but she did it. She talked quietly to her parents and to Cathy as if they were really there, could really hear her; and in a way, she knew they could. The family she had lost was still inside her, unchanged by time, frozen in her memory like a flower preserved in glass. They would have been a different family now had they lived. Their attitudes and feelings would have changed, their differences might have vanished or magnified; there was no way of knowing which.

That was what Teddi had to make peace with. She had always been a disappointment to her parents. They had never understood their rambunctious daughter. They had loved her in the way of all parents, but Teddi had always felt that their love sprang from obligation, not any particular attachment to her. She wasn't really sure they'd even liked her, and she knew with certainty they would have changed her if they could have.

So she sat in the sun and told her parents what she had done with her life. She talked about the good friends she had made and the challenges she had met. The little girl who had once brazenly climbed the Dry Creek water tower to find out if she could see England had now traveled the world. She had climbed mountains and scaled glaciers. She had tested the limits of earthbound speed in race cars and speedboats. She had soared the skies like an eagle. She had earned the respect of her peers, and her accomplishments, preserved for posterity, would live long after she died. Generations from now, people would still be able to look at her films and say, "This was Teddi O'Brien. This is what she did, what she saw, what she created."

The films weren't really a legacy, though. As Teddi

talked, as the experiences and emotions poured out, she realized they were a validation. They were her way of proving she was worthy of having survived.

"I know you'd have wanted Cathy to be the one," she told her parents, her voice choked with emotion. "I've always known it. If you could have chosen which of your daughters would live, which one would do the most with her life and make you most proud, you'd have picked her."

Teddi brushed at the tears on her cheeks. "And maybe you'd have been right. She would have given you grandchildren by now. She'd be the chairperson of the Dry Creek Civic League and the president of the PTA. Everyone would love her because she was sweet and kind and she had such high ideals." Teddi cleared her throat. "But I haven't done so badly, have I, Momma? Would you be proud of me, even a little, now?"

"Teddi, dear?"

Teddi nearly came out of her skin when she heard the thin-pitched voice behind her. She dashed at her tears, pulling herself together before she turned and found Myra Brick looking down at her.

"Mrs. Brick. Hello." It was all the greeting she could manage.

The frail old woman patted Teddi's shoulder comfortingly. "I'm sorry, dear. I shouldn't have intruded. I was just so surprised to see you here."

"It's okay," Teddi said, rising. "I came with some flowers."

Myra looked at the arrangements. "They're lovely," she said, then sighed regretfully as she looked at the small bouquet of roses she was carrying. "It's such a shame that cut flowers don't last."

"I know," Teddi agreed, still trying to dry her face. "But I've asked the florist to set out some artificial ones when these wilt away. I just wanted to put something alive and beautiful out here today.'' The tears threatened again, but she held them back.

"What a lovely sentiment, dear. I do the same thing every week, you know.'' She pointed over her shoulder in the direction she'd entered the cemetery. ''The senior citizens' van makes a trip out here every Friday. I always come to visit my Leo and bring him a sampling of whatever's in my garden.

Myra tilted her head to one side and peered at Teddi through her bifocals. ''Are you all right, dear?''

"I'm fine,'' she assured her.

"But you have a lot of catching up to do with them, don't you?''

Teddi didn't bother to deny that she'd been talking to her parents. ''Do you talk to Leo, too?''

"Oh, my, yes. He doesn't talk back, of course,'' she added with a grin, ''but I know he hears me. Nora and Bob can hear you, too.''

"I hope so.''

Myra seemed in no hurry to move on, and Teddi suspected the old woman was probably starved for someone to talk to—someone who talked back, that is. Teddi was surprised, though, when Myra began rambling on about Teddi's parents. ''You know, I remember when Nora and Bob bought this plot. My Leo was on the cemetery's board of directors, so he handled a lot of the sales.''

"I didn't remember that,'' Teddi replied.

Myra patted her arm. ''You were very young, dear, and much more interested in making sneak attacks on my garden than in practical things like cemetery plots.''

"When did they buy this?'' she asked. When her family had died, her aunt had made all the funeral arrangements, and Teddi had never wondered about the details.

"Oh, it was several years before the tornado. I don't recall the date, but I remember coming out here with Leo and your parents because I used to help with the paperwork—filing the deeds, recording special requests, that kind of thing." She pointed a crooked finger at a spot just behind Teddi, beside her mother's headstone. "I suppose you know that one is yours," she said.

Teddi felt everything inside her go very still. "Mine?"

"Your grave," Myra answered, as though she was saying, "Your hat," or, "Your shoes." She continued, "Nora and Bob bought four adjacent lots and specifically requested that they be buried in the center two, with Cathy on that side and you right there, by Nora."

"I didn't know that," Teddi said faintly.

"Well, Leo tried to argue them out of it, of course. No one had any idea that your parents or poor Cathy would be taken from us so suddenly, and Leo tried to tell them that when the time came, you and Cathy would probably want to be buried next to your own husbands. Splitting up a plot like that makes it much more difficult to sell later," she explained. "But they wouldn't hear of it. Nora said she wanted her girls around her so that she and Bob could watch over you both."

A flood of emotion almost doubled Teddi over, and she couldn't stem the rush of tears that coursed down her face. Her mother had wanted to watch over her. When she had carefully planned her final rest, she had wanted Teddi close. Surely that had to mean she really had loved her.

Myra put her hand on Teddi's arm. "Oh, dear. I didn't mean to make you cry again. I'm just an old woman who likes to reminisce."

"No, it's all right. I'm glad you told me," Teddi assured her as a smile broke through the tears. "Momma probably figured I'd need a lot of supervision, even in the afterlife."

"You're still looking at your parents through the eyes of a child, aren't you?" the sharp old woman asked.

"I guess so. But that's all I have."

"They loved you, dear. They didn't know how to cope with that wild, reckless streak of yours, but they loved you."

Teddi needed to believe that more than anything, but it was so hard. "They wanted me to be like Cathy."

Myra chuckled. "Well, you could hardly blame them for that, could you? Cathy didn't jump off roofs or climb water towers." She patted Teddi's hand. "They were just looking for a way to keep their baby girl safe. That's all."

Teddi felt a warm, curious twisting in her heart, like a key being turned in a lock. The door that swung open spilled out a whirling torrent of resentments and doubts that then blew away, leaving only a sense of peace Teddi had never known before.

"Thank you, Mrs. Brick," she said, brushing her cheek with the back of her hand to wipe away the tears.

"Whatever for?"

Teddi shook her head, unable to find the words. "Just...thank you."

THE THREE HOURS it took Teddi to drive back to the center were the longest of her life. She had found what she was looking for, and it was the sweetest realization of her life. She had thought the piece that was missing had been ripped away from her during that first chase, but she'd been wrong. It was something she'd never even had—the sense of being loved, of being *worthy* of love.

The reminiscences and speculations of an old woman weren't proof, of course, but Teddi didn't need anything carved in stone. She just needed to feel whole, and now, she did. For the first time in her life. All the doors were open. The sunlight was pouring in, and Teddi was ready to give Matt the guarantee he wanted.

It terrified her to think that he might not believe her. He was convinced that her past wouldn't allow them to build a life together, but she would find a way to convince him. Even if it took a lifetime to prove it to him. It would be time well spent.

She couldn't wait to reach Matt so she could get started.

The Bronco ate away the miles, with Teddi becoming more impatient the closer she came to Turner. Twenty minutes away from the center, though, she spotted something that compounded the excitement she felt. After fourteen chases, endless studies of clouds and countless hours spent reviewing films of developing storms, Teddi had learned to spot the difference between an innocuous bit of fluff that would eventually evaporate and one that was growing into a thunderstorm.

The billowing cloud she was driving toward had all the earmarks of the latter. She watched in awe as it bubbled into the atmosphere, dwarfing the few smaller clouds around it and finally gobbling them up like the hungry monster it was becoming.

That morning, Matt had predicted clear skies, but Teddi had learned not to be surprised by last-minute developments like this one. Sometimes they had days to prepare for a chase; at other times, chases that looked definite were called off. And sometimes, like now, storms blew up without warning.

Teddi was excited and disappointed at the same time. Matt needed promising storms like this and so did Teddi's documentary, but the timing couldn't have been worse. The brewing storm was some distance east of Turner and developing fast, and she knew that when she arrived at the center she would find Matt preparing to chase or already gone. She was about to burst with the need to tell him how much she loved him, but the middle of a thunderstorm wasn't the time or the place.

It was nearly four when she reached the center, and the cloud was hanging on the western horizon, billowing so high it dwarfed the Doppler radar dome. Hoping she wasn't too late for the chase, Teddi hurried inside and was astonished to discover that everything was business as usual. No one was hurrying through the halls, no one was barking orders. Puzzled, she stopped for a moment to look through the glass walls of Mission Control. Technicians were sitting around sipping coffee and soft drinks, leisurely doing their daily chores and barely paying any attention to their radar monitors.

Had she been wrong about the cloud? Was it just an ordinary cumulus that would float placidly overhead without uttering a peep? She couldn't believe it. She knew the signs too well.

She turned away from the puzzling sight in Mission Control and went looking for Matt. Every instinct she possessed told her that *this* was the storm they'd been waiting for, and it was only fitting that she be the one to give him the news.

WHEN MATT STEPPED OUT of his office and saw Teddi hurrying down the hall, it was all he could do to keep from retreating into his sanctuary. He didn't want to see her today, or tomorrow, for that matter. He'd cut his briefing short this morning just so he wouldn't have to be in the same room with her, and relief had flooded him when Bryce had told him she'd left the center on a personal errand. Knowing he wouldn't be running into her like this was the only thing that had allowed him to get through the day.

"Matt!"

He steeled himself and tried to remember that there were only five days of torture left. But when he forced himself to look into her face, the radiant smile he saw made those five days loom like an eternity. How could she be so happy after what had happened between them last night? How could her eyes be sparkling like fireworks? Why was she so radiant and so beautiful? And why did he still love her so damned much?

"What is it, Teddi?" he said shortly. He was in no mood to even attempt politeness, and he kept walking toward Mission Control.

Teddi drew a breath as he passed her without a second glance. The flash of pain she'd seen in his eyes when he'd first looked at her had been quickly covered up, but she had something for him that would take it away. Two things, in fact, but the professional one had to come before the personal one. She did an about-face and caught up with. "I have a suggestion for you that will save the center a fortune," she said.

Matt didn't even glance at her. Just the excitement bubbling in her voice was nearly enough to send him over the edge. "What?"

"You should scrap all that fancy radar equipment in Mission Control and put a spotter on the roof."

He stopped. "What are you talking about?"

"Look out a window, Matt," she said, grinning from ear to ear. "There's a cumulonimbus out there about the size of a small planet." She was exaggerating, but she didn't care.

"That's not possible," he snapped, though he knew very well it was.

"Be that as it may, there's a storm brewing on your doorstep."

Completely bypassing Mission Control, Matt hurried toward the parking lot with Teddi keeping pace with him. "Teddi, we sent up a weather balloon two hours ago, and everything was stable. The satellite feed at three o'clock showed no activity, and radar is clear. What you saw was probably just a cumulus."

"See for yourself," Teddi said as he barged out the front door and came to a dead stop.

It was ten or fifteen miles away, but there was no mistaking it. Teddi was right. A dynamite storm was brewing in his own front yard.

Matt whirled around and charged back into the center with Teddi at his side.

"Did I do good?"

He glanced at her and the joyful light in her eyes was more than he could resist. This was the same Teddi he had met in the California desert, vivacious and dynamic, with no shadows haunting her eyes, no self-doubt lurking in dark corners. Seeing her like this, so happy, so *complete*, he couldn't be angry with her. He could only feel sadness, regret and a crippling sense of loss. "Yeah. You did good."

"I'll tell the guys to get the van ready," she said.

He nodded. "We'll meet you out back in ten minutes."

They separated at a junction in the hall, but Teddi couldn't let him go.

"Matt!"

He stopped and looked back at her. "What?"

"This is the one."

Her smile was contagious. "I hope you're right."

She held his gaze, hoping he could see the love in her eyes. "When it's over, we have to talk."

But Matt shook his head and his small smile faded. "No, Teddi. There's nothing to talk about."

He disappeared down the hall, and it was all Teddi could do to keep from running after him to tell him how wrong he was. Instead, she held the emotions in check and dashed toward the editing room.

"Saddle up, men!" she sang out as she hurried into the room and made a beeline for the storage locker. "It's time to go to work."

Bryce looked up from the editing console and Griff removed a set of headphones without disturbing the baseball cap he always wore, indoors or out. "What's going on?" the older man asked.

"We're chasing."

"Today?" Bryce glanced at his watch. "It's after four o'clock. How can we possibly get into position?"

"There's a single-cell storm forming practically on top of us. Matt wants us on the road in ten minutes."

"I don't believe this," Griff muttered as he shut down the sound board. "Couldn't Mother Nature have given us a little warning?"

Teddi slung an equipment bag over her shoulder. "That's why they call it weather, Griff," she told him.

"What do you mean?"

She grinned mischievously. "Because you never know weather it will, or weather it won't."

Both men groaned, and Griff even threw his baseball cap at her in protest.

"Everybody's a critic," she grumbled good-naturedly as she tossed the hat back to him. "Let's just get loaded, shall we?"

By the time the teams were assembled, the cloud was a solitary giant dominating the landscape. It took nearly an hour to get into position behind and below the storm, because they had to zigzag back and forth on the country roads. By then, the mound of cotton candy had turned into a menacing curtain of blue-black ink. Matt called for the vehicles to stop, and both teams launched into their well-rehearsed routine.

Bryce and Griff recorded the procedure on film. Teddi got it on audiotape. Standing at the back of the van with her headphones on, she studied the storm, looking for anything different, anything that would make this chase special.

Through the headphones she heard the excitement in Matt's voice as he told them Pandora was finally reading positive. A tornado was forming in the clouds ahead of them.

"Fifteen minutes, maybe, but no more than twenty," he answered when someone asked how long they had. "Let's get ready to deploy!"

Teddi felt an instinctive jolt of fear, but she ignored it as she whipped off the headset and ran to the edge of the road, motioning for Griff to come in. She looked for Matt and saw that he had a map unfolded on the hood of the truck. Corey, Ryan and Gerry were gathered around him, plotting their strategy.

"We're going to deploy," she told Griff as he jogged up to her.

"Same procedure as before?" he asked.

"Same procedure," Teddi said in confirmation. "You stay here with Nate and the lead van. I'll drive Bryce to the drop spot." As she said it, a sense of revulsion welled up in her, because the real action was about to begin and she was reduced to being little more than a chauffeur.

"Teddi!"

She turned as Matt came running up. "Is it the real thing this time?" she called out to him.

His smile was dazzling. "If Pandora's right, it is."

"She's been right about everything else," Teddi reminded him.

"Those were negative confirmations. This one has to be positive."

"It will be!"

There was no time for Matt to be amazed by her enthusiasm, but he had to fight the urge to kiss her for it. "We're going four miles straight up this road."

"All right. We'll follow the deploy truck. Be careful!"

"You, too!" He ran back to the van, passing Bryce on the way.

"I'll see you later," Griff told her, but Teddi grabbed his arm.

She made the decision in an instant. In less than a week she was supposed to leave Oklahoma. This might very well be her last chance. "Give me your harness," she said to Griff urgently.

"What?"

"Your equipment harness. Take it off. Now!" she demanded. Time was running out. They had to get on the road fast and she didn't have time for amenities. Griff did as she asked, and Teddi turned as Bryce ran up to the van. "We're changing the procedure, Bryce. I want you to stay here with Nate. I'll do the deploy."

"Teddi, you're not serious," Bryce said, aghast.

"Yes, I am." She took Griff's harness and slung it over one shoulder, then grabbed his camera. "Come on! Let's move!" She jumped into the passenger seat of the van as Griff ran around the vehicle.

"Teddi..." Bryce protested, grabbing the door.

She swung toward him. "I have to know, Bryce!"

He studied her face. "Are you sure?"

"I'm sure."

Whatever he saw in her eyes must have convinced him, because he stepped back and closed the door. "Then go for it, gorgeous."

Just ahead of them, Corey jumped into the bed of the deploy truck and held on as it sped away with Gerry Hampton at the wheel. Matt and Ryan Sawyer were crammed into the cab with him.

"Teddi, are you really going to do this?" Griff asked as he put the van in gear and roared after them. "What if you freeze again?"

"I won't."

"Are you sure you should take that risk?"

Teddi looked at the truck and barely made out the back of Matt's head in the cab. She didn't have the right to take chances with his documentary, but she had to know. And Matt had to know, too. If she could do this, if she could conquer the fear once and for all, prove that she was whole again, Matt would have to believe she was capable of building a life with him.

"I can do this, Griff," she told him firmly, but the words echoed in her head as she remembered how many times she'd told herself that before the first chase. But she couldn't fail. She wouldn't let it happen again. There was too much at stake.

"You're the boss," Griff replied, and concentrated on driving.

Rain began peppering the windshield, and Teddi guessed that they had already passed the part of the storm that was building into a tornado. They were in front of it now and probably just to the east of it. She could see a heavy black rain curtain in front of them, obscuring the little town of Harvest that a sign said was four miles ahead. If a tornado did drop, that town was the last place Teddi wanted to be.

Just as they passed a gravel road that led to the east, the CB squawked and the deploy truck began slowing.

"This is it," Matt said over the radio. "That gravel road is our escape route in case we get trapped."

"We copy, Deploy One," Teddi replied. Griff put on the brakes just as Gerry swung the truck into a wide U-turn on the deserted highway. "As soon as I'm out, turn around and get ready to move us out of here," she instructed Griff.

"Will do."

The van came to a stop and Teddi jumped out, shouldering her camera. With her knees bent to reduce jarring, she moved forward, recording the deploy team as they scrambled around the truck.

Matt vaulted into the bed, darting a quick glance at the camera as he did so. He was so accustomed to being shadowed by Bryce or Griff that he hardly noticed them any longer. But when he realized it was Teddi beside the truck, he stopped.

"Teddi?"

"Just deploy the damned thing and get us out of here!" she yelled without pausing the tape.

Matt didn't have time to question her decision or the implications of it. If Pandora was right, they had only a few minutes left.

He went to work. His team was like a well-oiled machine, every movement they made compact and rehearsed. But the scene was also infused with incredible urgency. While Ryan and Matt released the safety clamps on Toto II, Corey and Gerry lowered the tailgate and unfolded the ramp that was hinged to it. Then they jumped into the bed, and together the four men rolled the three-hundred-pound instrument barrel down a specially designed track.

Staying well behind the truck, Teddi jockeyed for the best position as they lifted Toto II onto the ramp. The shot was spectacular. A fierce wind buffeted the men as streaks of lightning and the black rolling clouds of the advancing storm provided a breathtakingly dramatic backdrop for the shot.

Because she was the only one facing the storm, Teddi saw it first, a swirl of reddish dust in the distance that took shape quickly. The dirt was sucked upward, outlining a pencil-thin funnel. It was several miles away and Teddi was seeing it through her viewfinder, but it looked enormous. Terrifying. And it was heading right at them.

A jolt of horror rocked Teddi to her very soul, but she didn't lower the camera.

"It's down, Matt! It's down!" she yelled as she framed the men on the truck with the tornado in the background.

Teddi's heart thundered in her ears. Her analytical self knew that the shot was spectacular, but all she could think was that the tornado was coming for her again. This time, if it caught her, it would take Matt, too, and the thought was unendurable. He couldn't die until she told him how much she loved him! He just couldn't. Not even fate could be that cruel.

"Hurry, Matt! It's coming! Move it!"

Matt didn't bother glancing over his shoulder. If Teddi said there was a tornado bearing down on them, he wasn't about to question her. Unfortunately Corey couldn't stop himself from taking a quick peek. Perched precariously on the steeply slanted ramp, he looked behind him.

It happened so fast that Teddi wasn't sure how it happened. It could have been excitement or shock, or even the heavy gust of wind that blew up a pelting shower of dust. Whatever it was, it threw Corey off balance and he lost his hold on Toto II. The weight of the barrel shifted, and before the other men could compensate, it jolted off the track, smashing Corey's foot.

He howled in pain as he wrenched himself away and tumbled onto the pavement. He landed with a sickening thud, smashing his head.

"Corey!" Matt shouted, but he couldn't release the barrel or someone else would certainly get hurt, too. They grappled to control it as it toppled wildly down the ramp, until it was finally on solid ground. Rolling it on its bottom rim, they shoved it off the road, then clustered around Corey.

Griff came running up just as they were lifting him. "Get him in the van!" he shouted. He already had the doors open, and they placed him inside as gently as they could.

Through it all, Teddi kept the camera rolling because that was what she was trained to do. She had backed even farther away from the truck, trying to capture Toto II, the tornado, and the men in one shot. She lost the team as they carried Corey away, but when Matt came dashing back to the deploy truck looking for her, the power of the image she was recording stunned Teddi. The shot was only Matt and the tornado, and it was so magnificent she was paralyzed by the power of it.

"Teddi, come on! Let's go!" he shouted as he folded up the ramp.

And then the paralysis ended. With the camera still running, she ran for the truck. Matt grabbed her around the waist and practically threw her into the bed, then vaulted in himself just as Gerry sped away.

Teddi dropped to her knees and shouldered her camera again, focusing on the funnel ahead and to the right of them. It seemed the height of folly to be heading toward the tornado, instead of away from it, but the gravel road they'd passed was their best hope of escape. It would take them due east while the tornado traveled north.

The truck jolted as they turned, slinging Teddi to one side, and Matt grabbed her to steady her as she continued filming. With one hand gripping the side of the truck bed, he wrapped the other arm around her waist, his thighs bracketing hers as he pulled her against his chest.

For that moment, they were one person, bound together by a force more elemental than the tornado that played hopscotch across a field, lifting into the air, then dropping down again, time after time. Teddi zoomed in on it as it approached an enormous barn, then hopped over the structure like a child playing leapfrog.

A moment later, it defied gravity again. The clouds seemed to suck it upward, like a parent forcing a child to come home—and it disappeared.

Exhilarated and exhausted, Teddi lowered the camera as the truck slowed to a stop. She sagged against Matt, reveling in the feel of being totally connected with him—and with herself. He rested his chin on her shoulder as their heavy breathing returned to normal.

"I did it," she whispered when she finally found enough air to speak.

Matt coiled both his arms around her. "You certainly did."

Teddi felt an unexpected rush of tears. "I did it," she said again, not bothering to blink them back. In the last five minutes, she'd more than earned the right to cry with relief if she felt like it.

CHAPTER EIGHTEEN

THE HOSPITAL EMERGENCY was crowded that night. Just outside of tiny Harvest, the tornado had dropped again to plow through a few houses and businesses. Then it had leapt over Turner to pay one more visit on the countryside. Early reports suggested that casualties were light, but the nearest hospital, in Norman, was receiving a constant flow of people suffering from cuts, contusions and broken bones.

Teddi and Matt had driven Corey straight to the hospital in Griff's van while the deploy team met up with Nate to collect Toto II. Teddi expected them to arrive any minute, but it would be a miracle if they could even get close to the hospital. The emergency room had been nearly deserted when they arrived, but it filled up very quickly.

Matt was sick with worry. Corey had regained consciousness only once during the ride to the hospital, and that had been for a mercifully brief time. His eyes had been glazed with pain, and the possibility of a serious concussion was very real. He had a nasty cut on his head that Matt had clumsily bandaged using Griff's emergency kit, and there was no telling what other injuries he'd sustained in his fall. If anything happened to him, Matt would never be able to forgive himself.

He had notified the center about the accident, and they were getting in touch with Laura. There would be hell to pay when she got here, and Matt felt he had only himself to blame.

"Here. Drink this," Teddi said, handing him a cup of vending machine coffee.

Matt glanced at her face, then at the cup. "I don't suppose you have a shot of whiskey to go with this."

She shook her head. "Sorry."

He took it and sipped. "It's better than nothing, I guess."

Teddi sat beside him on the tiny sofa, and Matt allowed himself to be comforted by her presence. They had run out of waiting-room small talk and meaningless platitudes. There was nothing left to do but wait.

He closed his eyes and prayed, but a moment later he opened them again when he felt a featherlight touch on his hand. It was Teddi. She laced her fingers through his, looking at him tentatively as though to say, "Is this all right?"

Matt tightened his hand on hers and held on.

"Matt?"

He tensed and looked up to see Laura hurrying across the room, her face ashen and streaked with tears.

"Where is he?" she demanded harshly.

His own guilt made the accusing look in her eyes all the harder to bear. He got to his feet. "Corey's still in there. We haven't heard anything yet." When Laura started in that direction, he grabbed her arm. "Don't do that, Laura."

"Let me go," she said, trying to wrench away, but Matt held on.

"The doctor will come out as soon as he has any news."

She stopped struggling and glared at him. "Are you happy now? Is this what you wanted? It's just like before. It's a different hospital, but everything else is exactly the same."

Matt knew what she meant. "He's not going to die, Laura."

"Joe did."

"Corey isn't Joe, and not everyone who chases tornadoes dies. Why can't you understand that?"

"Because I had to raise Joe's son alone!" she shouted.

"No, you didn't," Matt said forcefully. "I was there, too, remember? Every step of the way. Who was at the hospital with you when he had his tonsils taken out? Who sat in the principal's office with you every time he got in trouble? Who taught him to play baseball and attended every Little League game he played? Who gave him the lecture about the birds and the bees?" He took her by the shoulders. "I did, Laura. That was me. I was there for Corey and I was there for you. And I'm here now."

He watched the emotions that played across her face as her anger crumbled, leaving only a mother's desperate fear in its place. She nodded, biting on her lower lip until it nearly bled, then lowered her head to Matt's chest.

He slid his arms around her, and together they waited for news of their son.

TEDDI MADE a tactful retreat when Laura came in, and now she watched them from across the room, amazed by what she was seeing. Obviously Laura needed her friend more than she needed someone to blame.

Teddi watched them sitting on the sofa comforting each other, and she tried not to feel shut out. They were a family in so many ways, and despite their differences, love had a way of binding them together. If Teddi's own family hadn't been taken from her too soon, she and her parents and sister might eventually have forged that kind of bond, too. Seeing Matt and Laura together only reinforced the feeling.

It also made her ache to tell him all the things that were in her heart, but she was beginning to think that the time would never be right. Until they knew Corey was going to be okay, there was no way Matt would be ready to hear anything Teddi had to say to him.

She waited, and a few minutes later a smile lighted her face when the doors opened and a nurse wheeled a groggy Corey into the waiting room. Teddi caught Matt's eye and gave him a nod. When he looked over his shoulder he was on his feet in an instant, pulling Laura up with him.

"Corey!" Laura cried, hurrying toward the wheelchair. She knelt beside it, gingerly giving her son a hug. He put his arms around her and cast a bemused glance at Matt that seemed to say, "Women, what are we supposed to do with them?"

Corey held her for a long moment, then finally kissed her cheek. "Okay, Mom. That's enough," he said, his face flushed as he looked around to see who was watching. "You don't wanna embarrass me, do you?"

Laura managed a tearful smile for her son and rose to face the doctor who had just joined the nurse. "Is he all right?"

"He's fine," the doctor replied, handing Matt the steel-toed work boot that had once adorned Corey's now heavily bandaged foot. "That probably saved him from some nasty orthopedic surgery. As it is, he's got some serious bruising and a couple of torn ligaments, but no broken bones."

Matt clenched the boot tightly. He'd never been so grateful for his own safety standards. "What about a concussion?" he asked the doctor.

"None that we can determine at this time, but I want you to get him home, keep him still and watch him closely tonight. If he has any episodes of vomiting or dizziness, get him back here immediately."

"They gave me six stitches," Corey said grumpily. "And they shaved the back of my head."

"Don't worry, the hair will grow back. You just stay off

that foot for at least a week," the doctor said. He handed Laura a prescription, then went back to the busy emergency room.

Laura looked at her son. "You scared me, Corey."

"I'm all right, Mom."

"Just don't do it again, okay?"

He shrugged his shoulders. "I'm sorry. I can't make that guarantee."

The words sounded painfully familiar to Matt, and he darted a glance at Teddi across the room. "Nothing in life comes with a guarantee, Laura," he said, hating the truth even as he spoke it. "It's not fair, but that's the way it is."

She searched Matt's face, then held out the car keys she'd forgotten she was clutching in her hand. "Will you take us home?"

Nothing would have made him happier. Almost nothing, anyway. "Of course." He took the keys and they moved across the room together. When he came to Teddi, he stopped. "You did a great job today. Congratulations."

"Thanks."

"I'll see you tomorrow," he said.

Teddi could only nod and swallow her disappointment as she watched him leave with his family.

IT WAS NEARLY MIDNIGHT before Matt felt confident enough of Corey's recovery to leave him and his mother on their own. He made a quick call to the Center and learned that Toto II had sustained a direct hit—another first for Matt—and the rest of his team had made it back in one piece.

There was nothing more he had to do before he called it a night. He'd arranged for two of the team to drop his car off at Laura's, and now he drove home, exhausted by the physical and emotional toll the day had taken on him. He'd never experienced so many highs and lows in such a short time.

And apparently he was in for a few more. When he pulled into his driveway, he had to slam on his brakes to keep from crashing into Teddi's Bronco.

How was he supposed to deal with this now? Whatever "this" was. He didn't have any defenses left, and he didn't know how much more he could take. She had been incredible today, like the old Teddi, the one he'd expected to film his documentary in the first place. The one he'd fallen in love with.

She had passed the ultimate test today, so what did she need with him?

He parked his car in the garage and looked around, but he didn't see Teddi anywhere. She wasn't in the Bronco or on his front porch, and the house was locked. Unless she included breaking-and-entering as one of her many hobbies, that could only mean she was on the back deck.

Trying not to remember what had happened there last night, he circled the house. The storm had passed completely, leaving a full moon and a sky filled with stars, so he had no trouble seeing her. She was sitting on the rail, waiting for him, wearing a flowing white dress that made her look like a silvery wraith in the moonlight.

Matt groaned and clenched his fists. He couldn't deal with this. He climbed the deck stairs like a man headed for the gallows.

Teddi stood. "How's Corey?" she asked when Matt didn't offer any kind of greeting.

"He's fine. The pain medication put him to sleep."

"And Laura?"

"She's fine, too," he replied wearily. "Look, Teddi, it's been a long day."

Teddi held her ground. "Do you think you can handle just a few more minutes for something important?"

Matt stopped at the top of the stairs and looked at her. "What?"

"This." She pulled a piece of paper from the folds of her skirt and handed it to him.

He squinted at it in the darkness, then stepped over to the wall and flipped a switch that bathed the deck in small pools of light. He looked at the paper, frowning. It was a certificate of some kind, computer generated, with dot matrix scrolls and curlicues. He was too tired to focus on the writing.

"What is it, Teddi?".

"It's a guarantee," she told him.

Matt frowned. He wasn't in the mood for games. "A guarantee of what?"

Teddi captured his gaze and held it. "That I will spend the rest of my life doing whatever it takes to prove that I love you."

Matt's heart turned over in his chest. It was all too much. "Look, Teddi, you did an incredible job today. I'm very happy for you. I'm sure you feel like you're ready to take on the world again, and you may be." He held the paper out to her. "But this isn't funny."

"It's not meant to be," she said, coming toward him, ignoring the certificate. "It's a promise, Matt. It's a commitment. It's my way of telling you how much I love you."

Matt had lost count of the sleepless nights he'd spent fantasizing about hearing those words, but he couldn't believe them. He didn't dare. "Don't do this, Teddi," he begged her, letting the paper fall to the deck between them. "Just…don't. What happened today in that chase—"

"This has nothing to do with the chase, Matt," Teddi said gently, her voice filled with infinite patience. She knew how hard it would be to convince him of the truth. "I went to Dry Creek this morning, because what happened between us last night made me realize I had to make peace with my past so that I could give you my future."

She took one of his hands in both of hers and pulled it to her heart. "I did that, Matt. I found what I needed, and I came running back to you to tell you that. If it hadn't been for that storm, I would have told you the second I saw you. I love you."

Matt felt Teddi's heart beating beneath his hand, an even, steady rhythm like the unending ebb and flow of a tide. He remembered all too well how beautiful she'd looked this afternoon. Like the old Teddi again, with no shadows haunting her eyes. Like now. She'd been looking at him with love this afternoon, but he hadn't been able to acknowledge it. He didn't know if he could now, either.

"Teddi, I know you think that chase today made a difference, but—"

"Of course it makes a difference," she argued, cutting him off. "If nothing else, it should prove to you that I can handle a tornado—or two, or three! I can handle a lifetime of tornadoes!"

God, how he wanted to believe it. "You say that now when you're feeling on top of the world, but what about later? Down the road when I'm chasing and you're waiting and wondering?"

Teddi raised her eyebrows. "What about the time you'll be waiting and wondering, Matt?"

"What?"

"Would you expect me to give up my career?"

"Of course not. It's too much a part of what you are."

"Are you going to be at home pacing the floor while I'm trotting around the jungles of Peru?"

Matt had a sudden image of Teddi in safari shorts, hacking her way through a green forest with a machete. The image made him smile, and the smile edged aside the doubts. "Yes, I probably would do a little pacing," he told her. "Either that, or I'd go with you."

Teddi saw the warmth that crept into his eyes, and tears suddenly burned in hers. "And you'd be welcome. We'd make quite a team. If you'll let it happen. I want to marry you, Matt."

She meant it, he could tell. But would she still feel that way tomorrow, or the day after? "Teddi, is this another challenge?"

"Hell, yes!" she told him. "It's the ultimate challenge. Have you ever known a marriage that wasn't?"

The pain of the past weeks warred with the love he hadn't been able to deny. And while his sense of self-preservation shouted at him not to believe her, his heart told him something else entirely.

Since it was his heart that had started him down this road to begin with, he knew which one he had to listen to. "Damn it, Teddi, if you change your mind..."

She let go of his hand and snatched up the certificate at her feet. "Here. It's signed. I'll have it notarized tomorrow if it will help. You want me to write it in the sky? I will. You want me to take out an ad in the *Times*? You want me to—"

"I want you to shut up and kiss me," Matt said, dragging her into his arms and silencing her in the most effective way he knew how.

When he finally released her and stepped back, he knew she was telling the truth. Teddi wasn't Laura. She never had been and never could be. She was one of a kind. She was beautiful, daring and impulsive.

And she was his.

Harlequin® Historical

From rugged lawmen and
valiant knights to defiant heiresses
and spirited frontierswomen,
Harlequin Historicals will
capture your imagination with
their dramatic scope, passion
and adventure.

Harlequin Historicals...
they're too good to miss!

HARLEQUIN SUPERROMANCE®

...there's more to the story!

Superromance. A *big* satisfying read about unforgettable characters. Each month we offer
four very different stories that range from family
drama to adventure and mystery, from highly emotional stories to romantic comedies—and
much more! Stories about people you'll
believe in and care about. Stories too
compelling to put down....

Our authors are among today's *best* romance writ-
ers. You'll find familiar names and
talented newcomers. Many of them are
award winners—and you'll see why!

If you want the biggest and best
in romance fiction, you'll get it
from Superromance!

Available wherever Harlequin books are sold.

Look us up on-line at: http://www.romance.net

HS-GEN

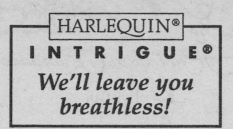

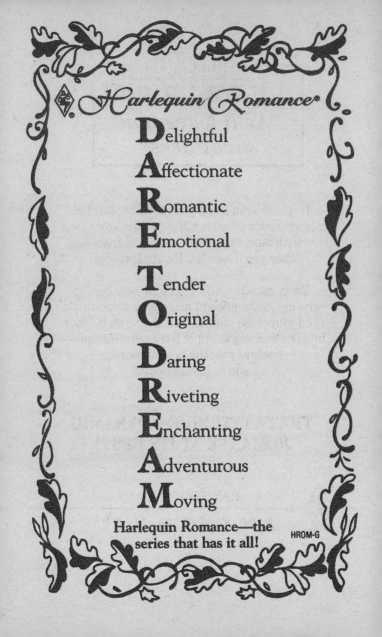

LOOK FOR OUR FOUR FABULOUS MEN!

Each month some of today's bestselling authors bring
four new fabulous men to Harlequin American Romance.
Whether they're rebel ranchers, millionaire power brokers
or sexy single dads, they're all gallant princes—and
they're all ready to sweep you into lighthearted fantasies
and contemporary fairy tales where anything is possible
and where all your dreams come true!

You don't even have to make a wish...
Harlequin American Romance will grant your every desire!

Look for Harlequin American Romance
wherever Harlequin books are sold!

HARLEQUIN PRESENTS

HARLEQUIN PRESENTS
men you won't be able to resist
falling in love with...

HARLEQUIN PRESENTS
women who have feelings
just like your own...

HARLEQUIN PRESENTS
powerful passion in
exotic international settings...

HARLEQUIN PRESENTS
intense, dramatic stories that will keep you
turning to the very last page...

HARLEQUIN PRESENTS
The world's bestselling romance series!

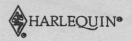

Not The Same Old Story!

 Exciting, glamorous romance stories that take readers around the world.

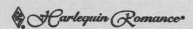 Sparkling, fresh and tender love stories that bring you pure romance.

 Bold and adventurous— Temptation is strong women, bad boys, great sex!

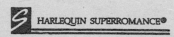 Provocative and realistic stories that celebrate life and love.

 Contemporary fairy tales—where anything is possible and where dreams come true.

 Heart-stopping, suspenseful adventures that combine the best of romance and mystery.

 Humorous and romantic stories that capture the lighter side of love.